THE GIFTED

THE GENOA CHRONICLES

JJ ANDERS

GRAYTON

THE GIFTED

DIGITAL ISBN: 978-1-945100-25-3

PHYSICAL ISBN: 979-8-682801-39-8

Published by Grayton Press

SUMMARY

The conclusion of the Genoa Chronicles.

For Tresstéanna and her band of gifted friends, the struggle for freedom continues. The queen of Valorna is still imprisoned within the giants' palace. Forced into servitude and charged with teaching the royal Grands magic, she and her friends hatch a plan to gain their freedom. But danger is around every corner, and her initial mission to return Genoa to her resting place deep in the Kylix becomes even more hazardous.

Kriston struggles to return to Tresstéanna's side and free her and the other gifted from the clutches of the giants. As the battle for freedom picks up speed, the prince's sanity will be tested as he struggles to keep Tresstéanna from harm.

To all those who inspire.

AUDIO BOOK LINKS

Enjoy listening along. Grab a copy of The Scholar, The Warrior, and The Queen on audiobook. Narrated by Marnye Young.

Links:
  Amazon
  Audible

PREFACE

The flower grew on a shelf of dirt nestled in a rocky field. Each black stone that settled around the blossom had sharp jagged edges. The vast field was devoid of any other life except the small precious flower.

Seven deep purple petals, completely round and delicate in appearance, opened to meet the two suns that shone over its desolate home. Its deep black center held thin yellow stamens in place as the sharp wind blew over the plant.

Sailvea, now a harsh planet, had once been ruled by two battling goddesses, each as powerful as the other. Both had set out to conquer and exile their trespassing sister.

The planet had seen years where battles raged amongst its inhabitants. Lives had been lost in war as elves, man, and magical creatures fought to banish the imposing enemy. Each faction fought for the protection of the goddess they served, while raising weapons against the other's creations.

Bettina had been the first star to fall upon the planet, which was nestled between two suns. She had started her new home, much like her many sisters who had fallen before her. They had dropped out of their place in the heavens and landed upon desolate rocks scattered around the galaxy. Bettina then built creatures of air and water. Lives were born into existence as loved bloomed upon the planet she called Sailvea.

Many years of peace and harmony passed before another of her sisters arrived. The goddess Bettina did not know if the arrival of Cargnet was planned or a mistake. But the results were the same.

Many years after the arrival of the second star, their creations clashed. At first it was just minor, secluded instances. A fight here or there was not much to worry about. And since the two stars did not yet know about the other's presence, nothing was done.

But soon, the small skirmishes became larger battles and then these battles became wars. Whole villages were demolished in attacks by the other faction. Whole colonies of gnomes and sprites were slaughtered. Man was pitted against other races, who also sought to eliminate entire species birthed by the rival goddess. This was something that the deities could no longer ignore.

Needing to protect their children, each goddess made Protectors who could ensure their offspring were safe. When they failed, other more powerful creatures called Seraphs were formed.

Each star made their own version of these creatures. One goddess used the image of large goat creatures with massive horns and strong horse bodies. The other goddess created huge cat monsters that were quicker and spryer. Each new version was larger or stronger than their predecessor.

But their creations had been to no avail. For whatever the rival star created, an equal and more challenging foe was formed.

For thousands of years, the once-peaceful planet of Sailvea remained battle ridden. Just as fast as the children of

either goddess died, new ones were birthed to pick up the struggle. Each generation was stronger, faster, and held more magic than the last, all born in the attempt to conquer their enemies.

But within this battle lust, both stars failed to see their limitations. For with each new generation of super beings, their own magic and life force was being drained.

The goddesses were so engrossed in their war against each other that they soon neglected their own surroundings and the planet they cared for. Volcanos erupted due to the unbalance of war upon the surface. The planet's water rose and flooding wiped away the soil, and quakes shook open the hard, rocky ground.

Soon Bettina found the simplest of conjuries difficult. Even creating a human drained away her inner spark. Fearing for her defeat, Bettina lashed out all her remaining power into one last warrior.

She created a creature so foul that she called the monster a Daemon. The birthing of the blood-thirsty beast left her very few remaining powers, but she was confident the creature would do her bidding.

The Daemon was a large beast with black skin hard as stone. Its eyes glowed red like lava and horns adorned its massive head. Razor-sharp teeth snapped at its victims. It would then cut them apart with its sharp claws.

Fearing for her own safety, Bettina created the Daemon to carry her corporeal globe on a thick chain around its massive neck. This allowed the goddess full control of the beast, yet it also exposed her to dangers.

Cargnet, thinking she was losing the battle after seeing many of her followers fall victim to the Daemon, soon used her last stores of power to create her own monster.

The Minotaur was just as large as the Daemon. Its massive ox-like head and horns were created to aid it in cutting down the enemy. Cargnet formed its strong body and built it for battle. Like Bettina's champion, the Minotaur also carried its goddess around its neck.

After destroying much of the planet and its inhabitants, the two monsters finally met on the flat plains of Rithnor. The battle raged for many years while the two creatures pummeled each other. In their struggles, they destroyed the landscape and any living creature for hundreds of miles.

Each blow laid upon their enemies would cost the attacking goddesses as well, as Bettina and Cargnet needed to repair their injured monsters to ensure maximum efficiency. But their focus should have been on storing up their own powers.

The complete destruction of the planet and the death of both stars was the inevitable result of the last battle. As the crushed globes fell to the ground, the magical life of both goddesses seeped out of the orbs. Their essence mixed and became one in the very place where, many years later, the Orwic flower grew.

Thousands of years passed as the wasted planet slept. Then the giants of Dezeilmex passed into this broken world and found the flower. No other living thing was uncovered on the planet, so the Nephilim dug up the strange flower and continued their journey, searching for a new home.

1

THE FEIER

Tresstéanna's frustration grew as she walked behind Belent on their way out of the Régorge Palace. This trip wasn't going as she'd planned. They weren't escaping, but instead were being led to the Feier Celebration. Surrounded by giants and in the presence of the Grands, there was little hope of escaping.

The giants' party, which was in celebration of the ending of the summer, took place on the last night of the Pythiá month. It was a party, she was told, that normally lasted the entire night.

Grand Cline and Grand Carrington had talked the other royal family members into letting Tresstéanna and her friends attend the party. This was unheard of, as the party usually only consisted of Nephilim, or giants.

Tresstéanna and her three friends, Belent, who was a sorcerer, and Shiarra and Leian, who were both wizards, were being led to the celebration location. Since the party was held high above the palace on the large Hessite cliffs, it afforded them a rare night out beyond the palace's confining walls. Walls that had successfully kept them imprisoned for over forty days.

Lanterns lit the path forward, which was a zigzag trail leading upwards to large landings above the palace. The trail went so high that, as the sun sank below the horizon far to the east, she could see all of the land called Midzark. Well beyond the massive Median Forest, she saw rolling hills of yellow sand. Mound after mound stretched beyond, and the setting sun appeared to turn the horizon into a sea of gold.

Kriston is out there somewhere, she thought as she lifted her skirts higher to ensure she wouldn't trip. The white gown reminded her of a wedding dress. Its billowed skirts had folds with gold trimming, and the tight bodice fit nicely. Despite the large sleeves and high collar, she thought the overall design was well done.

Her blond hair had been tied and twisted up in the front while the back was left to drape over one shoulder. Ribbons tied her hair in place, and their ends were left to trail down and entangle in her locks. Shiarra wore a similar dress and had her dark hair twisted in a thick braid.

Tresstéanna thought the men looked dashing in their white-and-gold suits. She glanced at Belent's shoes, as he was only a step or two above her as they continued their climb. She didn't know how long their pressed clothing would last, as the heat was intense along the cliffs.

The Grands too were dressed in fine clothing. Carrington wore a shimmering dress of gold. Pale pink ribbons adorned her hair, which had been coiled and looped atop her head. Jewels rested along her neck and brow and reflected the lights from any angle.

Cline wore gold. His jacket and vest held hints of pink in their lining and undershirt tufts. He also had jewels atop his brow in an odd crown-like fashion.

Maven Gorphen wore his usual robe, but tonight it was a

pale yellow. Jewels lay around his waist in a strange rope belt, and his unruly beard had been combed to lay flat.

Thoughts of Kriston and her missing friends far below kept her distracted on their long march upward. Before they reached the large landing where the party was being held, she heard the music and laughter filter down to them. The sound of flutes and a string instrument filled the night air along with the sounds of merriment.

Next came the alluring smell of foods. Something rich and spicy with a hint of sweet wafted towards her, making her stomach growl. The thought of food distracted her from her aching legs, which hurt from having to climb so many steps.

The main landing, when it was finally reached, was full of giants. The courtiers were all dressed in their finest tonight, and brightly colored dresses and suits filled her vision. The kaleidoscope of colors made it difficult to focus on any one person. Those gathered on the lower terrace swirled and danced about on a large wooden floor set in the center of the stone landing.

White and gold rugs had been laid out on the rock flooring, and large lanterns lit the massive area. Flowers of all sizes and colors adorned vases that sat on tables full of food. Ale was passed around in golden cups, and every giant partook of the food and drink.

Before being led to their tables, she noticed there were two higher landings, each only a short distance above the main shelf. Large stone staircases, which allowed for easy access to the main terrace, were filled with guests. More tables and chairs littered these levels, but the largest group of giants was collected on the lower terrace they currently stood on.

When they neared a large dais at the cliff's edge, she turned and watched as the sun disappeared completely beyond the horizon. Grand Cline then moved forward as the music stopped, and all eyes turned to him as he held his hands skywards.

"Tonight, we celebrate the Feier. On this, the shortest night of the year, we head towards cooler weather and longer nights," Cline said as a cheer arose from the crowd. Some giants raised their glasses as if toasting the shorter days while others stood with speculation on their faces. "The celebration also holds another joy for me and mine." He held his hand out to his wife, who immediately moved forward and took it. "We begin a new family, one that will carry on my name."

Again, some from the crowd cheered and saluted, yet she saw others turn and whisper amongst themselves. This raised her curiosity, and she kept a close eye on these individuals as Grand Cline continued to speak.

"For those who join me in celebration, this year will hold much. However, I stand before you an irritated man. Many times, harsh words have reached my ears, words of those who choose to oppose me." Cline's dark face held repressed anger, and his eyebrows lowered.

Feeling uneasy with these words, Tresstéanna braced herself. Her magic raised to the surface, and she linked it to Cline as she watched the inevitable unfold.

"Tonight, I will show you my power and all doubt will leave you." His words held the sound of threat as he continued to stand before the crowd.

With this statement, Tresstéanna unleashed her powers, which had been linked to Cline's thoughts. When her magic sprang forward, it emerged in a vision of the stars flying down to drop upon the crowd. The bright orbs and sparkling lights flung down as her magic mixed with Belent's and both of the wizards.

To ensure an amazing display, all four of the gifted

needed to flare their magic. Belent was charged with the swirling orbs of blue, while Leian used several electricity balls. He had them whizzing around the crowd like flies, zigzagging here and there. Shiarra was maintaining the flares of yellow and gold, which left the sparkling orbs and swirls to Tresstéanna. All these visions mixed and swirled around the giant leader as he stood, his legs widely spread and his hands up to the splendor of the mixed magic.

Unsure what was happening, the gathered men and women screamed in fear as they ran about while trying to flee.

Grand Cline marveled in his pretend power, a smile on his face, his arms held wide as his eyes glowed with pleasure. The four from Genoa continued to use their magic to maintain the deception. Yet seeing the lust for power and control in Cline's face, Tresstéanna finally felt doubt creep into her. Cline's dark eyes glowed white from her power, and when a new thought jumped into his mind, she was quick to read it and immediately was filled with fear.

"What have we done?" she whispered as the giants gathered before Grand Cline fell to their knees in either fear or reverence.

THE PAIN COLAB felt ran deep.

His young heart was heavy with sorrow as his body healed. Maraneal had been taking good care of him, and the deep gouges along his arms and neck caused by Biard the Wright's minions had closed. Most of the wounds had already turned to angry red lines that itched. Only a few cuts remained open, and those the pretty dark-haired girl kept clean and covered with a sweet-smelling salve.

He had been moved from the healing tent to one closer to the tent of Maraneal's family. Her younger brother, Manil, would sit and watch Colab when she was called away for other duties. The boy was only three years younger than him, but at thirteen, Manil seemed so much less experienced.

Of course, Colab had to remind himself that he was only sixteen. It had been Meshi who was the elder, wiser being. But since he shared all of Meshi's memories, Colab felt like he had lived longer than his sixteen seasons.

Manil would talk to him when he was taking over for Maraneal. The boy often talked about the large bees his people used for travel. It seemed Manil wished to grow up to be a trainer who worked with the young Mellifera and taught them to understand commands from those who rode them.

Colab would often listen to the lad as he spoke of his homeland, Midzark. When he mentioned the vast city Kós Kóvar, Colab had a difficult time understanding his descriptions.

"The walls are formed out of sand and water. We add the tall yellow grasses of our northern farms to ensure the bricks are strong," Manil told him one day as he helped Colab with his midday meal. "Once the bricks are dry, the building can start. Of course, now that the monsters are defeated, the bricks will be used to repair the damaged areas first."

"Do you know how many were lost?" Colab asked, trying not to think of his own lost friend, Meshi.

"Dad and Mum do not like to talk about the number lost around me, but Maraneal has spent most of her time aiding the injured here. Some have already made their way back to the city, after they were healed, of course," Manil said with a crooked smile.

"Has Svlain come to see me?" Colab asked as his thoughts

turned to the land nymph who had traveled with him from the mainland, Genoa.

"She came once. But she must spend most of her time in the city. There is much need for her."

"What of my other friends?" Colab asked as his eyes scanned the tent's opening. The soft bed he'd lain on for the past two days was near the flap leading out to the green of the oasis, but he yearned for movement. He had realized within the first day of his healing that this was the longest he had spent in one location since leaving his home along the shores of the Tentril Lake so long ago. Now, even the thought of traveling beyond the green of the oasis wore him down. This made him think of all the changes that had been thrust upon him.

First, he had left the Scarent home, a beautiful grassland settled along the lake's shore where the Lady of the Tentril gave his people guidance. They had been comfortable there, he and Meshi. They had been happy.

Then his leader, Mero the Push Tu, had sent him on a quest. Protect Kriston, his uncle, and find his future while aiding in saving their homeland. This quest had guided him on several paths, one that had led to his twin brother, Calob, who had been transformed into a monster by their father.

With Kriston's aid, they had returned Calob back to his natural form and saved Genoa by rescuing Tresstéanna, the queen. Once safe, she had been able to defeat the evil his own father, along with a diabolical wizard, had caused.

Once the land was safe, they had then set off on another quest. This one took them deep down into the Kylix, a black hole where monsters ruled. That adventure had led them into many dangers. Giant spiders, huge creatures called Protectors, and acid roots kept the group cautious.

Upon nearing the end of their quest, they had finally met a foe who ripped apart the group. The giants from Midzark collected anything magical. Their trapper had gathered the two wizards, Shiarra and Leian, along with the sorcerer Belent. Then they had kidnapped Tresstéanna too.

It was during these trying times that he had been separated from the main group. He had left in an attempt to track Belent and had successfully found the trail of the sorcerer. But he hadn't reached the man in time to save him from the grasp of the giants.

Then he had found the trail of the land nymph. Svlain had gone missing several days earlier, along with two of the dragon warriors. When Colab the Meshi had located her tracks, they had immediately set off to follow her.

They had emerged outside of the Kylix and found themselves in the new world called Midzark. In this land there were giants who were three times larger than any human found in Genoa. These Nephilim enslaved the smaller humans called Gi Jón. The slaves, known as Latria, lived a miserable life. They were traded like property and did the giants' bidding.

Colab the Meshi had just started to travel in this new land, still following Svlain's trail, when Genoa's ambassador, Rastel, a creature of Genoa's own making, found him. Completely invisible, the ambassador held many magics and knowledge about this land. One of the things known to him was that Colab the Meshi was needed for a different mission, a quest that would take him far from the Kylix and deep into the lands of this new world.

With the ambassador's aid, they traveled far to the east, beyond the Parós Plains and well beyond where the giants ruled. Far beyond the hot Rájpú Desert with its burning yellow sand and dry air. They had journeyed along the shore of the Márseille Lake and into the Khiosa Forest, where another Scarent named Biard the Wright ruled.

It was in this evil Scarent's fortress that Colab the Meshi

had struggled to complete Rastel's quest to retrieve the Ili Yeathía stone, a stone said to have formed from the goddess's tear. Biard coveted the stone and had hid it deep inside his fortress.

Their mission had been successful, but in their trek to obtain the Tear Stone, Meshi had lost his life. Biard's evil black Carron birds had ripped Meshi's small snake body from Colab's neck. The death of the Scarent snake should have also ended Colab's life, but he had been holding the Ili Yeathía stone. Its magic and power had granted Meshi's dying wish, a wish that had transformed Colab back into a young boy of sixteen.

Returned to his normal, human form, Colab had then almost died on his long journey across the Márseille Lake. Luckily, he had been found by Maraneal and her family. He had been able to provide Svlain and her new friends with the Tear Stone in time to prevent the full destruction of the vast desert city of Kós Kóvar.

But that had happened two days ago, and Colab still found himself healing from the Carron birds' attack on his frail body. No longer was he a Scarent, a creature with a large human form covered in thick scales and powerful muscles with an ancient snake wrapped around his neck. The loss of the symbiotic relationship he had shared with Meshi was the one wound he feared would never heal.

"Manil!" came a sharp voice from the tent's doorway. "Let Colab rest," Maraneal scolded as she entered the tent, a tray in her hands that held fresh bandages and water.

Colab felt guilty as he saw the young boy frown next to him. Maraneal was a very pretty girl of about sixteen. Her long black hair was tied in one thick braid today, and her dark eyes seemed to scold her young brother.

"It was my fault; I was asking about my friends," Colab spoke up to defend the lad.

"Yes, well, heal first," Maraneal said as she set the tray on the short table next to his bedding. "Manil, father requires your assistance." The boy jumped up and scrambled out of the tent without a backwards look.

"Now," she said, and Colab sucked in a short breath.

For some reason, he felt self-conscious around the girl. Her beauty was evident to him and so was his newly transformed body. He realized his once strong limbs had been returned to a normal boy's physique. Pink skin and small muscles were now foreign to him. Even the hair on his head felt strange.

"You will need a shave," Maraneal said as she moved her slender hands to unbutton his shirt. "How are you feeling today?" she asked as if she didn't notice his cheeks turn a bit pink at her touch.

"Um," Colab said and had to clear his throat before he continued. Before he could answer, she made a clicking sound in her throat.

"This one started bleeding again." He felt her removing the bandage along his left side and sucked in his breath as the dried blood ripped at his wound. "Sorry, let me just clean this." She bent her head over his wound.

Her concentration gave him time to study her further. For a young girl, she was quite apt at healing. Her hands were steady, and she seemed competent when she cleaned his injured body. She used salves that calmed the burning in the wounds and had a relaxed manner about her that put him at ease. Sometimes her dark eyes seemed to study him and other times they seemed to be laughing at him behind her thick lashes.

"There, is that better?" She moved to check his other wounds and, as her slender hands passed over his injured body, he burst out laughing. "Ah, you are ticklish!" she exclaimed with a smile as she moved her hands over a spot just above his left rib.

"What?" he said as he quickly grabbed her hand and held it away from his side, where his skin still tingled.

"Ticklish," she said as she tilted her head. "You know."

Unsure what she was saying, he looked down at where her hands had been. Instead of large snake scales, his pink skin had little goose bumps all over.

"You have never been tickled before?" she asked, and Colab heard caution in her voice. He turned his eyes to hers and felt sadness emanate from them. "Colab. What will you do now?" she asked as her dark eyes studied him. "Now that Meshi is gone," she whispered, and he felt the chasm of the unknown open wide before him.

KRISTON WATCHED the bright magical lights swirl around the gathered giants several yards above where he currently stood.

Desperation filled him as he saw his desire stand amongst the colorful lights, just out of his reach. Tresstéanna. Her white dress reflected the magic's colors as her pretty face was pointed upward. Her wizards stood behind her; their eyes also looked to the magic. Even from this distance, he could see Leian using his hands to emanate the electric balls.

"What are they doing?" Wizard Col asked from beside him.

"They trick the Grands," the slave Amándo said as he touched Kriston's arm. "We cannot stay here," he urged, yet

Kriston didn't feel like running and hiding from the vision far above him. In fact, he felt like drawing his sword and rushing up the vast stairs to fight for his life, and that of his love.

Seeing Tresstéanna so close after so long brought his emotions to the front. All the frustration he had felt for so many days tried to seep out of him. His feelings of helplessness and longing almost caused him to choke. His eyes burned on her face, so beautiful and so far from his touch.

How long had it been? The many nights when he had been trapped here in the hot world of Midzark and the days of fighting to gain passage into this blasted palace in his attempt to rescue Tresstéanna passed before his eyes.

Lonely nights without her had seemed to drag. Nights he had yearned for her, to talk to her, hear her tell one of her crazy stories, or just be with her.

"Come!" Amándo finally urged and gave Kriston's arm a hard tug. "They will return soon; we cannot be here!"

"Will they come back?" Col asked and helped Amándo drag Kriston from the large balcony they had been standing on. The balcony led into a giant-sized room with a table and chairs at its center.

"Yes, soon!" came Amándo's response.

With these words, Kriston came out of his daze and turned to the young boy.

"Where? When?" he urged, but the boy gave a shake of his head.

"Soon. After the party!" The lad continued to tug on Kriston's sleeve. "You cannot be seen by any loyalist."

The last word was said in a whisper, but its meaning was clear. Hiding was once again needed.

"Lead the way," Kriston said while the other dragon warriors fell in line behind him. Amándo turned with a nod and quietly walked down a darkened hallway.

No one needed to be told to be quiet; each passageway

they walked brought a threat of discovery. When they finally reached a small door, Amándo had them hide in a dark corner as he scouted ahead.

Kriston heard an odd ticking sound from somewhere ahead while darkness settled around the small group. Col had brought up the rear, and Kriston knew the wizard had his magic ready in case they were discovered. Yet previous battles against the giants had confirmed that a wizard's power wasn't much help against the large beings.

Stria had a knife in each of her hands, and Kip, Hilar, and Farin had their short swords out. Kriston too pulled his sword and held it ready as they waited for the boy to return.

The odd ticking seemed to keep time with his fast heart-beat. It felt like an eternity before the young boy came racing back.

"Quickly." Without waiting for their confirmation, Amándo turned on his heels and raced back down the hallway.

They passed large doors leading to darkened rooms. They raced pass giant furniture, their footsteps falling on thick carpets as they ran. When they reached a massive, closed door, Amándo rushed to open the heavy wooden entrance.

"Here," Kriston said, and he pushed the boy aside. It took he and Col pulling on the knob to get the door to budge. When it did open, Amándo rushed beyond, and they quickly followed him down the steep steps.

At the bottom of the stairs, Kriston was shocked to see they now stood in a normal-sized hallway. No longer where they dwarfed by the huge ornate walls, tall ceilings, and massive furniture. Instead, they now raced down bare wooden floors with empty walls.

Doors still lined the hallway, but these were normal sized, and all stood closed. Occasionally a room would have a light on, its glow shining at them from under the door. Kriston noticed Amándo would slow when they passed these. Again, no warning was needed for the group to be quiet as they moved beyond these occupied rooms.

Amándo led them down another staircase and past two more long hallways. Finally, the boy opened a door and quickly waved them inside. Only once the door was closed did he turn and smile.

"Welcome!" he said as he moved to the center of the room and turned up an oil lamp. The light illuminated a simple room where a table and chairs stood. "Come, sit. We have much to discuss."

"You said our friends will return!" Kriston urged as he closed the distance between them. "When?"

"The party will last two more hours," Amándo said after glancing at the clock then moved to a side table to pour drinks for everyone.

Kriston was unsure how much time this would be. They didn't tell the passing of time through numbers but the positions of the moons. He and his friends stood and glanced around. There were three doors leading out of the room, other than the one they had entered. One led to a small bathroom, while the other two opened into two smaller rooms that held bunks for sleeping.

"Where are we?" Col asked as he returned from looking in the back rooms.

"This is where your friends have lived for several days. When they return, they will come here."

Silence settled around them as Kriston took in his odd surroundings. He noticed the table with six chairs set about it. A small serving table stood against one wall and a hand-woven rug sat under the eating area. He walked to the small bedroom where there were wooden bunks. Each bed had clean linen and a dressing screen. Several dresses were hung on one wall from pegs and there were four shoes under the gowns of blue or golden brown. Fighting the urge to inspect the dresses to see which one Tresstéanna may have worn, he turned back to where Amándo now sat at the table next to Col.

"What is your plan?" Amándo asked as he studied Kriston.

"We have glides," Farin said and then proceeded to explain when the young boy looked confused. "Machines that will allow us to fly down to the forest far below."

Stria stood and unfolded her glide from her back. "Each can carry two people," she explained and then proceeded to refold the thin wings back into their hiding place.

"We have six. We can carry our four friends and two more," Col said.

"My sister must be one to go with you!" Amándo said quickly. "She will join us after her chores in the kitchen."

"Are there any more in the palace that will aid us?" Col asked.

Amándo shook his head. "None we can rely on. Loyalty can be bought, and after tonight, the Grands will not give up their gifted easily."

"What was it that we saw up there on the cliffs?" Farin asked as he took a sip from the cup Amándo had provided them.

Kriston had a hard time sitting still as the boy told them of Tresstéanna's plan to fool the giants at the party. Each word the boy spoke weighed on Kriston's mind. Fear and worry filled him when the lad finally finished his story.

"They had hoped to be rescued by now, or escape, but escape is impossible without aid," Amándo finished.

"Well, help is here," Col said soberly.

"I just hope we have not arrived too late," Stria mumbled from the corner of the room.

Amándo spoke of their friends' difficulty with the hunter, Káric. He told them how the little man had caused trouble for Tresstéanna but then was banished for his treachery. He was just finishing the story when a soft knock was heard on the locked door.

Weapons were quickly drawn as Amándo turned the lamp down then rushed over to the door. Madera, Amándo's sister, entered after a few quiet words through the locked door.

Kriston noticed the girl had Amándo's dark hair and eyes. Her young face was etched with worry as she twisted her hands nervously before her slender waist. Her dark brown dress was covered with a tan apron that was damp in several spots. She looked as if she had just finished washing dishes.

"Amándo, Paren is coming," the young girl quickly said, her dark eyes large with fear.

"Now?" her brother asked and, when she nodded, fear filled the young boy's eyes.

"Quickly, they must hide!" she hissed.

BRINE, one of the young brothers of Grand Cline, thought a party was a great place to scope out all the possibilities.

He was the next in line for his older brother's position, now that Fin had been banished several days ago.

Brine and his entourage had arrived well before Grand Cline had made his appearance. Brine's guards, each a loyal and well-paid friend, walked around him. There were three large military men behind and two in front. Each man wore hidden weapons and knew how to follow orders. His orders.

His second wife, Kristine, walked with her slender hand

on his arm. She was new, only four months into the marriage, but already trained well.

Kristine's long slender form was fetching in the dark green and white dress. He had been pleased when he'd noticed that her long dark hair had been left down tonight. The tresses shone in the lights while colored jewels adorned her neck and fingers.

She was his third cousin and had been raised to know her duties. Women, in Brine's opinion, should have no goals beyond pleasing their husband. This included public and private affairs.

He moved amongst the crowd as he aimed for the highest of the three balconies. Despite his yearning for full power of the palace, he preferred high ground and not center stage, unlike Cline. Brine knew that with a good vantage point, you could see trouble before it saw you.

As he settled near a low terrace wall, facing down at the lower levels, a smile crossed his thin lips. Much would be accomplished tonight, and if all was completed correctly, power would soon be transferred into his capable hands. As he waited for his fool of a brother to appear, his thoughts turned back to the path he had taken to get here.

Fin had been an imbecile! Brine had used his brother's power lust to his own advantage. Removing Fin had been as simple as having his new wife place a few thoughts into the head of one of Fin's mistresses.

The plan was only to whisper of the poison available in the hopes the mistress would take matters into her own hands. Brine had hoped the mistress would succeed in killing Cline and his recent wife, but when Fin and his whole clan had been banished instead, these results were acceptable too.

However, this had left Cline still sitting in the royal chair in the Régorge Palace. This was something Brine was getting tired of. And something, he hoped, would be corrected soon.

If tonight's plan was successful, then soon he would find himself settling in the powerful position of Grand. Grand Brine had a nice ring to it.

The smile on his lips curled into a snarl when his thoughts turned to the battles raging far below the palace. His brother had allowed the Latria far too many liberties. The slaves' rebellion was unacceptable, and something he would change as soon as power was his.

He had big plans, and squelching this revolution was the first thing he would do. The second thing he would do was to capture all magics for himself. For much like his older brother Cline, Brine too believed that the gifted held the key to power. And those who enslaved the gifted held that key.

When Cline finally arrived at the party with his entourage, Brine sat back to watch. With his brother's words of the expected baby, he showed no reaction. It wasn't until Cline spoke of power that Brine finally sat forward a little.

With eyes wide, Brine watched his brother call forward the very stars from the dark sky above. Lights of all different colors whizzed about the heads of those gathered that night. At first fear filled Brine. He was worried his brother had discovered his intentions. He feared the burning stars would leap at him and burn him where he sat, well before any of his plans could come to pass.

But as each star continued to fly about, he turned his attention to the gifted gathered behind his brother. There, the four stood entranced in the magic before them.

Brine watched with curiosity as the pale woman give a shake of her body when the closest star settled on his brother's outstretched hand. Dismissing the pale woman, his eyes moved to the other female gifted in the group.

'Yes, there were plenty of possibilities to see tonight,' he thought and a large smile formed on his face again.

Beyond the initial "fireworks" at the start of the party, Tresstéanna found the Feier Celebration dull.

Sure, the food was great. Soups, salads, and sandwiches started the meal. She assumed the slices of bread with spreads in the middle were meant to be finger sandwiches, but since each was about the size of her head, the delicacy was lost on the four from Genoa.

Next, they were served a large meat dish that had roots of various colors arranged around it. Again, the size of the serving was a weeks' worth of food, not a single helping. But since they had their own 'smaller' table, they were left to dish their own food onto the golden plates that sat before them.

Their table was nestled back and to the right of where Cline and Carrington sat. Two giant women came and set the food platters on their table. The women appeared to disapprove of their presence. However, since neither said a word, Tresstéanna could only guess the scowls on their faces were in objection to their presence.

When cakes and sweets finally ended the long meal, she guessed midnight had come and gone. By the time the food portion of the party was complete, her dress felt tight and her head swam from the ale.

Dancing had continued during the entire ordeal, giant women and men circling each other on the center terrace as the music played. The sound was mingled with laughter and the clinking of utensils or glasses. Tresstéanna found the music reminiscent of Earth's contemporary blues music, but with a bit more pep.

Since they were unsure what was expected of them after the last cake had been consumed, they remained at their table while the party continued around them. It was during this time she became aware of Shiarra and Leian holding a fierce whispering battle.

"I do not like it," Leian hissed, and Tresstéanna glanced his way. "His eyes have been on you since our display."

"We could ask," Shiarra whispered back, noticing that Tresstéanna was watching them. "Highest balcony, far to the right," Shiarra quickly said to her, keeping her own head down, contrary to her guiding instructions.

Not wanting to be caught looking, Tresstéanna turned back towards Belent, who sat on her left. "Trouble," she said softly but kept her head facing him, then moved only her eyes to where Shiarra had directed.

She was able to zero in on the offending man quickly. Leian was correct. The man was bluntly gazing at their table. His fancy robes and his entourage spoke of royalty. She guessed he was a relative of the Grands. Jewels adorned the woman sitting next to him, and servants hovered around the couple.

Despite all the movement between the man and where they sat several feet below, his dark eyes were fixed on them. More specifically, on Shiarra.

Speaking quietly, Tresstéanna gave directions for Belent to look at the man. He too moved only his eyes, and she saw worry fill the sorcerer's face when his gaze landed on the giant.

"Definitely royalty," Belent said, voicing her own thoughts.

"I think he's one of Cline's brothers," Tresstéanna said as her thoughts went back to her arrival in the palace. She had used her magic on the leader of the giants and seen into Cline's mind, gaining knowledge of his past, which included his family history. "I could be wrong, but I know Cline has a few more siblings hanging around the palace."

"He is not the one who was exiled," Shiarra said with a frown on her face.

"No. That was Fin," Leian advised while he tried to move his chair closer to Shiarra. Tresstéanna got the impression he was trying to block Shiarra from the man's view.

"Has he only been looking?" Belent asked, his voice filled with trepidation.

"One of his men disappeared a while ago, but yes, only looking," Leian replied.

"Leering is more like it," Tresstéanna hissed. She took a deep breath. "Cover for me." She closed her eyes.

She used her magic; it took a while and all her concentration. She found the trail to send her magic to the man difficult. She had to twist around all the giants that stood or danced on the floors between her and her target. When she finally found a clear path to reach the man, she called her magic forward. She only gained a fleeting impression before someone broke her connection by moving into her pathway.

"Yes," she finally said as she closed her magic away again. "His name is Brine. He's Cline's brother."

"Why was he staring at Shiarra?" Leian urgently asked.

Shaking her head, she turned to study the now empty place where Brine had been sitting. "I got a fleeting image of lust. But it's not what you think." She placed a hand over Shiarra's, which sat upon the table. "It's power he seeks, not you."

"Power?" Belent asked. Tresstéanna had a fleeting impression and knew what her friend was thinking.

"No, you can't disappear here. Not while all eyes are on us. Maybe you can seek him out after we return to the palace," she quickly said, speaking of Belent's ability to vanish. She gently placed her other hand on his as if trying to hold him in place.

"Do you fear another plot against the Grands?" Shiarra asked as the party continued around them.

"If Cline and Carrington are replaced, we would find ourselves back at the beginning," Tresstéanna replied with a shake of her head. "No, we must move forward with those we know." She scanned the party in the hopes of finding Brine amongst those still gathered. "The devil we know…" she whispered.

She got nods from both Belent and Leian. Shiarra continued to study the empty seat far above them. Tresstéanna's gaze joined Shiarra's on the empty seat, and a feeling of unease settled deep in the bottom of her stomach.

The party lasted till the first rays of sun rose from behind the very cliffs the celebration was held on. Several groups of giants still danced while other larger groups settled around tables or in plush chairs that were set on the first and third terraces.

Despite their concern over the leering Brine, the remainder of their time was spent watching the procession of partiers. Finally, when several couples started for the stairs, the tone of the party changed. Several people could be seen yawning, while others slumped in their chairs. After a long night, the party was finally coming to an end. When both Grands stood to leave, the group from Genoa took the hint and rose as well.

The stairs leading back down to the palace were made for both giants and normal-sized humans. The rungs were many and soon the distance between the two groups grew as the smaller humans had far more steps to traverse. Four giant guards surrounded Tresstéanna's small group, taking the large steps more slowly to keep pace with the gifted. Another six guards protected Cline and Carrington far ahead of the slower unit. She noticed that Maven Gorphen helped Carrington descend the steps as if she were made of glass.

As the Ingress Bridge came into view, the stairway opened up. Several branches of walkways and even more stairs snaked off the main trail. A line of giants could be seen far below them crossing the wooden structure as they entered the palace through the opened gate. The bridge's lanterns were still lit, despite the sun peeking above the mountains.

Even this early, the heat of the day threatened to take her breath away. The heavy dress and long night wore on her. Soon, Tresstéanna found herself longing for bed.

At first, she didn't take notice when a loud grunt sounded behind her. When a second sound came, she paused. When the noise changed to the sound of a man's gurgle in death, she quickly spun on her heels, ready for a fight.

Two of the four guards behind them already lay dead on the stairs. The remaining two quickly turned to raise their swords against several large dark figures. Long giant swords flashed in the morning light as Tresstéanna raised her skirts. It was so instinctive for her to join the fighting that she forgot for a minute she held neither sword nor bow.

"No, down this way!" Belent shouted and tugged on her arm as Leian and Shiarra fought their way down the steps towards them.

"We can..." Leian shouted but was interrupted by a giant's body slamming into him and Shiarra from behind.

Leian went flying towards where Tresstéanna and Belent stood, while Shiarra's fell to the stone steps with a muffled cry of pain. Her unconscious form disappeared under a giant's dead body as they landed several steps above them. The only thing they could see of Shiarra was her long skirt poking out from under the giant's metal armor.

Two giants rushed down the stairs at the small group. Screaming could be heard from behind them and by the time Leian gained his feet, leaning heavily on Belent, there were four giants surrounding the prostrate form of Shiarra. None of them had the insignia of the Grands on their armor.

"Shiarra!" Belent yelled as his right arm raised toward the attackers.

In horror, Tresstéanna watched as one of the giants bent down and detangled Shiarra's unconscious form from the dead one. Belent immediately sent a blast of magic at the attackers, but it bounced off their protective armor.

Leian quickly joined in the magical assault and together they had the armor of one of the attackers burning. But the other giant, who carried Shiarra, quickly disappeared down another flight of steps leading far to the south, away from the palace.

By the time the Grands' personal guards reached them on the steps, all the assailants had disappeared, along with Shiarra.

2

REUNION

Zain, healer and dragon rider, studied the view of Midzark as his friends moved out of the tunnel behind him. The air that hit him was hot, hotter than any he had felt before. Moisture dripped off the rock walls and turned to steam around him, making breathing difficult.

As sweat pooled at the base of his spine, he stood and thought about how this warmth was so different from the cave's coolness. The fluctuation in temperature was difficult for his body and mind to adjust to. Even the faint light caused by the sun rising behind the mountains was odd to him.

He was glad the group had decided to have Em, the ant, stay hidden in the tunnels. First, he doubted she would have been able to squeeze her large body down the narrow tunnel they had used to exit the Kylix. And second, he didn't think the ant would fare well in the heat of this place.

"It is not even the hottest part of the day," Timmons said as he placed a hand on Zain's shoulders. "This place is like a furnace midday."

Zain moved beyond the dripping water to the edge of the

cliff they stood on. To his right was a large forest. His eyes savored the bright green of trees, despite their enormous size and odd shapes. They reminded him of home. The cliffs reminded him of Faro, the sea cliffs where the dragons of his tribe made their nests.

When his eyes wandered down, he noticed they weren't very high up on the rock face. Only fifty feet separated them from the ground, but the trail down was a steep one.

Seeing movement to his left, he raised his eyes and noticed life beyond his surroundings. The whole valley before them seemed to be alive. Farmers with carts moved along a vast road before them while more people worked in the fields.

What grew in one square of the fields was vastly different from the next. One spot had bright orange plants while another held brown orbs lined in neat rows. Another appeared to be full of flowers, each petal blazing with bright colors.

"The Gi Jón work the fields. This should help us return to the Otomi fighter's lair," Seth said to both Zain and Toku. "Of course, we can wait to journey until after the heat of the day, while everyone rests."

Timmons' hand tightened on Zain's shoulder before it dropped off. "Nek, any noise from the palace?"

Quietly, a thin dark man stepped forward and shook his head. "Unknown. We heard quite a bit of noise from the cliffs as the sun rose, but nothing passed this spot and the farmers were not disturbed."

"It was Kriston!" Seth said, his youthful face full of eagerness. "Maybe he rescued them?"

Zain saw Timmons shake his head. "Not unless they met with no resistance. That was too quick since the time he departed from us." Timmons' face showed concern as his eyes moved to study the forest to their right. "And Kriston was attempting to complete the rescue using stealth, not force."

"It sounded like fighting to us." Another dark-skinned man came up to them, and Zain was introduced to Bail.

Zain had met Mett earlier when he had accompanied Seth inside the tunnel. Now, he studied the other new friends and found them interesting. They were dressed like farmers but carried weapons. Their speech was odd, and their manner was very stiff around him.

In return, these new friends studied Toku's slanted eyes with curiosity, but none voiced questions. This led Zain to think that Midzark didn't hold a diverse ethnic culture like Genoa did. This thought turned his mind to Svlain. He wondered how the land nymph was faring here in this different world.

"Where are we going?" Toku's question interrupted Zain's thoughts.

"Our travels are long; we should reach the river by tonight if we are lucky." Timmons handed Zain a water skin.

"You mean if we are not discovered," Seth said with a grim face.

"You mean discovered by these giants?" Zain asked for clarification as he took a drink.

"The Nephilim travel along these roads and fields too," Timmons replied. "But they are used by farmers, Gi Jón who work for the giants. This fact will aid in disguising us."

"Are they looking for us?" Toku asked, and Zain saw his friend's hand move to rest on his long sword handle.

"No, but the fighting has everyone on alert. Each road leading into the forest is watched. Most Gi Jón are denied access unless they have deliveries or are accompanied by their owners." Timmons grim expression spoke more than his words, and Zain found he grew worried.

"Then what is our path?" he asked, moving his own hand to rest on the handle of his sword.

"The Húriya people promised they would come, but until then, we should return to Mayson's group, the Otomi fighters," Timmons replied. He took the water skin from Zain. "This means retracing our steps, crossing many fields, and heading east until we reach the forest. Once there, we find the river and hope the Otomi fighters still hold the new bridge."

"You said Svlain was with these Húriya people?" Zain asked Seth hopefully.

The young dragon warrior nodded and smiled. "She was quite well the last time I saw her. She asked after you," Seth said with a wink. But Zain recognized something pass behind the man's eyes and apprehension filled him.

"Is she in danger?" Zain asked, taking both Seth's arms in a strong grip.

"She is the one who sent me to you." Seth's sober tone turned Zain's blood to ice. "She feared for you more than herself."

"What do you mean?" Zain asked, and his grip tightened on Seth's strong arms.

"Sash stayed with her. Colab was there too." Seth shook his head, and he reached out to pat Zain on his chest in a comforting move. "The city was under siege by monsters."

Seth then told Zain and Toku about the vast city of Kós Kóvar. He told of the children of Dreail rising up from the waters of the vast Márseille Lake. How the large monsters had attacked the city but had been held back by the warriors of the Húriya people. He told of Colab the Meshi's trials and how the Scarent snake had died while obtaining the Tear Stone.

"Svlain had the stone when I left her," Seth said. He

looked sternly at Zain. "Sash is with her and will protect her. She was insistent that I save you."

Fear for Svlain made it difficult for Zain to breathe. His steps were labored when the group finally moved down from the cliff's face. They moved into the vast fields where both giants and normal-sized humans worked in the distance.

As he walked, his mind raced with horrible images of all the evils that might have fallen upon Svlain. It wasn't the heat that made him sweat, nor the humidity, but fear for the woman he loved.

THE INGRESS BRIDGE was in chaos after the attack and kidnapping of Shiarra. Tresstéanna stood numb while Wizard Leian and Belent shouted to be heard over the noise. Both Grand Cline and Carrington were barking orders to Prime Magal as more giant guards surrounded the group.

"Track them!" Cline shouted, and Prime Magal gave a bow of his head and turned to order six guards to follow him.

Immediately, several more guards surrounded the group, but Tresstéanna knew the damage was already done. Her friend Shiarra was gone, missing, kidnapped. Whisked away in the turmoil of a monarch upset by deception and hatefulness.

She knew it was Grand Cline's brother who was responsible for her friend's kidnapping. She had seen it in the man's mind, what little she had glimpsed earlier at the party last night.

"I demand to go with them!" Leian shouted, and Cline

looked down at the three remaining gifted with shock and concern.

"No, you will return to the palace for protection. I will not have any more stolen from me," Cline said with authority in his voice.

"We are not your possessions!" Leian shouted up at the giant. "Shiarra was mine! Not yours!"

Tresstéanna recognized the grief and frustration in the wizard's eyes as a vein throbbed at the corner of his temple. Dried tears tracked his face while his clenched fists shook up at the Grand.

"Take them back to the palace!" Cline ordered as a guard stepped forward. As he approached the wizard, sparks flew from Leian's fists.

"If they touch me, they will burn!" he hissed between clenched teeth.

"Please." She laid a hand on Leian's arm as she addressed Grand Cline. "We can help locate her."

Pausing, Cline studied her for a moment then finally nodded. "What can you do?"

Before she could answer, Belent stepped forward. "Give me ten men, and I will find her."

"I will not let you leave the palace," Cline stated, but he stopped when he noticed Belent shake his head.

"I can do it from here." Belent turned to study the giant closest to him. After the sorcerer stared deeply into his eyes, he finally spoke. "Give me your sword."

The guard stood still, clearly unsure if he should follow the gifted man's orders. After receiving a nod from his leader, he removed his sword and held it crossways as he knelt in front of Belent. The giant held the blade so that it rested a foot from the sorcerer's chest.

Belent raised his hands inches from the sharp edge as quiet settled around him. His hands started to glow green. As the light grew, it dropped down and encircled the blade. The giant guard almost dropped his sword when he noticed the magic, but his curiosity must have been greater than his shock, because he held on to the weapon.

Everyone moved closer as the green light surrounded the weapon. They had been so intent on the glowing sword, that when Belent spoke, everyone was shocked that the sorcerer had already removed his hands. "This will help you locate our friend."

The large guard stood, his sword still held before him as the glowing magic faded from its sharp edges. Brown eyes turned from the weapon to look at the sorcerer, then back at the weapon.

"What do I do with it?" he finally asked.

"What is your name?" Belent asked as he studied the giant.

"Mayvers," the guard quickly replied.

"Well, Mayvers, the blade will glow green when you draw near to our missing friend. It seeks only Shiarra." Belent turned to address the Grands. "With this sword they can locate her."

Orders were given and Mayvers, along with nine other guards, were sent out to follow the sword's magic. The Grands insisted the remaining three gifted return immediately to the palace for their protection. To Tresstéanna, it felt more like being locked away than protected.

The walk across the bridge was short. Already the day's heat was increasing, and the long night was catching up to her. She thought quickly of Kriston and wondered where he was as the massive door of the Régorge Palace closed behind her.

Before they reached the small staircase leading down to the Latria quarters, Weston approached them. The head guard for the Gi Jón looked upset, his dark face grim as he neared.

"Forgive me," he said, turning to look at Tresstéanna. "Your quarters were disrupted while you were gone."

"Disrupted?" Belent quickly asked.

"The loyalist, Paren, took it upon herself to search your rooms," Weston replied with a shake of his head

Tresstéanna thought of their meager possessions here. Nothing in their rooms was even theirs. All the important items had been taken by the giants, including the Globe of Corpuscle and the Protector Adulario's eye.

"Luckily, she was thwarted by Amándo, who was in your rooms awaiting your return. But there was quite a scuffle when he refused her access to your private chambers." Weston's eyes turned sober.

"What do you mean? What has happened?" Tresstéanna asked quickly, thinking of their young friend.

"Paren and two others have accused Amándo of betrayal." Weston again shook his head. "She demanded to speak with the Grands."

"Not again," Leian said as his frustration seeped out in his voice.

"Yes. We took her last accusations into account and have instead restricted Paren and the two men to their own quarters. Unfortunately, they caused considerable damage to your common room."

"Damage?" Tresstéanna asked as a headache started to form behind her left eye.

"Most of the damage has already been repaired," Weston immediately replied. "I thought it best you were aware of this unfortunate event before you returned to your chambers."

Nodding, Tresstéanna moved passed the guard and proceeded down the steep steps leading to their rooms and prison.

The giant guards remained above while Weston followed the three down into the lower levels, which had been made for the smaller Gi Jón people. Turning down the last hallway, Belent grasped Tresstéanna's arm to slow her as Weston and his men continued.

"My lady, we must escape and go after Shiarra," he whispered as Leian moved closer.

"Yes, but not tonight. We are tired and must form a plan first." Her eyes were on the retreating guards. When their chamber doors opened, she saw Amándo jut his head out into the hallway.

After looking at the retreating guards first, he motioned his hands for them to quickly enter. There was no doubt in her mind that he wanted to relay the night's events to them.

As they entered the room, Amándo quickly shut and locked the door. His youthful face was full of excitement as he stood with his back to the exit.

"Before you begin, we know about the event here," she said as her eyes swept the room. She noticed the new chairs and a pile of rubble that she presumed Amándo had been in the middle of sweeping. The table looked untouched, but the water pitcher and glasses were no longer sitting on the side table where they usually sat.

"There are more important things to discuss," Amándo said as his smile grew, the broom still clutched in his hands.

"Can they wait?" she asked, rubbing a hand over the throbbing in her eye. It now felt like she was getting a migraine. She knew she needed sleep, or soon she was going to fall on her face from exhaustion.

"But I have come so far to see you," came a familiar deep voice from the door leading into the bed chambers.

Quickly she turned and saw Kriston standing in the door. Suddenly, the numerous days lost without him seemed to melt away as his handsome face smiled at her. Feeling her heart soar, she let out a loud whoop and flung herself into Kriston's arms.

THE GREETING between Kriston and Tresstéanna was not a private matter, much to her dismay.

She saw that worry and the passing of time had etched lines on Kriston's face. There were new scars too; one ran directly through his left eyebrow while another tickled his jaw on the same side. His hair had grown longer, and he still kept it tied back with a leather strap, but the locks now hung well below his broad shoulders.

His green eyes deepened as they studied her in the white dress. She wondered what he saw as he looked at her, but when he smiled, her heartbeat increased as she once again rushed into his arms.

When Tresstéanna finally noticed that the room behind Kriston was full of her fellow dragon warriors, she quickly scanned those gathered in the small room. Wizard Col, her mentor and protector for most of her life, was there, as well as Farin, Hilar, Kip, and Stria. Seeing her friends brought tears to her eyes as they all settled in the private common room. Laughter erupted as they told her the story of their arrival into the palace.

"We were delivered in padded boxes and came out smelling like fruit!" Kip said with a smile.

Tresstéanna was glad to see Kip's injuries from their prior travels inside the Kylix had healed nicely. She did notice that Kip's once-shaved head now sported a full two inches of hair.

This was something that also spoke of time's passing, which saddened her.

"We had hoped to escape before the Feier Celebration, but the palace is too well fortified," she said. Kriston's hand covered hers as it sat on the table. "Now I wish we had tried harder." Confused silence followed her statement until Belent spoke up.

"Wizard Shiarra was kidnaped tonight on our way back to the palace." To their credit the silence remained until Leian interrupted it.

"Do you have an escape plan?" he demanded, his face still filled with worry as he looked from one friend to the next. "You would not risk coming into the palace without a plan of escape!"

"We have," Kriston said as Col stood and walked back into the room they had been hiding in. "We had just arrived here when Amándo feared we had been discovered."

"Turns out Paren has been coming into the rooms each day and looking for anything she could use against you," Amándo said with a scowl on his face. "But tonight, I managed to fight off the intrusion before anyone could get into the back room where your friends were hiding."

It was then that Tresstéanna noticed the boy's blackened eye. Filled with anger at the injustice, she quickly stood and gently touched his face. "They hit you?"

"Do not worry for the lad. He gave much worse than he received tonight," Col said as he returned, carrying a glider.

The sight of the flying machine filled her with joy. Memories of her childhood freedom and the Cliffs of Faro raced into her head, and a large smile formed on her lips. Gone was the headache as excitement took over where the pain had been.

If it had been up to Leian and Kriston, they would have immediately strapped on the gliders and jumped out the nearest window. But Tresstéanna had to dowse the wizard's urgency to take flight.

"We need to locate the Globe of Corpuscle!" she insisted, reminding them that the globe was no longer in their possession. "Without Genoa, our mission has failed."

"I do not care!" Kriston insisted as Leian nodded in agreement. "I came here to rescue you."

"At least some of us should take the glides and escape," Leian voiced.

With a shake of his head, Col finally spoke up. "No, if anyone is seen escaping out of the palace, the whole mission will have failed. We must all stay hidden until we have our hands on the globe."

"The eye of Adulario is also in the box," Belent reminded her as they sat around the small table.

Tresstéanna then relayed the story of their discovery of where the globe and eye were being kept.

"Belent thinks the box is a portal," she said with a nod. "Once an item goes in, nothing of it can be seen until it is called for and retrieved."

"Where is this box? Can we get to it today?" Col asked as he scratched his chin.

Tresstéanna had been shocked to see that her wizard's head, normally shaved in a mohawk, was now covered in thick hair. She had been told that a shaved head made it harder for the Genoans to blend in with the Gi Jón. She had laughed when she noticed that he even sported a small beard. The facial hair was more silver than brown, giving her mentor an older appearance, but his eyes had still sparkled when he'd hugged her earlier.

"The box is kept in Maven Gorphen's rooms three levels up. They are at the base of the middle tower and very difficult to sneak into," Belent advised with a shake of his head. "But not impossible for one who can vanish."

"Well, it sounds like we have the start of a plan!" Col barked a laugh and slapped the skinny sorcerer on his back.

"This will take time," Belent said with a frown. "And keeping you all hidden will be difficult."

"Too bad so many of you came to our rescue," Tresstéanna said with a frown.

"We expected more fighting and less sneaking," Kriston said with a nod.

The group talked for several hours; midday was approaching before they spoke of retiring. By this time, Tresstéanna was so exhausted that she had dropped off to sleep while sitting at the table. When she felt her body being lifted, she jerked awake quickly. She relaxed again when she discovered it was Kriston carrying her.

"Just taking you to your bunk," he mumbled as he tried to lower her to the cot without hitting her head. In his defense, the bed was low to the ground, which made it difficult to climb into. He only banged her head once against the post before she asked that he release her.

Instead of crawling into the bunk, however, she sat on the nearby bench and looked up at him with a sigh. "I missed you so much." She grabbed his hand and urged him to sit next to her. After laying her head on his shoulder, she sighed again and closed her eyes.

"I hurt each day we were apart," he told her, causing another sigh to escape.

"Kriston, I have seen good and evil in this place." She was tired, but the discoveries she had made while enslaved within the palace swirled in her. She felt she had to share these thoughts and concerns now before any plans were made.

"Grand Carrington is not a bad person. At least, not entirely," she said as she tried to gather her thoughts. "I think, I mean, I hope we might be able to correct the injustices here in this place."

"What would you do?" he asked after a moment of silence.

She knew Kriston still held anger inside him regarding the kidnapping of her and her friends. But she had learned so much about the Nephilim and the Gi Jón, information that gave her hope this war between them could be settled peacefully.

"If Carrington could be swayed towards our plight, we might be able to correct the wrongs in this world." She tried to hold back a yawn.

"Sleep. We can discuss it when you wake." He gently kissed her goodnight.

Svlain was tired. The land nymph had difficulty concentrating and a weariness settled deep inside as she walked to her bed chambers.

After the monsters of Dreail had been banished, and well before the sun rose the next day, she had walked the entire length of the vast city of Kós Kóvar. She'd been shocked to see more than half of the city had been devastated by the battle. She knew the buildings wouldn't remain destroyed for long as there were already several people working on clearing the rubble.

Women used brooms and rags to sweep away the smaller debris. Men lifted the damaged wood and cleared away the stones, then placed them in piles. These piles were then picked up by other people with large wooden carts. Walkways twisted in and out of the large piles, allowing everyone access to their homes, whether they were still standing or needed to be rebuilt.

Svlain had been a constant and visual presence after the battle. This had been Ava's idea. The Zaeim knew that the Húriya people needed the reassurance of Genoa's land nymph. Ava had told Svlain that seeing her would make the people feel safer and comforted somehow.

Svlain could see the effect she had on those she stopped and talked to or just waved to on the street. Most reassured were the women and small children, but she couldn't doubt Ava's urgency about her being seen when she saw the results her presence had.

It sure made for a long day, she thought as she settled her tired body down on the soft bed. Before she drifted off, she had one last thought of Zain. His handsome face drifted in her mind as her brain finally shut down.

The vision felt more like a dream at first.

Mist swirled around and blocked her from seeing what she felt she needed to see. Odd dark shapes whisked in and out, yet none appeared to have any true form. Then, suddenly, she felt her body being torn apart. The next moment she was whole again, standing amongst the fog.

"This is needed!" came a deep and ethereal voice, so powerful and commanding in tone that it caused her to flinch. She thought the voice sounded like it came from the very depths of her soul.

With this command, the mist parted to reveal more blackness. So complete was the darkness that now surrounded her, that she didn't know she had been swept into it until the fog was left behind.

A soft glow emanated from ahead, and the darkness faded. As she neared the light, a small purple flower came into view.

Seven round petals made up the deep purple face while a black center held them in place. The stem was green and held one single leaf in the shape of a heart.

Shiarra woke from her dream confused.

She didn't remember what had happened to her. At first, she thought the dream was just that, a dream while she lay sleeping. Maybe it was a shadow, a nightmare from the time she had spent in the hated Pagilda mirror, the object the giant Maven Gorphen had trapped her and her friends in upon their arrival in Midzark.

Panic rose inside her before she realized she was no longer trapped in the mirror. She had been pulled from the glass, saved from the pain of being repeatedly pulled apart, rescued by her queen and friend, Tresstéanna, who had tricked the giants into believing they were friends and not enemies.

Taking a big gulp of air, she noticed the air was stale and unpleasant. Moisture and dirt filled her senses as her eyes flew open with more confusion.

A small light shone ten feet from where she lay. Its faint glow barely illuminated her surroundings. She felt something sticky on her face and smelled her own blood. When she moved, pain shot out along her left temple. When the dark room swirled, she quickly closed her eyes and tried to calm herself. Taking another breath, she tried to clear her mind and think.

The last she remembered, she had been walking down the steps towards the palace. She remembered leaving the party with Tresstéanna, Belent, and Leian. But that's all she could remember. Nothing of reaching the palace came to her mind, and she scrunched up her face while trying to think clearly.

Had they been attacked? If so, where were her friends?

Opening her eyes again, she tried to see into the blackness that surrounded her. Oddly shaped walls and the single light were all she could see. The small lamp was set on a bench, but no one was near.

After lifting her head slightly, she discovered she was lying on a pile of dry grass. When she sat up, the room gave a quick spin again, and she closed her eyes quickly.

It was during this time that the dream returned to her. The blackness and fog, even the commanding voice telling her that the flower was needed! She remembered the image of the deep purple flower with seven petals.

Unsure of the dream and its meaning, she opened her eyes again and tried to make sense of her surroundings. The odd walls stared back at her, giving her a fleeting memory of the Kylix.

The realization that she was in a cave came mixed with shock. Was she back in the Kylix? Were her friends somewhere in the darkness around her, maybe still unconscious?

"You are awake," came a deep voice, one she at first mistook for the same speaker from her dream. But this man's tone was higher, less commanding and more playful.

When the light moved, she noticed its glow illuminate a giant who stepped towards her. Fear filled her when she realized it was the giant from the party. The one Tresstéanna had said was Grand Cline's brother, Brine.

BELENT HEARD the conversation buzz around him. His mind and body were tired from their ordeal over the past few hours.

The celebration had been stressful, a party he and his

friends had had to perform at. Magic always took a toll, but that magic had been exceptional.

Tresstéanna and the two wizards had aided him in playing the part of teachers to the giants' leaders, Cline and Carrington. Despite them tricking Cline into believing it was him and not the gifted who had performed the magic last night, he still worried their ruse was discovered.

Trickery was not in Belent's nature and using his new gifts to trick felt wrong. Even though he and his friends had been enslaved, it still felt dishonest.

When they had returned to their quarters, he had been pleased to see the rescue party. It would be nice to return to their original quest of saving Genoa and returning her Corpuscle body to the cradle, then return home to Genoa, a land where magic and magical creatures were free, not enslaved like they were here in Midzark.

He watched as Kriston carried the sleeping queen, Tresstéanna, into the back room. Inside he smiled for the two. Their love for each other was apparent and, for a second, he thought quickly of his dead wife, Mala. Regrets and wishes passed inside his mind until the prince returned to the common room with a smile on his face.

Belent had vowed to protect the goddess, Genoa. That vow had also included protecting the one charged with Genoa's safe return, Tresstéanna. He now extended that oath to the protection of Kriston too. If Belent's new sorcerer powers could aid in the safety of either, then he would ensure they had their happy ending.

Kriston sat down and rejoined the discussion. The dragon warriors continued to ask Amándo about the palace and its daily activities. He knew they hoped to discover something that would aid in their escape. First, they had to gain the globe and eye, then they would try to free as many Latria as they could.

Once free, they talked about returning to the Kylix, the cave they had been traveling in before they had been attacked. The talk had turned to speculation about the cave when Belent's head started to buzz.

The vision slammed into him full force and doubled him over in pain. A deep voice spoke to him and a purple flower passed before his eyes, then the vision cleared. He discovered he was lying on the hard wooden floor with his friends gathered around him.

"Is Col awake too?" someone asked as Belent blinked to clear his eyes. He was shocked to discover tears leaking from them as he tried to sit up.

"No, stay down," someone commanded, and a glass of water was placed against his lips.

"I am fine," he insisted and found his voice a little shaky.

"What of Leian?" Hilar ask.

"Get away from me!" he heard Col demand. He smiled as the wizard continued to bark out that he was fine and demanding he be allowed to get up.

"I too am fine, please," he said as Stria's pretty face came into view above him. Her dark face was filled with worry and panic as she helped him return to his chair.

"What in the king's blasted name was that?" Col exclaimed, and Belent realized even the wizard's voice sounded wobbly.

"Let the lad up," Farin said. Belent looked over and noticed Kriston and Leian had been knocked out of their chairs as well. Kriston's pale face stared at him while Leian moved towards the table, with Hilar's help, while Stria assisted Belent.

"Took you too?" Col asked as he turned his gaze at the prince. Kriston nodded and was handed a glass of water. "He needs something a bit stronger!" Col barked and quickly handed Kriston his ale flask. "Here, this will put the color back in your ugly faces."

The prince took a gulp of ale and then handed it to Belent, who took a deep drink and then passed it to Wizard Leian.

"What happened to you?" Farin asked as warmth seeped back into Belent.

"A vision, one that apparently only affected magics," Col grumbled as he too sat at the table.

With this revelation, Kriston quickly stood and marched back into the bed chamber where Tresstéanna slept.

"You all saw a vision?" Amándo asked with wonder in his eyes.

Belent nodded and then turned as Kriston and Tresstéanna walked in. The queen's face was pale, and she leaned heavily on Kriston's arm. Her white dress had been replaced by a simple bed gown, but her hair was still tied to one side of her thin face.

Once again, the ale flask was passed around, and Belent smiled when the pretty queen took a deep swig. The strong drink helped put color into her cheeks, and he smiled when the delicate looking lady swiped her mouth with the back of her hand.

"Well, that was a kick in the pants," Tresstéanna said as she rubbed her hands over her eyes after passing the flask back to Kriston.

"Could that be Genoa?" Kriston asked, and Tresstéanna shook her head.

"No. It was... different. Stronger." The queen hesitated and turned to study Wizard Col. "Could it be?" she asked him and when she found no answer in her wizard's eyes, she continued. "I think it was Genoa's father."

3

PATHWAYS

Svlain's nerves were shaken as she stepped into the tent. She had spent the rest of her sleep tossing and turning and wondering about the vision.

What did the purple flower mean? Why was it needed? For what? These questions had kept her awake the rest of the night.

Her worries had increased when she found that Ava had had the same vision. The Zaeim was convinced the message was from Genoa, but Svlain had her doubts.

"This message felt different," she told her new friend as they sat around the Zaeim's table eating the first meal of the day, which consisted of small orange berries set upon thick oats drizzled with golden honey. Svlain was getting used to honey at each meal and appreciated the strong tea the Húriya people served. It helped wake her and made her feel refreshed, despite the little sleep she'd had the night before. "This was forceful, and very short."

"Have you had many visions from the goddess?" Ava asked when she handed Svlain a thick slice of honey cake.

"No, but I have been shown visions by someone who has

spoken directly to the goddess," the land nymph said as her thoughts went back to Tresstéanna. The queen's vision, given by Genoa, had been regarding the Kylix. This vision had been provided to her when she had touched the Globe of Corpuscle. This image was the only one she had ever known to be directly from Genoa, while all the other insights were formed from her gift as a seer.

In her seer visions there was never a speaker, only the images themselves. Most were events that might happen. But Svlain had learned seasons ago that her visions always had possibilities, that through her sights she could change the outcome.

This dream wasn't of an event, or even of what might happen. This was a demand.

"What should we do with this?" Ava asked, her dark eyes large and her tan face a shade paler than usual. If Svlain were to guess, she'd say the Zaeim was shaken from the vision, much like she was.

"I do not know, but I know someone who might," Svlain said, and rushed to finish her meal.

When the meal was consumed and she was dressed in a dark cloak to ward off the heat and the sun's rays, she and Ava made their way to the large beehives. The Mellifera could fly them to their destination faster than walking.

Now that the threat of the monsters born of Dreail was past, for now, Svlain felt a new urgency to be reunited with her friends from Genoa. She knew she would have to face the water creatures again but took comfort in knowing she wouldn't be alone in the next battle. At least she hoped so.

Yet she couldn't just abandon the new friends she had found in the desert people. They had stood behind her when even her origins had been in question.

These warrior people were now a part of her and her heart, and she felt torn between her original duty down in the Kylix and helping the Húriya people overcome the injustices of this world.

If she had known her queen, Tresstéanna, was fighting the same feelings, she might have been a little easier on herself. But as the large bee she now rode took off from the hot desert floor, Svlain berated herself for her thoughts.

She was still conflicted when the Mellifera softly landed in the cool shade of the oasis of Sparlynn. The young boy, Manil, was there to greet them. His face held the excitement of youth and innocence.

"Welcome Zaeim and great lady," the boy said. He bowed his head quickly. "My father awaits."

"Actually, it is Colab we wish to speak to," Ava said gently.

Nodding, Manil turned and beckoned them to follow him. Despite the rising heat of the day, the air was cooler under the palm trees of the oasis. Svlain used this walking time to collect her thoughts. She had her questions formulated as they entered the tent Colab had been placed in during his recovery.

The boy who had once been Colab the Meshi seemed better. Where the birds had attacked his head and neck, there were still angry red welts, but his wounds were healing. She noticed that skin and hair had replaced the large scales his body had once been covered by.

He was much different now than when he had been a Scarent. No longer did his limbs and joints stretch and move at odd angles. His eyes no longer shone red but were a soft green that held too many secrets and aged knowledge for a young man of sixteen seasons.

Colab smiled as they entered. Svlain questioned the smile, but then her eyes landed on Maraneal, who was sitting beside the boy. The pretty girl had one of her slender hands on Colab's forearm, and her body language spoke of more than a nurse tending to her patient.

This is good, Svlain thought and watched the boy and girl closely as she moved to stand next to Colab's bed.

"You look well," Svlain said and sat upon the low pillow next to the bed.

"I grow much stronger," Colab said and, with Maraneal's aid, he sat up in the bed.

"I see that," Svlain said after further study of the lad. "I seek your guidance."

Colab shook his head and his smile disappeared. "I no longer have any."

"Colab, you and Meshi were joined for many seasons." Svlain laid a hand on the boy's shoulder. "Do you not still hold his knowledge?"

She felt his shoulders tense as his head dropped. It was several quiet moments before he looked back up at her and finally nodded. "Ask."

"The vision," Svlain said. Colab sucked in a quick breath. "You had it too?" When he nodded, she continued. "What does it mean?"

"Rastel, Genoa's ambassador here in Midzark, spoke briefly of this land's troubles. At first, we... I mean, Meshi and I, thought he spoke of the pending attack from Dreail's children. But now I think his words ring true regarding more dangers than the monsters from beneath." Colab rubbed a hand over his hair. Svlain thought the boy did it as if confirming his hair was there, instead of the scales, but she said nothing.

"Who was the message sent by?" Ava asked as she moved closer to Colab's bed.

Svlain's hopes lowered when the boy shook his head. If Colab, with Meshi's vast seasons of knowledge, didn't know, then how would they ever understand. After he patted Maraneal's hand once, she was shocked to see him swing his legs over the low bed and stand.

"It could not be Rastel. The tone was different. But I do think the 'who' is as important as the content," Colab said as he walked slowly around the tent in contemplation. "The flower, we must find it."

"Where should we look?" Svlain asked as Maraneal walked over to Colab and steered him to one of the low pillow seats. She then handed him a drink and brought him shoes. As the girl bent and helped Colab clasp the sandals, an amused look passed between Svlain and Ava.

"Well, if we start another quest, we best first reunite with the others," Colab said as he placed a hand on Maraneal's shoulder. "Thank you for all you have done."

Colab tried to stand and looked shocked to find his way blocked by Maraneal. Svlain and Ava kept quiet as the girl gave Colab a stern look. Her hands were on her slim hips, and she was tapping her dainty foot on the soft carpet.

"Do not think you can go without me," she hissed, crossing her slender arms in defiance.

"I must. We must travel to where the others are, across the desert and into where the giants dwell." Colab shook his head. His soft green eyes held compassion as if he were speaking to a child instead of a girl his own age. "You cannot come."

Svlain's respect for the girl increased when Maraneal barked out a quick laugh and shook her head, sending her long dark hair swaying.

"Why do you laugh?" Colab demanded.

"I laugh because you actually think you can stop me," Maraneal said with another chuckle and a final nod of her head.

SHIARRA WATCHED with growing fear as the giant Brine walked toward her. His dark eyes held curiosity and something else she mistook for lust, but she was soon to learn was possessiveness.

Brine, like most of his brothers, held possessions in high esteem, always yearning for what others held, and most of all, yearning for what his brothers owned. Shiarra was just an item to him, a gifted who had been owned by his brother. And who now was his.

After the lantern was set on the floor, she cringed away from him as he rubbed his hands together, as if excited over a new toy. She didn't see any other movement in the darkness and knew there must be an exit to the cave they were in.

Hope was fickle. For one moment she envisioned herself racing out of the cave and into the wide openness, free. Free to return to her friends who might only be a short distance off.

Yet in the next moment, she remembered that she and her friends had thus failed to obtain freedom from these giants. Even in the palace they had not gained their escape. How would she then secure freedom from a cave she didn't know the location of?

"My brother," Brine said and Shiarra felt the loathing in the family term as the giant drew even closer, "would have kept you and your friends prisoner until your dying days."

Unsure of his intent, she kept quiet as she called her magic forward. She was not a helpless woman after all. She was now a full wizard. She knew her defensive magic couldn't cause much harm to a giant, but a well-aimed spell might cause discomfort.

"It has been my intention to free you and your friends, reset the balance so to speak," Brine continued as he held out a large hand, as if trying to aid her up from her lying position.

The word "free" had much effect on the wizard. When Brine had uttered the word, her magic died immediately as uncertainty took ahold of her. Did this giant just state he was freeing her? Releasing her from her captive's snare?

Thoughts raced around inside her mind as she studied the man's large hand. He held no weapons, no ropes to tie her up with, and no Remora bug to stifle her magic. If he was offering her freedom, at what price would it be given?

Knowing she needed time to gather information, she hesitated a moment more before setting her hand in his large one. He smiled and she studied his eyes. They still held secrets, secrets she would have to discover.

"Free?" she asked as he helped her stand.

Brine nodded then quickly released her hand. He picked up the lantern and beckoned her to follow him. The cave led to another smaller one, which then ran into a large cavern.

This large hollow had an exit out of the rock. At least she hoped it was an exit. The cave's opening was wide and had large wooden beams that blocked most of the span, but daylight could be seen beyond. The sight of tree branches and blue sky gave her some relief. It was at this time that she realized her time in the Kylix had given her a discomfort of being underground.

Casting a glance around, she realized that there were both Nephilim and Gi Jón milling about doing chores. This was something she found interesting. Did Brine enslave his own Gi Jón or were these loyalists who willingly served the Prime's brother?

"Come, you must be hungry," Brine said as he walked over to an alcove in the large cave.

As she slowly followed, she studied the layout of the area. Six large guards were positioned next to the cavern's entrance. She imagined there would be more outside but felt these six were enough to prevent her from fleeing out that way.

She noticed three smaller tunnels leading out of the cave, besides the one she had just stepped out of. Two had Gi Jón coming and going while the third only had giants moving in and out of it. This gave her pause, and her feet faltered as she followed Brine.

Maybe this was another exit. She quickly dismissed the thought. There were more giants within this tunnel than the ones guarding the exit. Fleeing out of the exit or tunnel were equally impossible to her.

Hurrying to catch up to Brine, she found him standing next to a small table. A Gi Jón woman was setting food at the table's center as Shiarra approached. The woman smiled quickly and, after bowing, turned to walk away without saying a word.

"Where are we?" Shiarra asked as she sat down. Since Brine hadn't made any move to walk away, she felt she might get some information from him.

"The Hessite cliffs hold many cave like this. Some are used by the Grands while others were abandoned years ago. This one," Brine said and swept his right hand out to indicate the cave behind him, "is too far from the palace to be much use. Except by me."

Any hope of escape dropped away as she saw how many giants and loyalists filled the cavern. If they were a large distance from the palace, then even if she escaped this cave, she would have to find her way in an unknown land. Knowing escape was no longer on the list, she felt boldness take over as her kidnapper stood above her and watched with intense eyes.

She was sick of these giants, sick of being held against her will, imprisoned for so long while the mission that was so important to her and her friends was placed in jeopardy. A mission that had already taken them away from their homeland. It had taken them deep underground where they had been in danger, attacked by monsters, mushrooms, and more.

Here was this new foe, standing over her like her life, her wishes, and her mission in this place didn't matter to him. She was just a pawn to him, an object to be used to gain power, or maybe to overtake his brother. As her emotions swirled around inside, her temper rose.

"Why have you brought me here?" she demanded as she glared at Brine, her fists clenched on either side of the plate set before her.

"My dear, you were brought here so we can formulate a plan to free you and your friends, the other gifted who are still in the palace." Brine knelt before her and placed his large hand on her shoulder.

By the time the sun started dipping behind the horizon far to the east, Zain held a deep loathing for this new land. The heat of the day had been enough to drench his shirt with sweat and fry his spirit.

He felt that he had drunk a lake full of water and still felt thirsty. His head was pounding with each step he took, despite him taking some Pedicel powder. The bright sun didn't help, though the hat Mett had lent him did keep the sun's bright rays off his face.

The land they traveled through, at first, was nothing special. Farmland stretched out as far as the eye could see, large fields where odd plants grew, some tall, some low to the ground, and all different colors than what he was used to seeing. Oranges and reds were most common, but here and there were tucked some black and blue bushes.

The odd-colored harvests were not the only differences. He felt he could never get used to seeing giants roam around.

But it was the heat that drove Zain crazy. It seemed to scorch his lungs as he took each breath. His eyes felt dry and the sweat that dripped into them did little to help.

Bugs the size of his fist buzzed around in the heat, trying to land on any exposed skin. Nek had provided a salve that kept the insects from biting, but it didn't stop them from continuing their annoying buzzing.

Timmons had thought that continuing their trek in the heat of the day was best. He hoped to remain undetected by the Nephilim guards and sneak back into the Median Forest well before dark.

It appeared the giants they saw out in the fields worked alongside the slaves. None had swords or weapons but instead pulled carts that held produce. They mostly traveled the vast roads while the smaller humans worked the fields.

Zain kept twisting on the path to gaze back at the cliffs and the massive structure nestled high above. His first sight of the Régorge Palace instilled awe in him. Awe and fear.

This was where most of his friends were. Timmons had told him that Kriston and the other dragon warriors were on their way into the belly of the beast, so to speak. If the two wizards, along with the sorcerer, couldn't aid their queen in escaping the fortress, then he didn't see how another handful of warriors hoped to help.

He felt reassured when Seth informed him of the glides they'd carried into the palace. They hoped these flying machines would aid in their escape.

But the sheer size of the place still gave him pause. The

large structure had five towers, one on each corner and a massive single one rising in the palace's center. Bright colors shone in the day's light, while numerous windows reflected the heat's rays. The water that ran behind, then below, the building seemed to add to its impregnability.

He had been told the palace was filled with more giants along with hundreds of loyalists, normal-sized humans who served the giants willingly. He had even been told these loyalists would turn on their own kin if it gained them a higher position.

Shaking his head, he turned his vision back towards their path. His inner thoughts veered to Svlain. The land nymph had been constantly on his mind since their separation.

He feared for her, yearned for her, and just plain ached. Seth's words about his last encounter with Svlain caused the sweat on his brow to increase. How had the slender nymph been expected to defeat monsters?

In his mind's eye, the large spiders and Draculae creatures swarmed at her helpless figure. Claws and sharp teeth snapped while they tried to rip into Svlain, all while he was far away, safely hidden in a hole that had been protected by large ants.

Frustration built in him until his hands hurt from clenching them in anger. He had to slow his breathing to calm himself and turn off his imagination. He turned his eyes back to his surroundings. He noticed the fields were becoming smaller. The countryside was now littered with bushes that looked to be covered with sharp thorns and cast little shade in the heat.

Large cracks in the dry ground had to be maneuvered to prevent tripping, and dust rose with each step and clogged his breath. The grass here was brown and dead. Zain felt the heat grow even more and wondered if he was just imagining the temperature rising.

He felt that despair was a step away as he took another swig from his water skin. After wiping his brow under his hat, he squinted into the bright desolate land.

"We are close," Nek said and changed their direction to the right a little. "Once we hit the shade, we will stop."

Zain saw Timmons nod his head as they marched on.

"Tell us about the Otomi fighters," Toku asked Seth as they walked behind Zain.

The young dragon warrior spoke to them of the freedom fighter's leader, Mayson. He spoke of the fighting that had taken place so far, and Zain felt instant respect for Mayson. Any man who would build an army to fight giants was a grand warrior in his book. Seth told them of the caves the Otomi fighters hid in, and how they had gained over half of the forest through their battles thus far.

"We had to rebuild the western bridge, but this allowed us to come and rescue you without using the bees," Seth continued. "Of course, we will need to secure the southern forest and block the Krack from the giants before we continue on our original mission."

Zain paused his steps. He felt Toku bump into his back before he moved again.

"Continue?" he muttered as he thought about the goddess Genoa's orb. "Cats!" he hissed and realized Seth was correct.

They would have to secure the tunnels and free all their friends before they could continue their search for the cradle. There was no way they could return the globe to the sacred structure with giants on their tails.

"Does Kriston have any idea how to secure the tunnels?" Toku asked. Zain slowed his steps to walk next to his friends.

"Well, not Kriston, but Mayson has one," Seth said, smiling. "He thinks we should blow up the entrance after we go in."

MARANEAL'S FATHER made quick work of gathering supplies, and, before the sun started its path towards the eastern horizon, everything had been prepared. Supplies and weapons had been strapped to the large bees, and water skins had been passed around.

Ava had already flown back to the city to gather her army. She anticipated they would start their trek across the desert to aid in the freedom of the Latria by the next morning.

The Zaeim intended to keep her promise to help the Latria who were trapped and enslaved inside the Median Forest, along with those inside the palace. Before she left, Ava had hugged Svlain and held a private conversation with the land nymph.

"We will send a first battalion on the Mellifera tomorrow. But the main army will have to trek across the desert. That may take an additional two days." Her face grew sober. *"Be careful my friend."*

"I will. Sash and Seth said most of the fighters were hidden in the northern part of the forest. Envod remembers where he took Seth. He will guide us there safely," she replied, speaking of the Mellifera rider who had flown her friends across the large expanse of sand a few days before.

Svlain found it difficult to say goodbye to the Zaeim. Her travels inside this land had been mostly with Ava. It had been the religious leader who had found her inside the Kylix and brought her out into Midzark.

Svlain had been lost inside the vast darkness of the tunnel that connected Midzark to Genoa when Ava had found her. Ava had then flown her across the desert on one of the large bees, befriending her and sharing her vision of needing Svlain.

She had been told they would reach the Otomi fighters' headquarters around sunset. The prospect of seeing her friends by the end of the day had her elated. This happy thought kept Svlain's worry at bay as they climbed up on the giant bees.

But the long journey gave her time to think. She hoped that Zain was awaiting her arrival inside the forest. She pondered how many days it had been since she had seen him and hoped he was well. She worried about Seth getting to him in time, before her vision could come to pass, the vision that showed Zain and Toku being killed by giants at the large steps leading out of the Kylix.

She was so caught up in her private thoughts and worries that she scarcely looked at the landscape far below her. The heat of the day was decreasing, and a golden sunset was lighting up the sky when they drew near the vast Median Forest.

Trees larger than any Svlain had ever seen rose above the sandy desert floor. Grasses and a marshy plain came first, then they were flying amongst the trees.

Svlain marveled at the greens and browns. The colors were so intense that she wondered if her eyes had grown accustomed to the pale golden sands of the desert. When a large green river passed beneath them, she felt its moisture hit her dry, hot face.

She took a deep breath, and her body seemed to soak up the welcoming water. The droplets were hot, but the feeling of them caused tears to form in her eyes.

Too quickly, they were once again flying amongst the trees. She started seeing homes on the forest floor and in the trees themselves. Rope ladders and bridges crisscrossed in and out of their route, causing Envod to guide their bee on a twisted path.

"There!" the guide said and pointed his left out to a rather large deck nestled between four large trees.

She noticed figures standing around the deck's edges. As they flew near, several torches were lit to ward off the pending darkness. Disappointment filled her when none of the dark faces gathered on the landing turned out to be familiar.

The bees settled easily on the massive deck and, with Envod's help, she disembarked. Colab came to stand next to her and she reached for his hand.

"Welcome!" a young lad shouted with a laugh. Turning towards him, Svlain smiled when she spotted Kiev.

"Kiev!" she said as the young goblin stepped out from behind the boy who had shouted the welcome.

"Svlain," Kiev said with a bow of his head. "Meet our friends."

The friendly boy turned out to be Max, the young brother of the Otomi fighters' leader, Mayson. She saw Cerg, who had come with Seth and Sash to Kós Kóvar so many days ago that it now felt like a lifetime to her. Sash had been alive then, before he had sacrificed himself to save her by throwing himself down into the waters to attack Dreail and allow her time to drop the Ili Yeathía into the deep waters.

They were taken into the nearest home for a large meal. Tables and chairs littered the room, which was wrapped around the tree's large trunk. Part of the building had even been carved into the wood.

The party atmosphere was disconcerting at first, but Svlain found herself comforted when Max and Kiev told entertaining stories. The two youths had formed a strong bond that she found endearing. It seemed that neither found their physical differences were a barrier to their friendship.

Kiev with his oddly shaped limbs and large eyes was alarming to most people at first, but the goblin had proven a true friend and a bright youth. Kiev had aided them in traversing the vast caverns known as the Kylix. He had proven himself both competent and friendly in their travels underground. These qualities had helped him become Wizard Col's apprentice after joining their band.

The boy, Max, was small of build and looked like his older brother, Mayson. Both had dark hair and eyes, but Max seemed to hold more humor, as if he still held wonder at everything he saw.

As the two friends told stories of battles against the giants, she found herself relaxing, even laughing at several of their stories.

Night had fallen outside the brightly lit home and the air turned cool inside the vast forest. When Mayson walked over and sat next to her, she turned her attention to the man. He wasn't much older than her, but she realized the age in his dark eyes, as if he had lived many more seasons.

"Your friends have reached the safety of the forest far to the south." Mayson's words had her leaning towards him.

"Who? Where?" she asked excitedly as Colab and Maraneal leaned forward too.

"The band that went into the tunnels, they reached the trees just after dark," Mayson said and held up a hand to stop any further questions. "They sent a bird, but the message was short. This is all I know for now."

Colab gave Svlain a reassuring smile before he returned to his conversation with Maraneal. Svlain took a moment to study the two, and a smile passed her lips.

A quick vision of the two growing old together passed before her eyes and the seer nodded her head. She had seen happiness and love in the short vision, one filled with family and children. A happy life awaited her friend.

Yes, it would do the boy good to learn to live beyond the death of the Scarent.

Suddenly weary, Svlain stood to leave.

"Are you tired?" Max was there tugging on her hand. "Come, we will show you your quarters."

With Kiev trailing behind, Max took her out into the cool air of the night and down a wooden walkway. When the trail passed between two trees, she stopped herself from glancing over the railing of the small wooden bridge. She knew they were high up in the trees and a swaying could be felt that made her uneasy. Clenching her teeth tight over the sudden fear of heights, she followed Max.

They descended a simple rope ladder and entered a wooden door. The room was small. It held only a bed and a table with a water pitcher and bowl. But the room was clean and the blankets fresh.

"There are clean clothes there," Max said and pointed at the foot of the bed. "When you wake, food will be ready. Maybe your friends will be here by then," the lad said with a crooked smile as he bowed and closed the door, leaving her to herself.

She washed the day's dirt off and found the soft clothing pleasing. After climbing into the comfortable bed, her weary body went numb as she fell into a deep sleep.

"Hello," came a sweet small voice.

"Hello," Svlain replied as the darkness that surrounded her faded. Faint light appeared, and she had the impression of her prior

vision of the purple flower. But the voice was female, not male, and the feeling of dread did not appear.

"Aunt Svlain?" the voice came again, and Svlain found herself squinting to see the speaker. As far as Svlain knew, she had no family. Who was this speaker who called her aunt?

"Who's there?" she asked. She looked around, but only the greyness was visible.

"It's me, Charlotte." The small voice sounded closer but still nothing could be seen.

"Who are you?" Svlain asked. She heard a deep sigh.

"Aunt Svlain, you have to help me save them," the voice finally said. "Stop the fighting and win the Grand lady over."

Svlain heard urgency in the small voice and her curiosity increased about the speaker. Was this a vision? Was this another dip into the unknown her powers provided?

"Save who?" Svlain asked and yet again tried to look into the grey fog.

"Everyone," came the response, and Svlain's skin prickled. "Befriend the Grand lady. Help her and hers to help everyone!"

With this the small voice grew strong and when Svlain blinked, a very young girl wearing a night dress stood before her. Long dark hair hung around a pretty face, but it was the girl's eyes that held Svlain's attention. She knew those eyes. Tresstéanna had them too.

When the girl smiled, Svlain returned the gesture.

"Save everyone," she said with another smile, and then she vanished before Svlain's eyes.

4

THAT WHICH HIDES

Biard the Wright was furious.

The Scarent sorcerer paced in his chambers nestled inside the home he had called Maglor. His strong legs ate up the ground as he walked around his rooms. One of his hands reached up and stroked the scaly fin that covered the sides of his head as his odd eyes narrowed.

It had been days since the thieves had stolen from him. Taken his one prized possession, the Ili Yeathía, the stone that held many powers.

A smile passed Biard's lips, showing his sharp fangs as he thought of the thief Rastel, who had been dispatched by his own powers. But even this thought gave him pause. Had he used his powers to kill the ambassador, or had the powerful creature used its own?

He remembered being confused at the creature's quick disappearance and thought back to what had happened when he had cornered it.

"Rastel," Biard said as his yellow teeth shone in the darkness. "You have failed once again."

"Failure happens when you do not try," Rastel said calmly,

invisible to any normal creature. His unseen form did not glimmer in the moon's light, but the Biard's eyes remained on him, nonetheless.

"You are a constant disappointment to your mother," Biard mocked as he remained crouched in his spot, his strong arms and legs coiled much like the snake he resembled. "Return what is mine, ambassador." The last title was given with a sneer as a large scaly hand was held forward.

"The Ili Yeathia was never yours," Rastel said calmly. The mellow tone infuriated Biard.

"I possessed it," Biard hissed and thrust his hand closer. "Return it to me."

"I hold not what you seek," Rastel said as several Carron, Biard's beasts, flew down out of the dark to perch on nearby branches or rocks.

"You have it. My creatures told me you took it from me. Give it." Biard thrust his hand closer to where Rastel stood, anger blocking his vision and turning it red with blood.

"You have been so busy chasing me that you have been blinded by the truth." Rastel raised one hand forward. "Yet know this: when my mother regains her full strength, you will be held accountable for your actions."

"You tricked me," Biard the Wright screamed, and his outstretched hand turned to a claw as he raced forward.

Rastel flung himself aside, then, using his power, shattered himself into thousands of pieces before Biard could regain his feet.

Despite not having any corporeal body, his voice spoke loud and clear as Biard the Wright sought to attack him.

"Biard the Wright, your days on Genoa are numbered."

Panic filled the powerful creature as this memory thrummed inside his mind.

Turning quickly, he marched to his inner vault. Using his magic, he passed beyond several traps and entered the outer vault. There were four vaults, one outer chamber, and two more secured, hidden crypts. The fourth had only been a hidden box under the inner sanctum's floor, but it now stood empty.

What he sought today was in the second chamber. Its walls were lined with magical possessions Biard had brought to this foul land many years ago. Crystals, wands, and even magical hats and swords lined his inner sanctum.

He marched to the back corner, where he kept the seeing glass called the Granulice, and stopped for a minute and studied the item. The large square chunk of ice-like crystal sat on an intricate golden stand. Its see-through form had small waves under its clear surface, as if waves of water were held within it. Upon seeing it, one would pay more attention to the golden stand than the crystal itself. But the glass was misleading.

Biard ran a hand over its odd square surface, and the rock started to glow from inside. This was the possession he had coveted most before he had claimed the Tear Stone as his own. Now, it would aid him in the stone's return.

Using his magic, he guided the glow to stretch out and fill the surface of the cube. Once the whole Granulice was aglow, he called forth his wishes.

"Show me the Ili Yeathía," he demanded, and hissed in anger when nothing appeared. After trying again, he demanded to see the thief Scarent.

Instead of the crystal showing him the Scarent Colab the Meshi, it showed him a young boy. The lad had short dark hair and green eyes. He was shown flying on one of the large bees known to build hives far to the east of Biard's homes.

"It is broken!" Biard hissed. He lifted his hand from the Granulice as his anger overtook him. Filled with rage, he went on a rampage. When the red haze of fury subsided, he found his vault in ruins. The Granulice had been knocked over and several more broken items lay in ruins.

Sweeping his hand over the mess, he put the room back to its former order and then turned on his heels and left.

As his impressive form marched through the vast stone halls of his fortress, the scowl on his scaly face had many of his Sleman and Carrons fleeing. The snake-like creatures slithered away while the black birds took flight out of the vast windows.

If the Granulice wouldn't show him what he sought, he would find it himself.

GRAND CARRINGTON SAT in her rooms high in the Régorge Palace and felt her emotions threaten to overtake her.

Loneliness, despair, sadness, and fear were the main feelings she could put words too. But underneath all these was a feeling of urgency. It beat with each of her heart throbs and sang out inside her mind as she sat quietly in her favorite chair.

Her feet were nestled atop the pretty cushion and her tea had been placed at her elbow. Looking around, she noticed the pretty bottles containing perfumes, powders, and dyes she used for her face. That day's jewelry, pretty yellow and green gems, still lay atop her dresser. Ribbons and barrettes littered the surface below the golden mirror in her room.

Her massive bed with its canvas cover adorned one wall, and thick rugs covered the floor. Her closet door stood ajar, and she saw all the colorful gowns she had. Reds, golds, greens, and more flashed before her as she thought of the yards of fine silks they were made of.

Plushness encircled her, yet the turmoil inside denied her

the deep calm she usually felt while resting here. Her eyes closed to her surroundings as she thought through the issues causing her discomfort.

Slaves.

Was it wrong to own another? To deny that living creature their own rights?

Love. Life. Happiness. The choices she took for granted on a daily basis had been denied to those who were mere floors below her.

Even now, there were those who ran around her home doing her bidding. Women and men who had no choice in their work, let alone their personal lives.

Unaware of her actions, she placed a protective hand over her stomach where her sleeping baby lay. Charlotte.

Her mind was so filled with turmoil that she was shocked when an idea formulated. Acting quickly, she arose and found her dark cloak.

Quickly, before she could talk herself out of her actions, she fled from her rooms, rooms she knew she was safe in, protected and well cared for.

She fled down the massive hallways of her home as if demons were chasing her. She was careful not to be seen, hiding when someone drew close and running when she found the way forward empty.

Finally reaching the large gates leading out to the open bridge, she paused. This gateway represented the barrier between safety and the unknown.

Could she? Should she? These questions cried out in her mind, but they were soon drowned out by the urgency of her unborn child's words.

We denied freedom to those who deserved it.

Grand Carrington found the courage to step out of the shadow of oppression and into the light. She slid quietly and unseen from the shadow of the Nephilim palace and disappeared into the darkness of the night beyond.

For the first time in her life, she breathed freedom for herself.

THE DARK FOREST that surrounded Zain and his friends was foreign to him. Sights, sounds, and smells assaulted his senses.

The animals that called the Median Forest home cried out odd and horrible noises. Screeches and death calls are what Zain compared the sounds to.

Mett warned him of the giant moths that called the trees home. Moths as large as a man.

"They are harmless, but when they silently swoop down from the trees, they can give you good fright," Mett warned with a smile.

"That is how they mate," Bail, who had been quiet during most of the trek, said with a smile. "They call silently to each other and use their massive wings to stir the air with their perfume. It is what lures the females out."

Zain wasn't sure if it was the moth's perfume or just the smell of the forest plants, but a heavy fragrance hung in the air. He found it too sweet and pungent to be pleasing. It swirled around him and his friends as they made their way slowly forward towards the vast Tabescent River.

Their pace was slower in the trees as the enemy held most of the western forest in their grip. Far east, where they currently traveled, only animals and an occasional giant army patrol roamed.

When they had first entered the trees, Zain had been overwhelmed by their sheer size. A sharp neck pain had been his indication that he had been gazing up for too long.

Nek had sent a note to Mayson, the leader of the freedom fighters by way of a black bird, something Toku had been immensely interested in.

"How do you train these birds?" Toku had asked the scout.

They had been told the Ennut birds were homing birds, that they sought their roosts, which the Otomi fighters kept high in the trees near their houses.

"When we carry them from their nests, they are able to fly home. And since they carry our messages, we take care of them and their young," Nek replied with a smile.

"So, they can only deliver a message to home, not the other way?" Toku asked as he scratched his chin.

"It is enough for us tonight," Captain Ray said as he urged them to continue walking in silence. Zain didn't know the captain's hesitation was due to the large Degurt, a giant lizard with sharp teeth that lived in the waters. One had attacked Kriston several nights before. But when Seth told them of this attack, Zain quickly looked around.

"Steer clear of the waters when we get close," Seth warned. "They also hide in the underbrush."

Zain had no wish to run into a scaled monster, so his eyes kept sweeping the path ahead. They ran into two more giants' patrols before they reached the safety of the Otomi fighters' first hidden camp.

"The Nephilim hold all to the south from here; only two of their small forts are west. We have held this line for the last three days," Bail said as they were greeted by the Otomi guards.

Once they were ushered inside the lines of the Gi Jón,

there was a quick discussion about proceeding or taking a break.

"We need rest. The path ahead is still long and treacherous," Captain Ray urged as he stood toe to toe with Zain.

"If our friends have escaped the palace, we should hurry and meet them," Zain said with urgency, while his mind thought only of seeing Svlain again. He had been told she and several Húriya had been spotted flying the Mellifera bees into the forest earlier that evening. This fact had Zain's heart racing and his feet wanted to catch up with it.

He argued for proceeding as soon as possible, but it was Seth who had him finally backing down.

"My friend, she will be safe with Mayson and his group until tomorrow," Seth said as Ray and the others moved off to find their beds. "We will rest for a time, until light, then tomorrow you can see her again."

Zain couldn't argue with Seth because the young dragon warrior had immediately turned his back and marched off, presumably to find his own bed. He found it hard to argue with someone who was absent. Shrugging his shoulders, he asked Mett where he could lay down and soon found himself fast asleep in the strange forest.

When Zain awoke it wasn't to daylight or even a friendly face shaking him to his breakfast. Instead, the sound of clanging metal woke the warrior quickly. Scrambling for his sword, he saw Toku standing nearby, his long staff in one hand and his sword in the other.

"They have breached the barrier," Toku hissed as Captain Ray came running up to them.

"Quickly. This way," Ray hissed as he moved to climb up a hidden rope ladder.

When arrows started whizzing past them, they all moved faster. One large arrow imbedded itself in the tree trunk inches from Zain's head, and he scrambled for cover.

However, no further arrows flew at him, making him think the prior one had been a lone rogue shot.

Zain discovered the next ladder was nothing more than a rope with knots tied every foot to give the climber an easier purchase. The three friends climbed with their weapons sheathed. Only their breathing could be heard above the sounds of fighting far below and the occasional whiz of a stray arrow.

Zain's eyes kept searching for the enemy but, so far, he only heard the sound of battle. Nothing below or above could be seen. Only the trees and branches filled his eyesight.

When they finally reached a landing far above them, it was to find the rest of their group waiting. Each held their weapons ready, and Timmons moved and quickly cut the rope Zain, Toku, and Captain Ray had just scaled.

"Quickly," Timmons said and moved to follow their guide Nek.

The man had them racing along the high rope bridges above the tree homes and walkways. Several roofs and wooden paths could be seen in the dim moons' lights. Zain couldn't be sure, but he thought it was Lazerith that shone above the leaves, somehow. Its yellow glow gave him comfort while in the strange land.

When the sound of fighting grew faint, Zain felt their pace finally slow. Several times they had descended one or two levels, but then they would quickly climb back up to the very edge of the tree canopy. Nek later told them that the higher pathways were scarcely used by giants as the branches were unable to hold their weight.

"The smaller rope ladders are only used by the Gi Jón people. We must only watch out for loyalists up here, but they should be considered equally dangerous," Nek said with a grim expression.

"If the ladders haven't been tampered with," Mett said

quietly, which had Zain worrying about falling to his doom by way of a cut rope.

As they drew closer to the river, Zain felt the moisture in the air increase. The sound of the waterfall was still far off, its roar barely audible above his own breathing. Finally, the temperature dipped to a comfortable level as they neared the river.

They were two floors above the temporary bridge that spanned the river when Nek motioned them to a stop.

"Where are the sentries?" Zain heard Nek mumble as he leaned forward to study the wide bridge.

"What is wrong?" Captain Ray asked as he moved to stand next to the guide.

"The sentries, there should be ten, five on this side and the others on the far end of the bridge." Nek shook his head and motioned for them to stay hidden. "I will go look ahead. Stay here. Only come if you hear me call to you," Nek said as he looked directly at Ray.

Ray nodded his head then motioned for the others to stay hidden. As a group they watched Nek quickly scramble back the way they had just come. Zain figured he would approach the bridge from another angle in case it was now held in enemy hands. This way his approach wouldn't give away their current hiding location.

Sweat dripped down his back as he watched the man's dark form disappear from his view. Turning, he studied the bridge ahead as if his life depended upon it, which, in fact, it did.

Hidden in the tree tops, the small band waited quietly. Zain's legs were starting to cramp from his crouched position, but he remained still, using this time to listen and think. It was several more moments before they finally saw Nek's figure slowly approach the bridge.

"He's not alone," Seth hissed as he crouched next to Zain.

Their guide appeared near the bridge; he was being followed by a very large giant.

TRESSTÉANNA'S DAY had been long.

After the shared vision, everyone found sleep impossible. They sat around the table during that day's high noon sleep time and discussed the vision's implications.

When she and her friends had finally gone to their beds, it had been well into the fourth hour of the long day. Darkness had already set outside the windows again. She was thankful that day's magical lessons had been cancelled because of the prior day's celebration.

Yet even now, after waking, as the bright sun peeked into the little window in her room, she found it hard to believe that the goddess's father had been the one to speak to them through a vision. But deep down she felt this to be true.

Cats, she thought as she followed Belent to the stairs that led up to the giants' section of the palace. *Genoa's father? Who would that be? God?* These thoughts left her head spinning, so she decided she would ask the goddess the next time she spoke to her.

For now, she needed to focus on her new task. The plan was a simple one. If all went well, by the end of the hour they would hold the Globe of Corpuscle in their possession. If their scheme failed, she might very well find herself back in the hated mirror.

This thought had a memory trying to surface in her mind. She tried to grab at it, but it flittered away when they reached the top of the stairs.

Giving one quick knock, Belent stood on the landing and waited for the giant guards to allow them to exit the slave quarters. They had sent a message earlier to the Grands asking for an audience and had been granted.

Their plan, which had been approved by all, had been to contact the Grands and ask about the status of their missing friend, Shiarra. Belent would disappear from Tresstéanna's side well before she reached the grand hall, at which time she would then be presented to the giants alone.

This was one of the flaws they had discovered while imprisoned here. The stair guards were told that slaves were coming and going, but never how many. Tresstéanna had requested an audience for her alone. She had excluded Belent and Leian on purpose. Yet the stair guards didn't know this fact, so when they were told the gifted were allowed an audience with the Grands, they assumed the ones at the top of the stairs had been summoned.

After leaving the slave quarters and passing beyond the guard's sight, Belent quickly disappeared using his sorcerer's skills. Seeing her friend use his magic still gave Tresstéanna a start, but she smiled as she turned to continue her path to the hall.

Belent's mission was simple—find the Greilk box then return to this hallway well before Tresstéanna was finished with the Grands. She had planned a long speech she would aim at Cline and Carrington and hoped this would give her friend plenty of time to conclude his mission. Using the Midzark clock, they estimated only half an hour's time would be needed

Since Belent had a great distance to travel, she slowed her pace as she walked. She hoped to use this conversation to try and convince the Grands to release her and her friends. She knew this would fail. If it was just Grand Carrington, she felt she would have a chance in succeeding. But Grand Cline was the chink in her chain.

Thoughts on how to turn Cline's mind from his traditional Midzark upbringing had kept her awake many nights. Only the plans regarding Carrington had ever resulted in a positive outcome. Each time she tried one of the schemes to adjust Cline's thoughts, they had resulted in failure. Some had even resulted in hostility towards the gifted.

Lessons had been uncomfortable after each attempt. Grand Cline had sat angrily through the classes after several attempts, almost sneering at them as they taught.

The very last attempt had resulted in Cline cancelling classes for the next day. This hostility had concerned the four from Genoa. They wondered if Cline was wise to their trickery and decided as a group they would focus their attempts at Carrington.

Yet even now Tresstéanna wasn't willing to quit her attempts to sway the two giants' beliefs regarding slavery.

When she entered the hall, she noticed two things that made her blood run cold. The first was that Grand Carrington was absent from the meeting. It was just her and Grand Cline present in the vast hall. Her steps faltered as she drew near.

The second thing that caused her concern was that the Greilk box lay in Grand Cline's lap. The giant's large hands rested lightly on the box's lid. She now knew that Belent's mission to locate and grab the box would fail.

The room was the same as her last visit. The two thrones stood high on the dais, but only one chair was filled. Grand Cline's face held a sour sneer as he watched her approach.

The doubt that grew in her was not a feeling she was used to. She was queen of Valorna, dragon warrior, and one of America's most wanted. She wasn't scared of anything!

This internal reminder made her square her shoulders as

she approached the giants' leader. She gave the formal bow of Midzark, as expected, and after straightening, found her pale eyes meeting the brown one's boldly.

"Since we are alone," Grand Cline stated as he studied her, "let us talk about magic."

Her feelings of doubt increased when Cline mentioned magic. After all, she was here to ask for a status regarding the search for Shiarra.

"Magic, my lord?" she asked, standing there and feeling more exposed by the minute.

"More to the point, your magic and my lack of it," Cline grumbled as he raised the box and gave it a gentle shake. "These items have failed to '*teach*' me the art of magic. I want you to explain to me why this is."

After clearing her throat, and with her heart racing inside her breast, she found her voice. She was pleased it sounded calmer than she felt inside. "My lord, the magic you have already shown has been great," she stated, trying to appease the man while stroking his ego. "You and your lady have shown great improvement since we started your lessons."

"No, what we have shown is patience in the lessons while you and your friends attempted to trick us with *your* magic."

She noticed it now. It pained her to admit it, but she saw the deception in the giant's eyes as he spoke the words she and her friends had feared. They had been duped, tricked by the Grand and used by him. Fooled into thinking they had conned the Grands when the whole time it had been *them* being deceived.

If Grand Cline had known no magic had been taught, then why had he endured the lessons? They had spent days droning on and on about magic and its properties. Did Grand Carrington know of their deceptions too?

So many thoughts filled her mind that her eyes became blind. It wasn't until Cline spoke again that her vision cleared, and she discovered the giant had dismounted the dais and was standing before her. His large form loomed above as he looked down at her.

Immediately, her warrior training kicked in and she quickly crouched in an attack stance before she could gain her thoughts.

"You are not what you appear," Grand Cline said with a smile. "But to date, you and your friends have been useful." The smile on his face had her resuming her original position as her mind raced into action.

"What do you know?" she hissed as a new plan tried to take root inside her.

"I know you have deceived me to buy time in the hopes of escape. I also know escape is impossible. I know you dearly wish to see the return of your missing friend. I too also wish that." Tresstéanna was shocked to see Cline kneel before her so he could speak to her face to face as he continued. "I know you have protected and shown my wife kindness. I know she believes in you and the other gifted."

Here Cline hesitated and turned to study the side door with a kind of longing in his eyes. When he turned back to face her, she thought she saw hesitation for the first time.

"The vision, the one of this land's future, was that true?" Cline whispered this question, and doubt filled Tresstéanna once again.

Standing firm to her resolution, she gave a small nod. "Possibilities have come to me. They are only that. The outcome can be changed." Here, her hopes to sway the Grands into releasing the Latria grew strong. "This current unbalance is causing discord in Midzark. It must be set right for this land to flourish."

When the brown eyes turned hard again, she felt her hope slip away. No, Cline would not be swayed on releasing the

Latria. But maybe Carrington and the unborn child could be used?

"After last night's display, my dominance over my people has been reinforced. With the kidnapping of the other female, however, there will be questions about my power." Cline stood once more and tightened his grip on the box he still held. "That is something I cannot have."

BELENT WAS PLEASED when his path was unhindered by giants or servants as he walked invisibly in the vast hallways of the Régorge Palace.

He had traveled this hallway once before, the first time he had roamed the halls while using his magic. At that time, he had been on a mission to locate an escape route. This quest, however, led him directly to Maven Gorphen's personal chambers.

He felt time ticking away from him as his feet flew down the massive hallways. Prior to his capture and imprisonment, he had kept time only by the sun's and moon's paths. Now, the Midzark's large clock, which sat in the classroom they had used each day, kept a blasted ticktock sound in his mind.

At first, he had found the constant sound unnerving. It was as if his life was being swept away before his eyes. Each tick matched his heartbeat and reminded him time was passing, flying from him while he was held against his will.

Days passed before he found the sound comforting. Instead of looking at the noise as a reminder that he was imprisoned, it now reminded him that he was, in fact, alive. Each tock now brought possibilities.

He, along with Tresstéanna, had found Midzark's use of a clock and calendar empowering. It felt to him that time had been tamed, defined and organized into segments.

He remembered that Anna had told them of how Earth had used clocks and calendars to delineate the passing of each moment. Prior to his time in Midzark, that concept had seemed unthinkable. For those who lived in Genoa, time had always been told by the position of the moons.

Now he found the ticking of seconds and minutes useful as he crept along the passageway of the giants. Tresstéanna and he had agreed upon a time allowance to ensure he gained access back down into the Latria quarters. If he was late, he may find access back into the locked floors impossible.

As he was a new sorcerer, his magic was still in its infancy. But its presence was something he took comfort in. He remained on the task, but his saddened heart betrayed him as he thought of returning to Genoa.

He missed his home; he missed his wife and child. But even when he returned to the lands of Genoa, he would never get to return to his family.

When he neared the Maven's private rooms, he brought his mind and heart back to the task. Gain the Greilk box. Hide it away from the Maven, bring it back to the queen, and then they could escape from the palace.

The next steps were beyond his thoughts at this moment. Only the box was his mission. As he neared the massive door, he hesitated before he reached for the tall door handle.

It was this hesitation that saved him from discovery. His hand was only inches from the knob when it gave a quick jerk and the door flew open.

"What do you mean?" Maven Gorphen demanded as he marched out of the rooms with the Prime Magal close on his heels. "She has gone?"

"I said we cannot locate her," the military man said.

These words gave Belent pause in his mission. Did Magal mean they could not locate Shiarra? Maybe they were calling off the search for the wizard. But if so, what of the magical sword he had given the giant named Mayvers?

Taking only a second to decide, he delayed his mission to enter the Maven's rooms and quickly and quietly followed the two. He estimated he had time for a small detour and hoped this one would net him information about Shiarra's location.

"Where do your men look?" Maven Gorphen demanded as they marched back down the long hallway.

"Most of the floors have been searched." Magal's words confused Belent and his steps faltered when he heard this.

Floors? Are they searching the palace for Shiarra? he thought and quickly moved to catch up with the two, who had continued down the hallway.

"What of her servants? What do they say?" Gorphen asked with worry in his voice.

It was this question that had Belent convinced the search was not for Shiarra, but for Grand Carrington. This discovery had new questions forming. Had they abandoned the search for their friend? After all, Magal had been sent on the important mission to search for Shiarra last night right after the kidnapping. Why had he returned to the palace? Maybe they had already located Shiarra. This could explain why Magal had returned already.

These questions overwhelmed Belent's mind, and he almost missed the conversation that was continuing.

"They stated she went to bed, but when they arose to dress her, she was missing," Magal said, and now Belent heard concern in the military man's voice.

Turning on his heels, Belent raced back to Maven Gorphen's room. If Grand Carrington was missing, this was not as important as his current mission.

He skidded to a halt in front of the massive door, raised his hand, and tugged on the knob. Finding it locked did not shock him. He expected no less from the Maven. He withdrew the tool he had whittled from one of the wooden spoons stolen from the kitchens.

The spoon was now the size and shape of a key lock but held no ridges. But in the making of the tool he had imbued it with magic, his magic.

Slipping the tool into the hole, he heard an audible click and the heavy door swung wide open. He quickly slipped in and shut the door behind him. Belent stood just inside the room and took a deep breath.

Time was running out.

Racing across the room, he found the second door and moved to unlock this closet. This is where the Maven kept magical items he was actively researching.

Most of the precious items were locked and kept in his official office. It was in that office the magical Pagilda mirror was kept. That mirror had imprisoned him and his friends the first day of their arrival in Midzark.

He unlocked the closet and scanned the shelves. He found Tresstéanna's dragon scale shield and snatched it up. Using the strap, he flung it over his back and continued his search.

The shelves were covered with odd items. Rocks and books littered the bottom shelf. He found a book with odd writing on it and when he moved his eyes beyond it, he was shocked to see the same book on the next shelf.

Thinking it was a duplicate book and not finding the box he sought, he looked on the third shelf and found the book again. Seeing it here stopped his search for the box, and he hesitantly bent to restudy the first shelf.

Finding the book there, he glanced up and noticed the book vanish and appear where his eyes landed. Unsure what this meant, he shook his head and stood to study the last and final shelf, where the book reappeared before his eyes a final time.

Placing one hand over the binding, he closed his eyes and focused. Using his magic, he transformed the odd shapes into writing he could understand.

"This is your book" was now written in the language he had grown up reading and writing. His magic told him the book itself was enchanted, but he sensed no threat from the book and after a small hesitation, he grabbed it and thrust it under his shirt.

After rechecking the shelves and finding no Greilk box, he relocked the closet and raced back to the door.

Counting his time as he quietly ran back to the meeting spot, he was pleased to see Tresstéanna had not yet returned. Their agreed upon meeting spot was beyond a sharp corner, hidden from the two giant guards that watched the locked door that led down to the Latria quarters.

The guards were not to protect the slaves but ensure none exited the lower levels without permission. Most Latria had daily chores that brought them above their locked levels, but these duties were mostly completed between two and four o'clock. Since it was nearing the eighth hour in a ten-hour day, most of the duties had already been finished. The palace was growing quiet, and its residents were settling down for sleep, which took place during the hottest part of the day.

As he hid and waited, his hand brushed over his shirt where the odd book was tucked. If he felt disturbed at himself for stealing the book, he shook this discomfort off by reminding himself the items in the closet had probably been stolen by the giants themselves first.

As the minutes ticked away, his curiosity grew. He pulled the small leather book from its hiding place and read the cover. It still held the odd title, 'This is your book.' No author or insignia was found on the side or back of the book. Opening the tome to the first page, he found the foreign language, but after blinking once, the words transformed. Without the use of his magic, he was able to read the words, which were now in his own language.

"Her deceit was discovered. Return to your friends downstairs."

Pausing, Belent thought it odd a book would start with these strange words, so he continued reading.

"Go now, use your magic and disappear. The door will be opened in twenty seconds."

A thought occurred to the sorcerer as awareness filled him like a drug. This book, was it talking to him?

"Yes! Go now!" The written words had the tall man quickly shutting the book. Using his magic, he disappeared and then raced around the corner.

5

FOLLY OR FOE

Grand Cline liked to think he was a patient man.

He had bid his time in the many long lessons given by the gifted. During the teaching, he hadn't been idle. He had used the time to gain knowledge of the magic he so desperately sought. He yearned to discover how magic worked, its deep hidden secrets that had eluded him and his kind for many years.

But after the third day of those lessons, he knew without a doubt that he and his kind would never gain magic. Never feel the flow of power course through his body to be released through a shower of sparks and color. Never feel the power of it inside him.

He didn't know if it was a fault of the gifted and their training, or if it was something lacking in him and his kind. The latter seemed more possible as he had tried hard, in and out of the class, to replicate the small tasks they had been assigned.

When Carrington had been able to produce magic, his belief had wavered until he asked her to duplicate it outside of the classroom. She had tried to light many candles in their bed chambers and failed at every attempt.

When she'd admitted that she didn't know how she had performed the magic, his suspicions had been confirmed.

No giant could perform magic.

The Maven had voiced this concern long before the four gifted had been presented to them. His years of study in all things magical had formed this conclusion. The Maven was convinced magic was lacking in the Nephilim race.

Now, this confirmation resulted in a horrible impact on him emotionally. Depression was a pain Cline tried to overcome. It ate away at him like a cancer, ripping out chunks of his personality until he was drained and empty.

Even now, as he knelt before the small gifted woman, he felt the loss of something he'd never had. But he knew that power could still be his, through this female and her friends. He may not wield magic from his hands, but magic would still bend to do his bidding.

"Those who stole your friend, they would have me and my wife banished. Control would change hands and you and your friends would be ordered to do their will." Cline hissed the last words, and he saw the fear in Tresstéanna's pale eyes. "I would not be able to protect you."

"Protect?" she asked as hesitation now filled her face.

"Yes, protect. The Latria quarters have been used to keep you from those who stole the other woman," Cline said, his words spoken carefully. "My men seek to return her, but until she is found, you and your kind are in danger. The magical show you presented last night was impressive. However, I was told by my Prime that, before you were brought to the palace, he had seen your gifts in battle."

Silence hung in the large room as Cline stood once again and looked down upon her, deep in his own thoughts. He had admired the way this woman stood tall. She had an elegance in her stance, but he suspected her form also hid a fighter. She moved with grace born of those with power, and he quickly had a fleeting thought that she might have held a position as a ruler. Even now her eyes burned with defiance.

"The gift of magic cannot be mine. It does not appear to do much harm against us Nephilim, but it could." He lifted the box and the woman's eyes grew large with longing. He did not know exactly what the items in the box did, what magic they held, and part of him didn't care. What he did know was that each time the box had been presented in class, it had been this woman who had withdrawn the red ball. Each time she held it, she cradled it like a loved child. This act betrayed the importance of the orb.

This ball and the pretty jewel within the box were two items Cline had forbidden the Maven to touch or research. It had been his deep understanding that these two things were valued by the gifted. Valued and revered. Now, when his hand brushed the top of the box, he noticed something else in the woman's eyes.

Desire.

"Do these items really increase your gift?" Cline asked as he held the box up as if to open it. When she took a small step forward, he smiled. "Would they assist you in locating your friend?"

When she remained silent, his temper grew. He had known this woman would not serve him freely. Her kind never had. He had to take a deep breath to stamp down his anger.

Changing tactics, he nodded and held the box out. He saw uncertainty in her blue eyes at his gesture.

He nodded and knelt once again. "Consider it a gift. Both items you seek are in here. I give them to you with the understanding that you use them to find your friend. Return her to us here in the palace, and you and yours will be given the highest position and rewards. You will become my advisors in all magic. You and yours will want for nothing."

Mistaking the woman's smile for acceptance of his offer, he allowed her to take the box from his outstretched hands with a nod.

ZAIN CROUCHED next to his friends from Genoa as they watched the makeshift bridge far below them. The Otomi fighters had laid a long rope ladder across the span of the Tabescent River. Large rocks kept the water bubbling as the liquid moved eastward.

The sun's rays hadn't yet reached them, but its light faintly illuminated the empty bridge and its surroundings. The trees were taller here near the bank of the river. Many homes had been built in the tall trees, some sitting on top of the next. Yet none had been built on the ground. Zain wondered at this but was quickly told about the dangers of the Degurts, a creature that lived in the river.

This explained why the bridge and the homes had been suspended well above the water. No lights shone in the huts that surrounded them; the only light was from Nek's lantern.

Nek stood feet from the end of the roped bridge and looked back up. He waved and signaled towards where Zain and his friends still hid. His lantern shone on the cloaked giant that stood next to their guide.

They couldn't see any weapons on the giant and as Nek continued to wave to them, they all understood the way forward was clear. None hesitated as they left the safety of their hiding place to join the guide down below.

Quickly descending the ladders and nearing the bridge, Zain was shocked to see the giant was a woman. A long gown covered her figure under the cloak, which was pulled tight to hide her facial features.

Upon seeing them, Nek nodded once then turned and guided them across the bridge. Quickly and quietly they moved across the rope ladder. Nek didn't give any explanation for the unexpected giant but moved silently ahead of them.

The missing sentries were found on the far side of the structure. They told Nek that their instructions had been to take up guard on the northern shore. This guarding position was only used during fighting, in case they needed to cut the ropes that held the bridge.

"We did not see you until you showed up on the far side," one guard said as he eyed the large giant. "We knew you, but not her." He jabbed a finger at the newcomer.

Nek nodded but again gave no explanation regarding the large woman. Instead, he ignored the giantess and motioned for the guards to draw near. "We need an escort to the base," he demanded.

Ten large men and three giants came forward just as the heat of the day began to climb towards a ridiculous temperature.

Plans were made, and Zain watched as their water skins were refilled and food passed around. He was given a large round cake and, after giving it a sniff, determined it was more bread than cake. He took a bite and found the center full of meat and roots. The flavor was pleasant. He finished his and was quickly handed another.

Before they continued their journey, he had eaten two more of the round meals and had another two in his pockets for later. Seth bragged that he had eaten six, but Zain felt four was enough to keep him going for a while.

Their travels now kept them on the jungle floor. There was no need to travel up and down the ropes in an attempt to escape detection. The northern part of the forest was strictly in the hands of the Otomi fighters. This made travel easier and gave them a faster route.

Before the sun had finally peeked over the top of the Hessite cliffs in the west, they were nearing the headquarters of the resistance. Zain took comfort that his journey that day was nearing an end. His leg still pained him when he failed to rest it regularly, and a deep ache was setting in.

He was imagining a good long rest when a shout arose high above the group. The voice was familiar and his heart leaped in his chest. Glancing up, he saw Svlain quickly descending a rope ladder a few feet away.

Forgetting his exhaustion and discomfort, Zain raced to catch the land nymph as she jumped into his arms. Her green hair was tied back in a braid and her dress was foreign to him, but her smile warmed his heart.

Without hesitation she hugged him tight to her and snuggled into his neck. She smelled of flowers and a deep rich spice that was unfamiliar to him. He sighed with comfort and realized she felt like home in his arms.

"I have missed you," she whispered.

"When you two are done," Seth said, earning him a sharp elbow in his gut from Timmons, who had a little more patience than the youth.

Drawing Svlain away, Zain made sure to keep an arm around her as they faced their friends.

"This is Mayson," Seth said as his dark eyes scanned the trees above them. "He is the leader here."

"Welcome." Mayson greeted the newcomers with a smile. "You are all welcomed."

Zain watched Mayson's eyes land on the giantess, but Seth's urgent question had all turning his way.

"Where is Sash?" the dragon warrior demanded of Svlain as he continued to look for the large warrior. "Is he still sleeping?"

Zain felt Svlain tense beside him, and his heart sunk. He feared her words, but released her when she moved to step forward.

"Sash was true to his word. He protected me in a time of great danger. He threw himself down into the waters of the lake and attacked Dreail. His sacrifice gave me time to find the heart and drop the Ili Yeathía into its depths." Svlain's left hand reached for Seth's as her right continued to grasp Zain's. "He was swallowed by the monster that Dreail had become."

Her words brought silence as several heads bowed in remembrance of the large warrior. Memories of Sash filled Zain's mind. His large arms and quiet manner had been a constant in their travels underground in the Kylix. Zain hadn't known the man well, but another of his countrymen had been lost to this journey and sadness filled him. It was a sadness that he felt far too often lately.

Ray's voice of excitement broke the silence as he rushed towards the rope ladder.

"My king!" Ray said as he reached up to help a young man gain the floor of the forest.

"Ray," Svlain started to speak but stopped when Colab stepped forward after his descent.

"I am not Calob but Colab. Meshi was lost to me and, through the Ili Yeathía, I was returned to my normal form," Colab said with sadness on his face.

Zain saw the sadness and understood the loss. When a pretty girl descended the ladder behind Colab, Zain's eyes picked up the boy's subtle change. When the girl laid a hand on Colab's arm, Colab placed his over hers.

So, even though there was sadness, there was healing here as well, Zain thought and moved to stand next to Svlain once again.

"Tell me, how were your travels?" Mayson asked as he turned once again to study the group.

Nek stepped forward in response and spoke to his leader, but he didn't speak of their travels.

"We have met with a surprise on our trek today," the guide said as the cloaked giantess finally stepped forward from the back of the group.

In Zain's rush to see his friends, he had all but forgotten about the mysterious woman. Now, as she drew closer to Mayson, he was reminded of her presence.

"Great leader of the Latria, I present myself to you in the hopes that our people can resolve this conflict and peace can fall upon this land," the giantess said as she reached up to lower her hood.

The few Gi Jón standing around the group gasped. This put the band from Genoa on guard, but when Mayson spoke, the confusion finally became clear.

"My lady, Grand Carrington of the Nephilim. Your presence here is unexpected," Mayson said as Zain turned to study the giantess with new understanding.

Here was the wife of the leader of the Nephilim, the man who controlled the large palace and had enslaved his friends. She was before them willingly, unarmed and unguarded.

Grand Carrington stood tall, her dark brown hair braided in neat rows and piled upon her head. Gone were the brightly colored folds of dress, and no ribbons decorated her hair or garb. A small golden crown had been woven in the locks, and it sat on her brow above dark eyes that studied Mayson with intent determination.

It wasn't Mayson nor the giantess that made the first move, but Svlain herself. She quickly released Zain's hand

and boldly walked towards Grand Carrington. The land nymph never hesitated as she neared the large woman.

Carrington's eyes studied Svlain with curiosity and shock, no doubt having never seen a land nymph before. Zain watched with growing concern and almost took a step towards Svlain to protect her. But before he could act, Svlain bowed deeply and looked up at Carrington.

"My grand lady," Svlain said with a smile. "You are most welcome. I am Svlain, land nymph from the mainland we call Genoa, and I am your humble servant." Her words shocked Zain as she continued. "I have been foretold of your arrival."

Doubt crept into the giantess's eyes as she looked intently at Svlain.

"I myself did not know of my intent to be here until a few hours ago. Who told you of my arrival?" Carrington asked with speculation.

Svlain stood tall to answer, and Zain saw shock cross Carrington's face when she received the answer.

"Charlotte told me."

Kriston paced back and forth in the locked small rooms in the lower part of the Régorge Palace. To him, it seemed forever since Tresstéanna and Belent had left.

It infuriated him to have her gone from his side now, after all the time and many battles it had taken to get to her. He had made a promise to himself to keep her safe and within his sights once he got into the palace. Yet now here he was stuck in a room while she walked away from him and into danger, once again.

But he'd lost the argument about this plan hours ago. A plan that allowed Tresstéanna to dance with danger while she tried to gain the Globe of Corpuscle, the very orb and essence that was the goddess Genoa herself.

Belent and even Col had been hopeful their plan would work. The sorcerer would use his magic to render himself invisible and hunt up a box that supposedly held the globe and other items that belonged to them. The eye of Adulario was also said to be inside this box.

As he walked the short distance across the room again, his frustration rolled off him like smoke. His companions had left him to his pacing, which he was thankful for.

Farin and Hilar inspected the glides, and Kip and Stria sharpened their weapons. Patience filled their faces, yet Kriston knew they too counted the time using the blasted clock in the corner of the room. To Kriston, the ticktock the thing made seemed to mock him and his feelings with each sound. Finally, when the little points on the clock aimed at the odd symbol Tresstéanna had shown him, he walked to the door and placed his ear against the wood.

Nothing.

Turning back, he saw his friends studying him. Wizard Col had a pained look on his face but when the wizard stood, Kriston shook his head.

"They will come." Conviction was in Col's voice but did not show on his face.

"I will go out and see if I can discover anything," Amándo said, and he slipped out the door quickly, leaving the group to wait in silence.

Before, Kriston had felt that time slipped by slowly. Now it appeared to stand still. Even his heartbeats betrayed him as they kept an odd time against the noise of the clock. Sweat poured down his back as evil predictions ran through his mind. Predictions of foul endings where he and Tresstéanna were doomed to be apart forever, cast asunder by fate and life itself.

When the door did open it was to Belent, not the young slave, Amándo. Kriston was so shocked to see the sorcerer that Wizard Col moved quickly to grasp the man in his iron grip before Kriston could even move forward.

"Where is she?" Col demanded and his words burned with fear.

"She has not returned?" Belent asked and some of Col's fear poured into his pale face.

Kriston was able to finally move and closed the short distance to Belent. Spinning the sorcerer around to face him, he tried to hold his emotions in check.

"What has happened?" he demanded and was frustrated to see the man shake his head and pull a small book from his pocket.

"Now is not the time to read!" Col hissed and almost knocked the book from Belent's grip.

"No, it will tell us," Belent said quickly as he moved the book away from Col's harmful hands.

"Tell us?" Kriston asked and looked at the book with confusion. "How?"

"I do not know. I found it and it helped me get back here safely." He opened the book and studied the odd writing.

"It is in a different language; how can you understand it?" Col demanded as he glanced over the man's shoulder to look at the book's pages.

"I just do," Belent said as his fingers ran along the odd shapes on the paper. "She is safe. It says she was in a meeting with Grand Cline."

"We already know that!" Kriston said with frustration. "What we need to know is where she is now!"

"She is on her way. But we must remain here when she

returns," Belent said with a shake of his head. "We must not escape yet."

"What do you mean?" Col asked as his dark eyes turned to look at the book again. "What does it say exactly?"

Belent cleared his throat and held the book tightly in his grasp. "It says all will be revealed by the coming of night."

"Night? We must wait that long?" Stria asked from her place across the room.

All eyes turned to see the morning's rays still growing strong outside the room's window. Even now the heat was trying to beat back the coolness as the palace's vents started to pump in the chilled air caused by the waterfall underneath their feet.

"Why night?" Col asked.

"I asked and it keeps saying it depends on what page is turned. I do not know what it means. Probably some form of book humor," Belent said with a shake of his head.

"Yes, but where is Tresstéanna?" Kriston demanded once again.

"I am here," Tresstéanna said from the opened doorway. Amándo was standing slightly behind her with a smile on his face.

Kriston strode across the small room with a single step and had Tresstéanna in his arms before the others could move forward. The fear melted from him and was quickly replaced with relief, along with a small amount of anger.

"What in the king's name took you so long?" he hissed into her hair as she tried to shuffle the small box to one side.

"You're crushing me," she said with a laugh and, after he pulled her back a little, she stood up on her toes and placed a gentle kiss on his lips. "I'm back and nothing bad happened. In fact," she said and turned to the others in the room, "I have been victorious!"

"The box!" Wizard Leian exclaimed with wonder as the box was held aloft for all to see. "Is she inside?"

Tresstéanna nodded and moved to set the box on the round table. Kriston moved closer as the lid was opened.

"How?" he asked as Tresstéanna reached in and pulled the large Globe of Corpuscle out of its small depths. Next came the deep blue eye of the Protector. Kriston's own eyes grew wide with wonder at the box's magic.

"The only thing missing is my shield," Tresstéanna said regretfully, a grim expression on her face.

"I think this is yours," Belent said as he pulled her missing shield from his back. "I found it in Maven Gorphen's rooms and liberated it for you."

Her squeal of delight had them all smiling as she hugged the golden shield to her. "Now we can go," Tresstéanna said and looked at Leian. "We can go and find Shiarra ourselves."

"No." Belent quickly spoke up. "We must remain until dark."

Turning, Kriston saw Tresstéanna's face harden and knew she was preparing for an argument. Stepping quickly between the two, he placed a hand on her arm. "There is something you need to hear."

THE GIANT MAN named Mayvers held the now magical sword aloft as it glowed bright green in his hands. He remembered that the first time it had glowed, he had dropped it.

But that had been yesterday morning. That day, he and his men had followed the glowing magical sword. It had taken them up into the Hessite cliffs and far to the south.

Up and down their path had led them, over the rocks and even down into the farmlands south. Sometimes it glowed faintly, other times it burned bright even in the daylight.

Before midday, they had caught up to the Prime and his men. Upon hearing of the magical sword, the Prime had left three of his men in Mayvers command, then quickly returned to the palace to resume his duty in protecting the Primes.

Mayvers found himself now leading the expedition to locate and return the gifted witch to the palace. This was something he had felt confident in doing, until the hidden cavern had been located.

The caves had once been used as food storage for farmers. Several sheds and grain silos stood against the rock's face, confirming this. Yet, instead of being used to store food, it appeared these caves were now occupied by the Grand's brother and his followers.

Mayvers knew of Brine; he had seen Cline's brother every day in the palace. He had heard of Brine's will to overthrow the Grand and sit upon the very throne his brother occupied.

Mayvers had never been one for politics, but he was good at following orders. And at the moment, Grand Cline sat upon the throne. This meant that Brine and his followers were enemies, not allies.

"Three of you cover that crack to the left. I will take six with me. The remaining three will hang back and only rush forward when I give the signal," Mayvers instructed as he eyed the wooden structure that hid the cave's opening. He knew the cave well. It held three large rooms and a hidden exit that was now covered by his men.

Once his men were hidden and in position, he took his six and boldly marched forward, not even hiding his approach. Well before he was prepared, a shout rang out from the darkness ahead.

"Halt." Even without being told, he knew arrows were pointed at him and his men.

He may not play the political game, but he knew the ins and outs of the military. One never questioned orders. One didn't even question where the orders came from.

"Replacements," Mayvers said with conviction. He knew the guard master on duty would check the roster, if they had one. He hoped he could manipulate the roster to fit his plan.

"What replacements?" came the reply and suddenly Mayvers had doubts regarding his idea. He knew Brine's current wife was the lady Kristine. Maybe he could use this?

"Sent by the lady. She has determined more guards were needed," Mayvers replied, again holding himself with confidence. With each passing second, he could feel his men start to grow uneasy.

Finally, the order to proceed sounded, and he felt the dampness of sweat roll down his back. Falling back on his military training, he advanced to the dark opening, worried that at any moment he and his men could be cut down and their mission and lives would be lost. When they entered, the guards lowered their weapons, and Mayvers breathed a quiet sigh knowing his plan had succeeded.

"Report?" he barked at the young guard stationed just inside the wooden structure. He noticed the cave's entrance six feet to his left but dared not look at it yet. Keeping his eyes directed to the guard, he listened to the report that nothing had transpired during their watch as he smiled.

"How many are on station?" Mayvers demanded and was pleased when the count of less than twenty was given to him.

"More were promised; however, you and your men are the only relief we have seen," came the response.

Nodding, Mayvers felt his men draw closer. Giving them a quiet signal, he had them fall back and wait. When the young guard finally finished his report, Mayvers dismissed him and his men in the promise they would take up the post.

When his men were set beside the doorway, more blocking the way out than preventing anyone from coming in, he moved into the main chambers. He noticed his goal before he took a single step into the cave. The gifted woman was sitting at a small table, eating. However, his luck at finding her so soon ran out quickly. The Grand's brother, Brine, knelt next to the small woman.

Unsure how to proceed, he took up a post next to the cave's wall and thought of his next steps. While he waited, he watched the woman. When doubt crept into her face, he wondered how long it would be before Brine would leave his new possession alone.

BIARD THE WRIGHT had traveled far in the darkness of the night. His Scarent legs were long and good at keeping a fast pace.

He traveled light. Only his magic was needed now. He would track down the Scarent and kill him. Kill him like he had killed the ambassador Rastel.

With this thought, Biard's steps faltered and doubt crept into him. Had he killed the creature? Remembering Rastel's last moments kept that doubt in the forefront of his mind as he continued his journey.

When he reached the shore of the Márseille Lake, he automatically turned west and headed towards his foe. However, only a few steps later he stopped. His magic sensed a difference in the waters of the lake.

Turning, he looked closely at the turquoise water. Looking far out to where the water met the sky, he didn't notice anything, yet his gift told him something was there.

He reached out with his magic, his long snake-like arms stretching towards the unseen and his eyes wide. It took time. The sun continued to rise to his right as he felt for what was hidden.

Finally, when he was able to locate what was different, his anger grew. The magical barrier was made of bits of light, much like the Ili Yeathía had been made of. Bright little lights flickered above the surface of the waters as it kept the monsters below at bay.

He could sense the creatures far below, blocked now by the magic that had made up the Tear Stone. His stone!

It had been broken, ruined, and used up to keep simple-minded creatures from destroying those weaker than them. His anger was so intense, he flung his magic out at the surrounding area. It burned the sand, flashed against the waters of the shore, and sizzled up at the very air.

When his temper finally subsided, the surrounding area was charred and smoldered with fire and smoke. Biard stood amongst the remains, a sneer on his lips as hatred filled him.

They would all pay for his loss. The stone had been his, not theirs. He had possessed it the longest and now he would never have it again.

Turning from the waters, he moved along the shore, intent on hunting those who had destroyed his stone. In his twisted mind, he saw Colab the Meshi's image as he moved west.

6

THE PRICE OF FREEDOM

Tresstéanna listened to her friends as they explained the strange message from Belent's new book. After they were finished, her first thought was to continue with their escape plans. She wanted to run to the nearest window and use their glides to float down into the forest far below.

She wanted to be free.

"Maybe some of us should take the globe, use the glides, and fly away from here?" she urged, but her shoulders dropped when she spotted Belent shake his head.

"It says we must all stay," Belent said gravely.

"What else does it tell you?" Col demanded. "Does it tell you why?"

Another shake of his head had frustration building in everyone.

"How do we know we can trust it?" Kriston asked, his green eyes looking suspiciously at the small item held by the sorcerer.

"It was correct when it guided me back down here," Belent said as he held the book aloft for everyone to see.

"It could be a trick," Col stated. He too eyed the item suspiciously.

"There is more," Belent exclaimed as they all stood around him.

Tresstéanna still felt the need to rush to the nearest window. She felt that escape was the forbidden fruit just out of her reach. Before, prior to Kriston coming to her rescue, freedom hadn't been so close. Now she saw it slipping away from her. Pain and frustration settled deep inside her chest.

However, as Belent continued, this pain was replaced by a feeling of concern.

"Grand Carrington is missing," Belent said to the room as he set the book in the center of the table. "I heard Prime Magal tell Maven Gorphen."

Leian rushed forward. "The Prime was supposed to be searching for Shiarra!" the wizard exclaimed, fear and anger mixed on his pale face.

Belent nodded and turned to look at Leian. "I thought of that too, which is why I followed them at first." Turning, Belent placed a hand on Leian's arm and smiled. "The book tells that Shiarra is safe. It says she will return to the Kylix before we do."

Quick questions were shouted at Belent before he could hold a hand up to stop them. When silence settled around the room again, he finished, "I know nothing more than that regarding Shiarra. But when I followed Maven Gorphen, I heard that they have searched the whole of the palace for the missing giantess."

"What does this have to do with us?" Kriston asked as he sat in the nearest chair. When he gave a hard tug of Tresstéanna's hand, she landed softly in his lap.

"We've been trying to recruit her," Tresstéanna said. She turned to look at him. "I, that is all of us, found she was the most susceptible to thoughts of change. Thoughts and visions were presented to her regarding freeing the Latria." When she recognized confusion on his face, she continued. "She was starting to doubt the tradition of owning the Gi Jón." Confusion still filled Kriston's handsome face.

"And?" Col asked.

"Well, it won't be easy to escape. Then, once we do, we still have to get down into the Kylix without the giants recapturing us. Then we have to fight and win against Dreail." She studied her mentor with sober eyes. "We can't do all that while trying to stay one step ahead of the giants."

"You mean to win them over," Col said with a smile.

She nodded and turned to explain more. "If we solve this civil war, free the Latria once and for all, then maybe we can gain allies that would put some weight behind our fight against the last Protector."

"Would they fight with us?" Stria asked.

"Maybe. Carrington is pregnant. She worries for her child, and so do I. If we can't stop this fighting, we will never gain the Kylix without the giants on our heels."

Tresstéanna turned to study Kriston again. She so desperately wanted to tell him of the vision of the future, their future. But now was not the time.

"I feel friendship is needed over fighting now," she finished, leaning into his arms.

They talked until Amándo's sister brought word of the missing Grand. Madera was flushed with excitement and worry as she rushed into the private rooms.

"They are saying she was kidnapped by the Otomi fighters," the young girl provided. "Now the palace has sent many guards down to join the battles in the forest."

"There is no way the fighters could gain access to the palace," Amándo said with a shake of his head. "I have spent years trying to escape. None have even gained entrance, unless sold or traded into service of the palace, in all this time. How could they have taken her from here without anyone knowing?"

"You think she ran away?" Tresstéanna asked with worry.

"It is be possible," Amándo answered as he scrunched up his face, deep in thought. "She could have left on her own. But where would she go?"

"She's gone to the resistance!" Tresstéanna said as she stood quickly to pace the room. "Think about it. We've been planting the seed in her mind that peace is needed to prevent the destruction of Midzark. She must have gone to talk with the fighters, to make peace."

Turning around the room, she was suddenly filled with worry for the giantess. Would these freedom fighters harm the lady? What if they did, what if they killed her? It would be her fault. She was the one who had nudged Carrington into believing that slavery was evil, that the fighting needed to stop to save this world. If harm came to this woman, it would be her fault.

"No," Amándo said. He grabbed her arm gently, interrupting her thoughts. "I can tell what you are thinking, but I do not think they will harm her." He shook his head. "Mayson and his men might use her appearance to their advantage, but they would not cause harm to her. That would destroy all we stand for. We wish to live as equals, not dominate the Nephilim."

"What does this mean for us?" Col asked as he returned to his seat next to Kriston. "If Cline is sending his guards out into the forest searching for her, what will they do if they find her in the presence of the fighters?"

"Maybe the palace is less guarded now than before?" Kip suggested. Hope filled the eyes of her friend, and she felt horrible having to extinguish this flame in their minds.

"No. There are many guards here in the palace. Many protect the Grands, but most live here. Even if he sent half his guards, there are still too many for us to defeat." Turning once again, she looked at Genoa's globe and a new thought occurred to her. While it formulated in her mind, the talk continued around her.

"What if..." she said, interrupting Col, who had been speaking. "What if she knows."

All eyes turned to the globe, which she was currently pointing at. She felt the room grow quiet as she stepped towards the table.

As her hand slowly reached to touch the globe, she felt everyone hold their breath as her fingers brushed the cool surface. Her eyes dimmed as the goddess started to communicate with her.

"Child," Genoa said inside her darkened mind. "Much is at stake here."

"What do you ask of me?" Tresstéanna questioned quickly. She was pleased that the goddess was speaking without images, which always made her a little queasy when they zipped past her.

"I felt my father's presence. First I must know what has happened."

So, it was Genoa's father who had pressed the flower image upon the gifted, Tresstéanna thought as she quickly relayed the information to the goddess.

"He showed you the Orwic flower?" Genoa said, and an image passed before Tresstéanna's eyes.

The world she saw was beautiful. Orange and purple trees and grass filled her vision. Strange yet beautiful creatures flew or crawled amongst the foliage. The air glowed with a blue haze, and more creatures filled the sky.

"This was Sailvea," Genoa said and the image changed. It was a devastated world now—no plants grew and no creatures stirred. Only rocks and fire filled her vision now.

"This is currently Sailvea," Genoa said as the image sharpened on the small purple flower many miles away. "This is the Orwic flower made by my father. He created it upon the death of two of my sisters. They fought each other and destroyed all they had created by way of their battles."

The darkness returned as Genoa told her of the evil creatures her two sisters had created. How the monsters had carried the corporeal globes of her sisters while doing battle. She spoke of the devastation her sisters had caused their children.

"The flower was a memorial to their lives and those they had created. Any who hold it will be granted their wish."

"Why were we shown this?" Tresstéanna finally asked after the image had gone dark. The answer provided to her sparked fear deep down inside.

"You spoke of a book," Genoa said, not answering her question. This evasion frustrated Tresstéanna for a moment, but she finally answered the goddess.

"Yes, Belent holds it."

"It sounds like the Trialth book. It will serve him well."

"So, we should trust its guidance?" she asked, still unsure why the book wished for them to wait.

"Much depends on what happens in this world. We have far to go still to return me to my resting place," Genoa said as the image of the cradle once again flashed before Tresstéanna's eyes.

"I will not fail you," Tresstéanna urged.

"I have heard the plight of this land's people," Genoa said. "They grow dear to my heart."

With these last words, the communication ended, and

Tresstéanna was once again standing at the table. Kriston was next to her with concern on his handsome face.

Reaching up, she brushed her knuckles against his face and smiled. There was much to tell him. Some she would have to keep from him.

MAVEN GORPHEN WAS BEYOND CONSULTING. The old giant tugged on both his beard and what little hair remained on his head as he paced the Grands' private chambers.

The rooms were vast and at the front of the palace. High expansive windows lined one wall, giving the main room an open feeling, yet heavy drapes lined each window, allowing one to close out the heat and light when needed. Rugs and tapestries were scattered about the space, along with three couches and four large chairs set around a short table. Two long tables filled with food and drink sat against the far wall. Four doors branched off the room, leading to private bed and bath areas. Flowers filled large vases and bright fruit sat in bowls around the area, giving off their sweet smells.

Gorphen gave a hard tug of the hair behind his left ear, and tears threatened to spill from his eyes. He was glad his anger kept them from falling, but even this feeling could not stop the fear he felt for his daughter.

Where was she? Was she safe? Was Cline correct in his assumption that the horrid fighters far below the palace held her captive?

Stopping, he turned to study the man who had married his little girl. Cline looked worried, but whether his concern was for his missing wife or the fighting going on down below was unknown to Gorphen. Maybe he should do his own investigation?

"Where has the Prime gone?" Gorphen asked as Cline turned his dark eyes towards him.

"He went to relieve his patrols for sleep," Cline said with a wave of his hand.

High noon had come and gone and still no word came to the leader's private chambers. Gorphen hadn't eaten his last meal nor slept during the hot hours of the day, so consumed with worry for Carrington that his appetite and rest eluded him.

As he continued to pace about the vast rooms, his mind raced with troubled thoughts. If the guards failed to locate her, what could he do? This thought disappeared when he remembered the skinny gifted man holding his hands over the guard's sword and infusing it with magic. The sword and guard had yet to return, but the magic for locating someone had already been shown to him. He wondered now if they could use that same magic to locate his daughter.

Maven Gorphen, like Grand Cline, knew that magic was lacking in the Nephilim. All the magic shown the other night high on the cliffs during the celebration had been that of the four gifted. The deception had been good but incomplete. For like the Grand, Gorphen had also tried to wield magic outside of the classroom.

He had attempted many spells to no avail during his time after class. Nothing had worked for him, nor Cline. Even Carrington doubted her abilities, yet his daughter had been slow to understand why the Latria gifted would betray them. She still questioned the magic she had been shown. She valued the teachings more than her husband and her father.

Gorphen knew he couldn't complete magic, but he knew where those that wielded it were located.

"Send for the gifted," Gorphen shouted, forgetting he was

in the Grand's presence. When the guard near the door hesitated, Gorphen turned to look at Cline. After scratching his chin hair, Cline nodded, and the guard quickly disappeared.

"What do you have in mind?" Cline asked as Gorphen continued his pacing.

"Have them locate her," Gorphen said as he tugged on his hair again.

The minutes ticked away as he paced across the vast rooms. When the three gifted finally came, they entered the room with confusion and hesitation.

Gorphen quickly waved them in and moved to stand near Grand Cline, who sat in a chair set on the far side of the room. After the three bowed to Cline, he motioned for Gorphen to conduct the meeting.

"You," Gorphen said, pointing to the skinny dark-haired man. "Bentel, you made a sword magical so it could seek your missing friend. Could you do something like this for my daughter?" Gorphen was so intent on his question, he failed to notice the man wince at the mispronunciation of his name.

When Belent nodded, Gorphen quickly stepped forward. "Do it!" he demanded promptly, so sure his wishes would be completed that it took him a moment to realize the man was shaking his head.

"I will not complete magic that would put anyone at harm." Belent's words had confusion filling the Maven.

"Harm? What are you talking about?" he demanded.

"What would you do if Grand Carrington was found in the company of the Gi Jón?" Belent asked.

"So, she has been captured by your kind!" Cline hissed as he stood.

Belent shook his dark head as the pale woman with an odd name stepped forward.

"We don't know. What we know is you have accused the

Latria of taking your wife. We know this is impossible and think she left the palace on her own. Free and seeking answers to questions that have eluded you and your Maven," the woman replied. With her words, anger crept into Gorphen, overtaking his fear.

"You dare deny me!" he hissed and had thoughts of throwing the three into the Pagilda. "My daughter would never choose to leave the safety of the palace on her own!"

"Has she asked you any questions about the Latria?" the blond-haired gifted man asked quietly. "She has asked us many questions, questions that made us think she worries about the vision she had."

"The vision you forced upon her!" Gorphen shouted, and noticed the woman take a step back. He smiled when he saw her frown. "Yes, I too know about your deceit. That vision was fake!"

To her credit, the woman stepped forward and stood tall before him. When she shook her head boldly, Gorphen reached out to grab her by her arms, intent on shaking the truth out of her.

However, a second before he laid his hands on her, her eyes turned white. As his fingers brushed her, he felt the sizzle of magic as his vision swirled. When he blinked, he noticed a small child stood before him.

"Grandfather," the girl said. Her dark eyes and long hair shone in the afternoon light.

"Witch!" Gorphen hissed, still unaware he was inside a vision.

"Grandfather, tell me a story," the girl demanded with a pretty pout on her lips.

"Lies," Gorphen hissed, yet doubt crept into him. The child was the image of his own daughter, but the nose was different. Her dark hair was braided in a thick strand that hung over her right shoulder. Small flecks of freckles were scattered across her cheeks and thick eyelashes closed when she blinked and looked up at him.

"Tell me of our bond with the mainlanders," the girl said and *pouted again with her pretty little lips. "Please, Garpa. Please!"*

It was this word of endearment that had tears leaking out of Gorphen's eyes. Doubt flew from him as he studied the true image of his granddaughter.

When the vision ended, Gorphen discovered he was on his knees before the pale woman. Tears ran down his cheeks, and Grand Cline was rushing to his aid.

"No!" he shouted and waved Cline away. "I am well." Turning, he studied the lady before him. "Who are you?" he hissed, and watched the pointed chin rise a fraction.

She replied, "Someone you should not have imprisoned. But someone you should befriend."

"Is it not too late?" Gorphen asked, shocked to realized he cared deeply what her answer would be.

When a smile passed her lips, he took a deep breath he didn't know he had been holding in. Her eyes once again were blue, and he thought he noticed relief and hope in their depths.

"No," was her single answer.

"Was…" Gorphen had to clear his throat to continue his question. "Was that real?"

A single nod provided him with his answer, and he bent his head in relief. "What of my daughter?" he pleaded.

"That I do not know. But with your help we can find out," Tresstéanna said, and the large giant got up from his kneeling position.

As Shiarra followed Brine around the enclosed encampment, her suspicions were confirmed. This man held little respect for those he deemed less worthy.

He did call each person by their name, but his treatment of them was similar to his brothers. He ordered them about or ignored them if the Gi Jón was not serving him. Brine even dismissed several of his own men as if they held less importance.

Brine walked about the cave and showed her his "progress," as he called it. Maps and scrolls were shown to her about lands he now owned. Nephilim and Latria alike were listed by name. Shiarra wasn't sure if those listed were considered property or supporters. She guessed Brine didn't know this distinction either.

She noticed animals were listed as well, along with several farms that declared they would only send their supplies to Brine and his men. She even noticed several maps of other, smaller caves that were being used to store weapons and supplies.

None convinced her this man would be successful in gaining the whole of Midzark's support, let alone hers. She saw his interaction with the few people her size inside the cave and realized she now found herself in a different prison than her previous one. But this one was missing her friends.

Knowing this, she kept her thoughts from Brine. He seemed to want to sway her, please her with what he felt were important facts. She didn't doubt he expected her to sign an allegiance to him within the hour, pledging her magic to do his bidding and follow him in overthrowing his brother.

Disillusioned though he was, she also feared Brine's reactions if she denied him her loyalty. She did not miss the fear in the eyes of several of Brine's supporters, both giant and normal sized. They were scared of this man and the power he wielded over them.

As they drew near a pile of boxes, one of the guards caught her eye. She had seen this giant enter the cave while she had been sitting at the table. But as of yet, he had only stood against the wall while the others moved about completing various chores.

He was clad in armor like the other Nephilim, his head gear on and his sword sheathed. But unlike the others, his eyes remained locked on her as she moved about the cave with Brine. A deep uneasiness settled in her as the dark eyes remained fixed on her form. Alarms rang inside her head as she was shown another box of supplies, as if their presence would sway her.

"See, there are many weapons here that my men will use. Once we have the palace locked down, we will have full access to the weapons stored there. My control over the court will be complete once I have banished my brother from the palace walls," Brine said with a gleam in his eyes as he turned to her.

Moving her attention quickly back to Brine, Shiarra nodded.

"And how will you be gaining the palace?" she asked, and a red glow crept into Brine's face. Unsure if it was anger or excitement, she held her breath when the giant stood before her.

"You do not need to know those plans," Brine replied as he rubbed his hands together. "But know this—before the sun rises tomorrow, I will sit upon the throne."

"And you need my magic for this?" she asked, trying to ignore the feeling of the guard's eyes on her.

"Only a small bit," Brine replied. He led her back to the table. As a large chair was dragged over for him, she made a show of settling herself, but her eyes discreetly met the guards. When he moved to raise his sword from his sheath, her fear increased. When she noticed the blade glow with magic, she sucked in a quick breath.

What was this guard doing with a magical sword? Who was he and who had sent him? These thoughts quickly came into her mind, but then so did the answer. "Leian," she whispered. She caught the eye of the mysterious guard and sent a secret nod to him.

This was a friend, or at least a guard of the palace sent to find her. If the sword had been empowered by magic, that meant Belent had done this. The sorcerer was the only one she knew who could complete such a task. Endowing magic upon an object was difficult and required a wizard to use elements and long spells. However, she had seen Belent quickly use his magic on items before with none of the normal fuss of time and tools.

Her mind when to the small bracelet worn by her queen, Tresstéanna. She had also carried a knife and bow made by the sorcerer. But she knew those items had been taken from Tresstéanna when they had been captured.

Her friends had sent this guard. That was all she needed to know. She slid her chair slightly so she could see the guard over Brine's shoulder, her attention divided as Brine started speaking once more of his plans for her.

She watched the guard looking around the room and worried he was alone. One giant against so many would not win a fight, no matter how skilled he was. Even if she used her magic to aid him, he would eventually be cut down.

"Once we are in, you can blast the Prime. He would be the only Nephilim present beside my brother." Brine talked as if Shiarra were listening to every word he said. As he leaned forward to continue, Shiarra saw another guard approach the first one. When a small word and nod passed between the two, she realized he was not alone after all.

"The hardest part would be if we cannot gain entrance for my men. I have very few inside the palace at this time. Most are here or in the other caves," Brine said, unaware Shiarra's attention was elsewhere. He once again produced the map showing the other caverns and tapped it with one of his large fingers.

The giant continued listing out his very simple and devious plan. She noted his plan included disposing of all loyalists along with the giants, as if the Latria had a choice of who they were enslaved for. Shiarra watched the guard motion towards several new arriving guards. When they took up position around the cave, she held her breath. She counted only four and grew concerned this was all that had come to aid in her rescue. But when two more emerged from the back cavern she finally understood.

This giant, the one sent to rescue her, was smarter than she'd first thought. She guessed that his men had already secured the back entrance. Infiltrating all of the exits of the cavern was smart, and it appeared they had yet to be discovered.

When the infiltrator finally made his move, it was quick and efficient. Shiarra watched as the magical sword was drawn and brought down on the nearest of her kidnappers. As the kidnapping giant fell, she raised her own defenses against the nearest of Brine's guards, who was currently being dispatched by another of the subversives.

Then she blasted her magic towards Brine. The red flares bounced off the man's chest, but she continued to use them to distract him. She was grateful her rescuers had already disabled the others, as her magic didn't have much effect on the giants.

Brine stood sputtering angry words as she swirled fire and sparks in front of his eyes. When she noticed the infiltrator and his men nod in her direction, she lowered her hands but stood ready in case she had been mistaken.

"Well done," Mayvers said with a nod. He sheathed his magical sword. "I see why the blond gifted is crazy for your return."

"Leian!" she whispered as the giant turned to issue orders to his men.

"If they want, they can return home," was his answer to the question his men asked about what to do with the Latria found in the caverns. "They probably miss their family as much as I do."

Turning back to Shiarra, Mayvers studied her as he introduced himself. Brine remained standing, but his face had turned a dark purple as anger ate away in him.

"How dare you attack me!" Brine insisted as he raised himself to his full height of about fourteen feet. "Do you know who I am?"

After nodding, Mayvers squinted one eye and looked at the man. "I do. Your brother will have a few words for you before the day is finished."

Turning back to Shiarra, Mayvers nodded. "Shall we?" He pointed to the exit with a smile.

TRESSTÉANNA HAD KNOWN many facts in her odd life. One of those facts was that things were not always as they appeared to be. She herself had never been as simple as how she presented.

As Anna, she looked like a normal earthling. Yet her tall thin form had hidden much during her travels in the USA.

She hid her past, which she had been oblivious to until her arrival on Genoa. She hid her feelings, the longing to understand where she had come from and the yearning to find family. A family that maybe longed for her return, people who maybe loved her. But mostly, she hid her magic.

As Té, she had hidden little while being surrounded by her dragon warrior family. Yet even she had secrets, including from her mentor and father figure, Wizard Col. She had hidden her fear. Being a warrior, a fighter who rode the backs of dragons, left little room for fear. Yet when she thought of the duty to join with the missing parts of herself, she did fear.

It was a deep panic, one that would keep her awake far into the night. Sometimes it would be so intense it would clog her breath. Her mind would race about the possibility of becoming something other than who she was. Someone who was—different.

As Tress, she had many secrets. Her appearance had been of a young queen, pale and royal. One who ruled in her missing parents' stead and had portrayed the very body of leadership for her people. She sat upon the throne her father had once used, calm and regal in appearance as she ruled the lands of Genoa, who gave their allegiance to her.

However, inside she hid her discord. She knew there were spies walking next to her, infiltrators that slept in her home and portrayed themselves as friends. Spies who wished her ill in their minds as they smiled at her.

So, as she stood there and looked at a father desperately worried about his missing daughter, she knew this giant was more than what he had shown her up to now. The worry was genuine, of that she was sure. But she still felt darkness lurking beneath the surface of this man.

Maven Gorphen's dark eyes held tears as he knelt before her. Lines formed on his bald forehead and around his eyes, which had dark circles beneath them. His hands shook as he grasped her slender arms, as if reaching for hope.

"I can see if a vision of her will come to me. But the Grand must recall his guards from the forest. All fighting must stop." Grand Cline quickly stood and she turned to boldly look at the leader of the giants. "If your wife is down there, then any fighting in the forest will put her and your child in danger!" she hissed as she stood tall.

"You would have me surrender to the slaves?" he demanded.

Gorphen stood quickly and approached the Grand. "She only requested the fighting stop. Nothing was said about surrender. She is correct—if Carrington is down in the forest, she could be caught in the fighting," Gorphen said with concern in his voice.

"Only until she is found," Tresstéanna said and studied the leader. "Grand Carrington may be safe. Any vision I have might confirm this."

"You expect me to trust you?" Cline sneered, "You who have lied to us at every turn?"

"I have never enslaved you!" Tresstéanna scolded boldly. "But know this, every lie I told held parts of the truth. They were spoken to aid you in your mission. If we wished, we could have worked to overthrow you! Allowed Fin and his followers to poison you and yours." She noticed hesitation in Clines face and pushed her magic at him. "Even now, my actions are done to bring your family to you. Do I wish freedom? Yes, but that freedom will be with you still in power of the Régorge Palace."

"Why?" Cline asked as he took a step towards her. "Why aid us at all?"

"My reasons are my own." She pulled her magic back, magic she had been pouring towards the two men in small dosages. Magic that she hoped would help convince them of her trustfulness.

Much of what she was saying was true. She and her band needed to return to their original mission, to return down into the cave, free from pursuit of the giants. Free to finish their quest to return Genoa to her place of rest and return her homeland to its formal glory. At least she hoped.

Cline gave her one final look, then marched to his door. After giving his order to withdraw the troops back to the Ingress Bridge, he closed the door and returned to his seat.

Maven Gorphen stood with anticipation as Tresstéanna closed her eyes.

Darkness turned to grey as the vision came to her.

Carrington stood tall upon the Ingress Bridge. The woman's long dark hair was unbound and swirled in the night's wind.

Carrington raised her face upward and Tresstéanna saw movement behind the giantess. Hundreds of Gi Jón rushed up the cliff face to stand at her back. Some flew on massive bees while holding lanterns. which made the creatures look like large lightning bugs. Others carried weapons and marched along the cliffs. The flames from all the lanterns gave the night an odd glow, and Tresstéanna quickly turned to glance at the palace as a voice shouted down at the gathering horde.

"Húriya and Latria," Maven Gorphen shouted from far up on one of the corner towers. Massive lamps set on the walls of the tower illuminated the Maven. She panicked when she noticed Carrington's father raise the Globe of Corpuscle above his head. Hatred and pain crossed his face as he stood there.

"Father!" Carrington shouted in panic as she raised her arms, her hands outstretched. Gorphen stopped his movements and looked down upon her. Hope and joy filled the old man's face, but his eyes grew large with shock when sparks flew from Carrington's upraised hands. Flashes of blue magic flew from the giantess's

hands and raced towards the palace with a blinding speed that shook Tresstéanna.

When the vision was ended, Tresstéanna stood shocked as the implications of the vision filled her.

"Magic," she whispered as both Cline and Gorphen demanded answers from her.

7

THE CIVIL IN WAR

Gado the lizard felt the air that surrounded him with his long tongue. His golden eyes swiveled around and showed him two different angles of the cave. He knew that vision could be deceiving, so he stuck his tongue out once more.

The taste of the cave felt off.

He and the Protector Leewana had taken up posts near the Krack after their friends had disappeared out of the cave. They had seen the small band from Genoa several days before and had been asked to await the group's return here.

But Gado did not like waiting.

Most of the time he waited alone. The Protector would fly down into the darkness and be gone long periods of time. When she returned, she would call to him, and he would once again make himself visible to her.

"Dreail's children grow restless," Leewana advised Gado in her flowing voice. The Protector was massive. Gado had first feared the large lady. Her horns had intimidated him and when her wings moved the air, the lizard had disliked the stirring.

"Do they make their way here?" Gado asked as his eyes darted around in the darkness again.

"They have attacked the settlement, but with giants there, they met resistance," Leewana replied. "I was able to dispatch the spiders and serpents and block them in the water, for now."

"What will they do next?" Gado asked. His tongue darted out once again.

"They amass now. But I fear well before the next cycle, they might gain the cliff's face."

"What should we do?" Gado asked as the cavern around him turned ominous.

"You must go find our friends and warn them," Leewana said with urgency. "I will hold the creatures off as much as I am able, but our mother must be here to aid in this fight."

Understanding the urgency, yet hating the thought of leaving his home, Gado the lizard nodded his small head and disappeared. If he had to travel in the land of the giants, it was best to do it invisible.

STILL SHAKEN, Tresstéanna slowly walked back down the stairs leading to the Latria quarters. She was accompanied by the loyalist guard Weston and her two friends Leian and Belent. She was being helped down the stairs as her mind spun with the vision she had been shown.

With each step, she thought back to how she had lied to both Cline and Gorphen about her vision. She'd told them that Carrington was safe, hidden inside the forest. She could honestly presume this was true, because in her vision the grand lady had seemed fit and well.

When asked if the vision showed her why Carrington had fled the safety of the palace, Tresstéanna shook her head.

"I don't know," she said truthfully as she felt the drain of using her magic take her over. She rubbed her head, and Gorphen drew closer to her, curiosity written on his face.

"Maybe she worries about security since the other gifted was stolen?" Cline hissed, and Maven Gorphen turned quickly back to his son-in-law. This seemed a logical answer, and Gorphen was quick to jump on this idea, forgetting Tresstéanna completely.

"If she fears for her safety then we must protect her!" Gorphen insisted. He urged Cline to send his men into the forest looking for Carrington.

"No!" Tresstéanna shouted, once again drawing attention to her as she leaned against the wall. Her energy drained a bit more, and she quickly closed her eyes as the room spun. "She is safe while the forest remains empty. Withdraw all your troops, send them out of the trees until she returns. If your troops are not battling the resistance, then they have no cause to be near her and will withdraw to their headquarters."

"Are you sure?" Gorphen asked and once again grabbed her arms, this time more firmly as fatigue almost overtook her. Leian and Belent drew near and helped her stand.

"You cannot know that!" Cline insisted, but doubt crept over his face. Her single nod was all she could handle at the moment and, once released by the giant's grasp, she slumped back into Belent's arms.

The two giants argued for a while, their voices a dim echo as her head buzzed and her vision swam. At one point she heard a sharp call but ignored it as the afternoon heat tried to suffocate her.

When a large glass of ale was put in front of her, she took a deep drink and thanked the Latria guard, Weston.

"I am to return you three downstairs, my lady," Weston said, concern filling his dark eyes. She took a quick drink and the glass was taken from her by Leian.

She felt Weston place one hand under her elbow while the other was grabbed by Belent. When her vision cleared, she glanced around and was shocked to see they were already out in the hallway.

"What happened?" she asked, embarrassed about her frail condition but knowing only food and rest would restore her.

"Grand Cline and the Maven will discuss much, and your presence is no longer needed." Weston continued to guide them towards the Latria quarters.

After descending the long stairs, she felt a little stronger. As they neared the door to their chambers, she quickly thanked and dismissed Weston. She was worried he would open the door to her rooms and discover the small band of dragon warriors hidden within. Luckily, Weston nodded and, after bowing, turned and retreated back down the long hallway to resume his duties.

Kriston rushed to her side when the doors had finally closed behind them. Concerned words and then cakes had been thrust upon her after she had taken her seat at the table. Three large slices of bread and two glasses of water, then one of ale, had the color slowly filling her cheeks again.

Upon relaying their adventures to the rest of the group, speculation and ideas were passed around, along with the ale. Night was settling outside the windows as the talk continued.

"Magic?" Belent questioned as he stood and paced the length of the room. "You saw it come from her own hands?"

She nodded as Kriston's large hand continued to run

gentle circles on her back. His concern was touching, and she felt his hesitation to leave her side as the talk continued.

"You think Genoa has given this woman, this Carrington, the gift?" Kriston's question had all eyes turning to Wizard Col. "Is that possible?"

"She is the goddess," Col said as his brown eyes moved to look at the Greilk box, which currently protected the orb. "She told you she grows fond of these people."

"Yes, but to give a giant magic, a creature not of her own making?" Kriston spoke up.

"Why not? Have we not seen the wonders of her powers ourselves? Even now her children wander our homeland and the Protectors guard the Kylix. If she had not been stolen all those seasons ago, she would still be creating miracles." Belent nodded his head and turned back to look at the group. "You said Carrington was with the Gi Jón. Can we get a message to them?"

Amándo had then been quickly dispatched to his rooms in the hope he could communicate with the freedom fighters far below the palace. The rope bucket had been replaced so communication could continue, but it was no longer left tied to the window. After each use it was brought up and hidden in a drawer.

Minutes passed and the young boy failed to return. Ideas and thoughts spilled about the room like wine, yet still they seemed no closer to the truth than before. Had Carrington come into true magic somehow, and if so, was it the goddess Genoa who had bestowed this? Was Tresstéanna's vision far into the future or would this image play out within the next day? If the vision came to pass, what would the outcome be?

Carrington had been shown to travel with the Otomi and Húriya fighters. Did this mean they had been successful in changing the lady's ideas of slavery?

When Amándo finally returned to the room, the day had

finally ended. Darkness stared back from each window and a faint cool breeze blew into the rooms.

The boy looked excited and shaken at the same time. His dark hair was a mess, and his young sister trailed behind him. Her long hair was tied up on the top of her head. Small locks had come undone and the front of her apron was wet. Tresstéanna guessed the girl had come straight from her chores in the kitchen.

"She is there." Amándo's words had everyone standing in excitement as questions were thrown at the boy from all directions.

When Amándo held his hands up to stop the bombardment of queries, the room fell silent again. His eyes found Tresstéanna, and a smile crossed his face. "Grand Carrington is there. She approached the Otomi fighters earlier in the day. She arrived at headquarters the same time your friends did."

"Friends? Timmons?" Kriston asked, and the young boy nodded his head.

"I was told the land nymph had also arrived from Kós Kóvar." Here the boy grasped both his hands before him as his smile spread even more. "They are coming!"

Confused by his statement, Tresstéanna walked over to the boy and looked at him. "Who is coming?"

"The Húriya people!" he exclaimed. "Their army comes to aid us in our fight!"

Ava the Zaeim of the Húriya people stood and watched the large yellow moon Géémon rise in the darkened sky. Below its yellow glow, the city's army marched across the hot desert. Even with the moon's glow, the desert seemed dark tonight.

The moon named Sedona was far to her left. Its constant presence in the sky gave her comfort. She studied Camma as it too glowed; it was pale white tonight on the desert's horizon. Yet the moons and their lights failed to brighten the hot sands and the dark travelers tonight.

She felt the desert somehow reflected her own feelings as she watched the procession on the dunes. Black was her mood as doom once again settled over her and threatened the fate of her people.

As she watched the procession, she thought back to her city's victorious battle against Dreail's monsters. There had been much to do after the battle. Caring for the injured and laying to rest the dead had been the first order. The rebuilding of homes and public places was next. But first, they needed to ensure their land's safety. This now included aiding the quest of those from the mainland.

The diminished army that marched before her was only one fourth of the city's total forces. A little over two thousand military men trudged through the hot sands towards the forest of the giants. This new battle was long overdue and might cause the end of the Húriya people. Far too long had they allowed the giants to steal their kin, enslave their loved ones, with no resistance from those who lived across the desert.

Yet even now as she urged her army on, she feared that they were going into a battle they could not win. The history stories confirmed her people's inability to triumph over these foes.

Since there were not enough Melliferas to fly across the desert without causing considerable harm to the hive, the large army had to walk. But several Mellifera riders would join them once the sun rose again.

Walking meant they had to wait and start their journey after the heat of the day subsided. Even now, the desert still held the day's heat on its skin, causing sweat to flow and water skins to quickly empty.

The oasis of Sparlynn had been reached promptly and then left behind. She guessed if they continued their march, they would make it to the next oasis before tomorrow's heat rose. Even with their quick pace, Ava felt that they were traveling too slowly.

She worried for her new friend Svlain. The land nymph had reassured her she would be safe until Ava and her army arrived. Yet doubt kept Ava company tonight as the stars twinkled in the dark blanket above her.

"My lady," Pothel said as he approached.

"We make good time," Ava confirmed. She awarded her first in command with a small smile.

"Yes, Commander Switz is pleased with our progress," Pothel replied.

"I hear worry in your voice," Ava said soberly, turning to study the man.

"My lady, I grew up hearing stories of the Nephilim and the many battles we lost to these oppressors," Pothel replied quietly.

She nodded and then realized that Pothel probably couldn't see her movement in the dark. She remembered the stories her parents had passed down to her of the vast battles against the giants and took a deep breath. These stories had at one time been fantasies to her. Stories told to children to scare them into behaving and nothing more.

But when she had grown old enough to ride on the back of the Mellifera, she had seen for herself the vast jungle. She had witnessed the large homes nestled inside the trees and the giants who dwelled there.

It was then that she had seen the smaller Gi Jón enslaved by the Nephilims, forced to do the giants' bidding. After this, she no longer considered her parents' stories of the olden days to be fantasy.

Now the tale of Spaknik's sacrifice to free thousands of Húriya seemed so real to her, and the tale of Bian and Varra's sad love story now seemed heroic.

It had been these stories, these sacrifices, that had shaped and built her into the adult she now was. As Zaeim, she was awarded several liberties. Her magical gift had helped her gain this position, but it was her passion for freeing the Latria that held her close in the hearts of her people.

Most of the people in Kós Kóvar told of having family who were trapped over the vast desert they now marched across. Loved ones imprisoned and forced into labor for the giants, sold or traded based on their owners' wishes.

As her eyes traveled over the marching men below, she could pick out men with missing loved ones—uncles, aunts, and even cousins who had disappeared while traveling the desert. Rumors kept the missing alive.

After her appointment to religious leader, she had taken a battalion out, using the bees, and scouted for the missing. When these lost family members had been spotted from the air, hope bloomed in the desert for the first time in years. Attempts had been made to free the enslaved with some successes. Yet most of their attempts resulted in the capture of the whole regiment sent to free the Latria.

If a bee fell from the sky, it usually fell slowly, spiraling down towards the ground if its wings were unharmed. This usually kept the rider safe. But this was a fact the Nephilim knew. So when a Mellifera carried a rider, the giants would launch arrows at the bee. The Húriya who survived the fall were immediately forced to work on the farms or sold to the giants living in the jungle.

This was why, after many failed attempts, she had called off the rescue attempts. The Shéza had been quick to blame her for the failures and insisted the attempts continue. Luckily, the army commander refused to send out his men and Berrit, the leader of the desert people, had quickly moved his campaigns on to another endeavor.

Svlain's arrival in Midzark had confirmed, in Ava's mind, that the Midzark way of life was about to change. Ava had asked the land nymph once about the mainland and when no mention of slaves was told, she was filled with hope. Could they change Midzark? Could they force the giants to give up their dominating ways?

Finally, when the last man had walked past her, she and Pothel moved to follow. As she walked next to her friend, her steps faltered as she felt a tug of her magic. Reaching out, she grabbed Pothel, who had stopped next to her, just as her eyes turned inward to a vision.

The creature traveled quickly in the darkness. Cloaked, its true form was hidden from her seer eyes, but the powerful way it moved and its sheer size told her this was a dangerous foe. She watched as it raced along the many deep tracks made in the sand as hatred filled it and kept it company.

As the moons dimmed and morning came forward, it reached its foe and overtook them. Flashes of red and black came from its hands as it killed all it found in the desert.

"Colab the Meshi!" it hissed as it killed man after man. "I come for you!"

An image of herself flashed in her mind, and she horrifically saw her own death before the vision ended.

Svlain's interest in the giantess went much deeper than their physical differences. She was sure this mutual interest was something even Carrington felt.

After the introductions, Mayson asked that she and Carrington, along with the others from Genoa, join him in his headquarters. The treetop home was giant sized and only three stories above the forest floor. There was large furniture that had been set about and mixed with wooden chairs of normal size, making the home feel welcoming to both giants and small humans.

Svlain was so glad to be reunited with Zain, but duty and her curiosity kept her focused on the large woman. Zain remained close to her, and she took comfort in his presence.

"My lady, would you care for a drink? Perhaps some food?" she asked with a bow of her head.

"Please, water," Carrington asked and one of the Gi Jón rushed to bring drinks and food.

"Please sit, there is much to discuss." Mayson motioned towards the sitting area.

Once everyone had settled in chairs, and food and drinks were brought, Mayson and the others sat quietly. Timmons and Seth, along with Captain Ray, were settled near Mayson, while Toku, Zain, and she sat closer to the large woman. Since none of them had seen much of the giants, getting a chance to study one so close was too much to pass up.

Svlain found it hard to keep from staring, but she kept a smile on her face as she waited for Carrington to speak. Maybe she would tell them why she had traveled out of the safety of the palace and come to the enemy's door. Svlain hoped whatever the woman said, she would bring news of her queen, Tresstéanna.

"First, I want you to know your friends are well,"

Carrington stated after taking a delicate sip from the large mug she had been provided. "They have been treated fairly and have been well tended to by the loyalists."

"They are still held against their wishes," Seth said grimly. He was quickly hushed by Timmons, but most of the other dragon warriors nodded in agreement.

Carrington cleared her throat and continued, "This is what must be discussed."

Mayson leaned forward. Svlain noticed eagerness in his eyes, but his face remained solemn. "We are willing to listen."

Carrington nodded and turned her eyes back to Svlain. "I have been provided several visions from your lady, Tresstéanna. One vision showed a child." The woman place a protective hand over her stomach. With this motion, Svlain gained a little insight into this woman's reasons for being there.

"What did the vision show, my lady?" Svlain asked gently.

"It showed destruction and death," Carrington replied with a sob.

If Svlain had been looking at anyone but Carrington, she would have seen every man in the room grow uncomfortable when the giant woman started crying. Tears were not something warriors were used to dealing with, but luckily Svlain's eyes remained locked on the woman.

Standing, Svlain reached Carrington's side quickly and placed a small hand on the woman's forearm. When she handed Carrington a cloth, Carrington's tears increased.

"Such kindness," she cried. "Such kindness from those whom I have wronged," Carrington said between sobs.

"My lady, you are here, we will listen," Mayson said again as he shook his hands before him as if wishing to damn the tears from Carrington's eyes by waving them dry. "Please."

It took moments before Carrington's sobs subsided.

Svlain patted and spoke comforting words to her until she was once again quiet.

"Thank you. Much has happened between our people, but this I feel is the first step towards healing," Carrington said with bright yet still wet eyes.

Though the tears had stopped, Svlain felt that the emotions were still on the surface. Kindness and compassion were needed now.

"Please, can you tell us of the vision?" Svlain asked as she remained standing near Carrington's chair.

After another sniff, Carrington relayed the image Tresstéanna had shown her. "Your woman provided this vision, despite the deception that the magic had come from me." Carrington waved a sodden cloth before her with a smile. "No matter the deception, the vision spoke truth. This I felt. My daughter"—here again the hand moved over the woman's stomach—"speaks to me from the future."

Carrington's eyes turned to Svlain. The land nymph thought she noticed hope within their dark depths.

"You spoke to her too?" Carrington whispered.

Confused by Carrington's question, Svlain tilted her head. "My lady?"

"Charlotte!" Carrington urged. "I intend to call her Char-lotte. She has already been in one vision. Did she not speak to you as well?"

Svlain grew still as Carrington's words sunk in. Ideas churned around inside her head. In one idea, she thought of lying to Carrington about her vision. Making the child a giant instead of normal sized might help solve the issues within this land. But would deception bring positive results or harm the true mission?

She felt no good would ever come from treachery. Worried about the harm her words could cause, she paused for a long moment before her conscious took over and finally shook her head.

"No, my lady. In my vision it was a small child, one of my size." Svlain stepped closer to Carrington's chair. "She urged me to aid you and save everyone. To stop the fighting and help you and yours."

More tears leaked from Carrington's eyes, much to the dismay of the men gathered near. But through the tears, Svlain saw a smile form on Carrington's lips.

"If it wasn't my daughter in your vision, then it was one named for her." Carrington's eyes moved up as the smile spread. "Charlotte is correct, the fighting must stop. The slavery, the injustice caused by the Nephilim, must end now! Those who are not free shall be given their freedom, free to live as they wish. No longer held against their wishes. Those kept as workers, in a setting they have no control over, will be compensated. Those inside the palace shall be set out, allowed to live with family and loved ones. They will be paid for the years we have unjustly kept them from their own. I will ensure that Nephilim and all Gi Jón will be equals!"

The conviction and finality in Carrington's words had everyone inside the room immediately standing to applaud her words. Both the free and the enslaved alike felt the truth in her speech as Carrington sat, now a giant amongst friends.

AVA WATCHED the black-cloaked figure rise above the sand dune as fear blew threw her like an icy wind. Her magical vision had saved her and her army—at least she hoped it would.

As she lay quietly in the sand on her belly, her body all but covered by the special canvas, she watched and prayed. Only her head was exposed, something she could quickly rectify by lowering the eye flap, rendering her once more invisible.

She knew the dark creature held magic; she had seen as much in her vision. But the desert people also held small amounts of the gift, and they were using one form of it now to disappear.

The mirage had taken years to develop. It had been tested numerous times and it was years before they had finally implemented the canvases. But she now felt it had been time and resources well spent. The simple trick was a combination of skill and magic that allowed those who called the desert home to vanish. No sight, no smell, nor sound, not even their breath could be detected by an enemy once under the cloak.

Now as she lay there watching for this new foe, she hoped that its simplicity would allow them to go undetected by the evil creature. Doubt crept into her as time ticked away and only the wind moved.

A part of her feared that this monster that followed them would be exempt from their minor magical skills. Yet as she noticed the dark figure march quickly past her hidden people, she took a deep breath of relief. She knew her fear was real, for she had guessed who they had just escaped from.

Biard the Wright. The very creature who had destroyed Meshi the Scarent. She had been told by the boy Colab that Biard was a powerful sorcerer. The sorcerer had mixed with another powerful creature, a Scarent. Colab had told her that even the goddess's ambassador, Rastel, was fearful of this creature.

Unwilling to move from her hiding place yet, she studied

the spot where the dark figure had disappeared. As the moons continued their march across the sky, she shook her head.

"He was not fooled by our canvas," she finally interjected and stood up as the tarp fell back to the sand. "We are not what he seeks." Fear welled inside her for her friend Colab.

"The boy must be warned," Pothel voiced as he too stood beside her.

Her eyes went once again to the sand hills far to the west as she took a deep breath. "Yes."

Pothel nodded and slowly her army reappeared from their hiding places. Men dusted the sand off their weapons and cloaks while she continued to look to the west.

"My lady," Commander Switz said from her side, his words interrupting her deep thoughts. She turned to face him. The man stood rod straight, despite one foot being high on the top of a sand dune while the other had sunk deep into the grains.

She nodded to him, and he quickly barked out orders for the march to continue. Switz had been her first choice for this mission, one the council had quickly agreed to. Jobie, the newly appointed Shéza, along with the other council members, had stood behind Ava and her request to march to the aid of Svlain. After all, the land nymph had saved the city and its people in their time of need.

The council's agreement was something Ava was grateful for, if not a little unused too. After all, she had spent years being the city's Zaeim under a leader who wished only for fame and comfort.

Shéza Berrit Ká Neptan had only wished for personal gain. He had used the position of city leader to his benefit only. These benefits did not include religious leader's insights, magical or not. But Berrit was gone, killed in the first attack by the monsters that had crawled out from the bottom of the Márseille Lake.

Luckily, the remaining city council members had been fast to vote upon a new Shéza. Jobie was a wise woman whose late husband had served in the military and whose children were also part of the city council. One son was a high military leader, while her only daughter aided families out on the eastern shores. Ava knew the woman and her children and respected them all.

Jobie had immediately seen the wisdom in sending aid to those enslaved in the west. Some of the council members had voiced concern that dipping into the Nephilim's domain would return the Húriya to danger. Doom would follow if they awoke the giants' anger.

It had been said that the giants would attack the city if Kós Kóvar sent its armies into the jungles. Arguments had ensued regarding the debate but in the end, Jobie had swayed the majority.

Ava was glad Jobie had insisted Commander Switz join in the march. Switz was a man Ava respected. Her father and Switz had been friends years ago. Even now Switz respected the position that Ava held, despite her young age.

Commander Switz had called five different battalions to the march, each with special strategic skills. Three were usually stationed on the northern shores of the lake, where they protected the farmlands from the large lizards that attacked the fields and people. One battalion was usually stationed inside or near the oasis of Sparlynn, while the other two came directly from the walls of Kós Kóvar.

The number of personal friends that marched with her was small. She had insisted her young friend Bonita, her apprentice of sorts, stay behind. Bonita showed potential in the use of magic and would easily step into the Zaeim position if Ava failed to return to the city.

Ava had tried to convince Pothel to remain behind too, but he had been stubborn in his conviction that she would have need of him. And she had to admit, she did feel more comfortable with him beside her.

Much rode on their march west. She knew there were many Gi Jón who called the forest home. She understood most were slaves, traded and sold like livestock. She also understood that some of these people were more loyal to the giants than their own kind.

These loyalists, as the Latria called them, could be dangerous. They would trick you into believing you were friends, then they would turn on you. It was said they would trade in your secrets for better homes or even slaves of their own.

As she moved forward, her thoughts turned back to the overall mission. Free the slaves and return those who wished to go back home to Kós Kóvar. But if their battles with the giants were not resolved, letting in loyalists, hidden as Latria, might be the downfall of her home. If a mole gained entrance into the city, there was much they could do to harm those who lived there.

"Greetings, sister," came a deep voice next to Ava. The words and their closeness had Commander Switz and Pothel spinning on their heels, looking for the speaker. Switz had his sword raised and looking for danger before Ava could calm them.

"Rastel?" Ava asked as she peered into the darkness before her.

"Yes, sister. I am here," Rastel, the ambassador to Genoa, replied, causing Ava to smile.

"Welcome, brother." Tears threatened to fall from her eyes. "We thought you gone."

"No, even the Scarent sorcerer cannot break my magic," Rastel stated. "Mother still has need of my skills."

"It was you?" Ava asked as understanding came to her. "You hid us from the Scarent."

"Yes. Your trick assisted. Evil and anger blinds the creature, with my help," Rastel spoke.

"He will hunt Colab," Ava murmured as dread filled her again.

"Meshi's sacrifice will hide the boy. But others are in danger of this creature."

"What must be done to protect them?" Ava asked. In her mind's eye she once again witnessed the horrid vision of the annihilation the creature was capable of.

"He must be sent out of this world," Rastel replied. "And the giants have the means to do this."

8

THE UNDERDOG

To Shiarra, the air outside of the cave had never smelled so sweet nor so fresh. The heat was still intense, but the cool night's wind helped calm her as she took several deep breaths.

As the giant named Mayvers led her safely out of the vast cavern, she paused a moment to appreciate the air and the freedom it represented. But she knew both would be short-lived, for she was destined to be imprisoned once again. Yes, not in a cave, but instead inside the palace, which was still a structure not of her choosing.

After a quick discussion with his men, Mayvers turned to look down at her. His solemn stare caused her to move her eyes away from the moons above and right into his lantern-lit face.

The giant's grim expression indicated he had received news he didn't care for. She watched him rub a hand over his sword's handle as he took a deep breath.

"The few loyalists of Brine's have fled; it was not my orders to bring them back, and I have no issues with the Latria," Mayvers said as he knelt before her, his expression still dark, something she wondered about. "I am a man of orders. Structure is key to my life." He tilted his head as if he were trying to make her understand his words. "In my world, there are rules and those who provide them. Yet…"

The long pause caused Shiarra to step closer to him. Was this man just a tool sent to bring her back to the palace or was there more hidden behind his brown eyes?

"Surely you see this world changing before your very eyes," Shiarra hinted but noticed no reaction in the man.

"Change is inevitable," Mayvers said with a wave of one massive hand. "My men and I don't question our orders, those were clear. We question the reason behind them. Carrington, I mean Grand Carrington, has disappeared. It has reached my ears that she is believed to be with the Otomi fighters. It is said she went of her own choosing."

"Carrington?" Shiarra asked, her concern for the woman immediate. This feeling was something the wizard instantly tried to categorize, believing it was because the woman was pregnant. Yet Shiarra had to finally admit it was more than that. She had grown fond of Carrington, much like Tresstéanna had. After days in close quarters with the three giants, out of all of them, the four from Genoa had been charmed by Carrington the most.

"She was once promised to me," Mayvers murmured, and Shiarra saw sadness in the man's face as his hands brushed the handle of his sword again. "Despite her new stature, she is still special to me."

When he stood and drew his magical sword, Shiarra quickly took a step back.

"This found you, now I ask, can you make it locate her?" Mayvers pleaded while his men gathered closer behind him.

"What of Brine?" Shiarra asked as the younger brother to Grand Cline stood, bound and brooding, between two of Mayvers's men.

"Gene and Pire will be taking Brine back to the palace. They will tell of our paths crossing the path of Grand Carrington. They will explain that we followed her tracks to ensure her safety." Mayvers said with a nod of his head. "Can you? Can you make this sword track her?" The pleading tone of his voice sounded desperate, and Shiarra considered his request for a moment, then had to shake her head no.

"No, I do not hold the magic within me that can accomplish this, however…"

Her last word had Mayvers leaning closer. Hope filled his face as he drew near.

"However," she repeated, "I believe I know where to find Grand Carrington. She may be with my other friends, friends who are hidden within the forest."

"Can we reach her?" Mayvers asked quickly, his expression still sober, his lips frowning, as his dark eyes studied her intently.

"It might be dangerous for you and your men." She turned from Mayvers to face his men. "I cannot guarantee your safety."

"We go where he goes," one man voiced as the others all nodded in agreement.

After several moments of silence, Shiarra slowly nodded her head in agreement. She had no clue where the Otomi fighters' headquarters was. And what little she knew of this land was based on what she noticed from the palace windows far above the forest. She knew the palace sat upon the very cliffs the Kylix opened out from. The mountain the palace sat upon was the one that separated Genoa from Midzark. She had seen the forest and the falls drop down into its midst. She knew, thanks to Amándo, that the river divided the fighting. She remembered that Amándo's bucket dropped on the northern side of the river, so that would have to be her starting point. Which didn't help, as they were currently on the far southern side of the vast river.

"Very well. First, I must be taken to the river." Mayvers returned his sword to its sheath, then nodded to the others. His agreement caused her to release the large breath she had been holding.

"This way." Mayvers turned and walked down the cliff ledge away from the cave she had been held in. Brine and his new captors followed them until they reached a large rope ladder.

Brine and the two guards continued walking along the cliff's path off to the right, while Mayvers moved to climb down the massive ladder. The rungs dropped down into the forest from a dizzying height, one that had Shiarra questioning her safety.

"It is quite safe. There are smaller rungs on the side," Mayvers said. He climbed onto the top of the ladder backwards and held a hand for her. "I will stay near you if you are frightened."

Just as he'd said, there were smaller wooden rungs on either side of the large ladder. These smaller steps were made of metal or iron and held firm beneath her feet. She made sure to not cast a glance down, as the height was quite extreme and made her stomach flop about.

Bugs buzzed around her as the heat of the night lessened the further they moved downward into the forest. The shade of the trees helped reduce the heat, as did moving away from the rocks of the cliff's face, which seemed to radiate the sun's heat.

Branches had been kept away from the ladder, so she didn't have to worry about being scraped from them. But the climbing down did wear on her muscles, and her arms soon ached from holding tight to each rung.

It felt like forever before her feet touched solid ground

again, and she felt relief when dirt lay beneath her feet. Her arms felt heavy and sore as she stretched her shoulders and back.

When she finally turned from the ladder, she saw the tall trees stretch high above her. Dark brown and grey trunks rose out of the soft dirt. Their height gave her a feeling of being small and insignificant.

Large green plants with odd curled leaves littered the immediate area and gave an eerie feeling to the land. Mist hung on the forest floor as the darkness of the night helped hide much from her eyes.

"The river is a long way from here. Will you be able to keep up?" Mayvers asked.

After giving him a nod, they started their walk. Mayvers and his men attempted to match her pace, using smaller steps and pausing often to allow her to catch up to them. She was thankful for this because it took four of her steps to match one of theirs.

She could no longer see the moons and was unable to gauge the travel of time. Mist swirled around the tree's trunks, making the odd ferns appear to be monsters that surrounded them. Each fern leaf looked like an arm reaching out for its victim. More bugs buzzed around her, and the smell of dirt and spices hung thickly in the air.

She felt fatigue trying to take over and used her magic to boost her energy. This lasted awhile, but soon she was worried about falling behind.

Mayvers must have seen her slowing and called a halt to their travels. She was glad for the short rest. As she dropped to the nearest rock, she felt sweat dripping along her back and realized the once-white dress now had unattractive stains.

Water was provided as she tried to wipe some of the dust off her gown. She lifted the bottom of the dress and tucked it in to the belt to try and prevent it from catching on branches. It gave the dress the odd appearance of puffy pants. But this seemed to work when she tested it out by standing and walking around in small circles.

Thoughts of a soft bed seemed far away as she tried to catch her breath before Mayvers urged her to continue their travels. Darkness encircled them once more as the forest remained unchanged. She questioned if Mayvers knew which direction they were traveling in. More than once she tried to spy any of the moons through the thick foliage high above her head. She worried they were traveling in circles and tried to spy any indication they were on the right path.

No tracks or walkways were apparent. Even the rope ladders and homes she had seen from the palace windows were missing in this part of the forest. Concern grew in her as they continued to walk. She found it difficult to keep her mind from roaming and concentrated instead on each step she took.

They had just adjusted their path to the left when Mayvers called a quick halt. He raised one of his massive hands and bent and twisted his head in concentration.

Distant sounds could be heard from the underbrush, rustles and crunches that had everyone else stopping and drawing their weapons. Mayvers's eyes darted around and when he drew his sword in haste, Shiarra quickly raised her red magic to the tips of her fingers.

She was unsure if it was friend or foe out in the dark forest and found herself praying as she prepared for battle.

AMÁNDO'S and his sister's elation about the Húriya people coming brought excitement back into the room. Tresstéanna felt the joy fill the air as the two young people hugged everyone and smiled. Happiness leaked from their very bodies, infecting the others as they rushed around the room.

"The Húriya people!" Amándo exclaimed with a shake of his head. "They are really coming!"

"Who are the Hurry ya peoples?" Stria asked.

Her question was answered by Madera. "The Húriya," she explained. "These are our ancestors, the free ones who live across the great desert."

"They live in the wonderful city of Kós Kóvar!" Amándo said as he danced about the room, unable to contain his joy.

"Our friends went to the city," Kriston said with a nod as the young boy rushed up to him, excitement all over his youthful face. "They told of its wonders and said the army promised to join our fight after they dispatched the monsters they were currently doing battle with." The boy looked amazed at Kriston's words.

"I have heard of these people my whole life but have never seen them or the great city. Though sometimes, at night, I imagine I can see the lights from the city shining across the great desert like a beacon of hope."

Everyone in the room turned their eyes to the now dark windows. Night had set while they had been waiting for Amándo to return.

"It is night," Kriston said and now all eyes turned to Belent.

The sorcerer nodded and moved to take the magical Trialth book from under his tunic. Tresstéanna had noticed her friend had taken to keeping the small book there. Genoa's words returned to her—*It will serve him well*—and she nodded when the sorcerer's eyes locked with hers.

She found it interesting that Belent did not need to

voice his questions for the book to provide him with an answer. As soon as Belent opened the book, he started to read.

"The rot of this world is falling away. Much more is at stake than your freedom," Belent said as everyone gathered closer to hear the book's words. "A powerful foe draws near and must be vanquished from this land. You know the tool needed for this; within the tool's shimmering confines you will find what the father has shown you. Take heed, if emotions run too high, they may destroy all."

Belent turned the page and shook his head when it appeared blank.

"But should we escape now?" Farin voiced the question that was on everyone's mind.

It was not Belent or his book that answered. Instead Tresstéanna shook her own head and spoke up.

"No," she said, and all eyes turned to her. "No, we need to get into Maven Gorphen's rooms." Even as she spoke, fear welled up inside her.

"The mirror," Belent said, and she saw the same horror fill his eyes. Even Leian's eyes now held fear as he stood to pace the room.

"The flower must be within the mirror," Tresstéanna stated. "The vision, it showed the same greyness we had seen inside the mirror."

"You cannot know this!" Leian said as he twisted his hands together and paced the room. "It could mean something else."

"No," Belent said, his voice shanking with fear as he looked at the wizard. "She is correct. I should have seen it earlier, but fear clouded my mind."

"What mirror are you three talking about?" Col asked. Tresstéanna saw impatience on his face.

"The Pagilda mirror," Amándo answered quietly. "The

place where the Maven places dangerous or unknown items, including people."

"Amándo, have you ever seen anyone else pull objects from the mirror, besides the Maven?" Tresstéanna asked quietly.

"No. I fear this object and never go near it when I am in his rooms," Amándo answered truthfully, shame covering his face.

"So, we know where the flower lies. We also know where we need to place this new 'powerful foe,' but who in the king's name is this new enemy?" Stria asked as her eyes moved back to Belent. She quickly peeked at the book herself.

Everyone was looking at Belent when the outer doors were thrown open. Time seemed to stand still as Tresstéanna watched the already full room flood with more people.

Before she or anyone else could raise their magic or weapons in defense, they were apprehended by the palace guards. Kriston's sword was taken from him, as were the dragon warriors' weapons, including all of Stria's hidden knives.

Tresstéanna felt stupid. She and her friends had been lulled into feeling safe in their little rooms. After all, it had been almost two days since Kriston and the others had snuck into the formidable palace. She realized now, too late, they had grown lax in their defenses. Not that it would have mattered. It had only been a matter of time before they were discovered.

"I told you!" The screeching voice raised the hair on the back of Tresstéanna's neck as she turned and saw Paren, the loyalist, march into the room. "The kitchens reported it to *me*, and I knew something was wrong!"

Weston, the head of the Latria guard, slowly walked in behind the woman, his face dark with anger. Weston nodded his head, and when his eyes met Tresstéanna's, she under-stood the anger was not directed at her or her friends, but something she didn't quite understand.

"Weston," she said and took a small step forward. She stopped when several swords pointed in her direction. After clearing her throat, she turned to study her friends. She knew where she needed to be, knew the steps required of her, and realized she feared more for her friends than for herself.

"This is now a matter for the Prime," Weston said as chains were brought into the room.

Tresstéanna saw the look in Col's eyes and, with a subtle wave of her hand, told her wizard to stand down. Facing back to Weston, she nodded and held her wrists out.

"We will go." Turning her eyes, she studied Kriston. It was then that she noticed Belent had vanished. Hiding a smile, she sent a wink at Kriston. "Quietly."

Svlain's eyes grew heavy as the night wore on. Talks between Grand Carrington and the Otomi fighters' leader, Mayson, were deep and exceptionally long.

The man and woman were so intent on their conversation that they rarely noticed when food or drinks were refreshed. Even most of the guards had disappeared, either to bed or duties.

Svlain and Zain stayed behind while Toku and the others, except Captain Ray, moved off to find their beds. Ray stayed behind, as Mayson kept asking his advice regarding locations of new battalions. Svlain came to understand that Captain

Ray had quickly become important to the freedom fighters' strategic planning. He and Mayson's man Cerq spent most of the night with their heads bent close while pondering a map. Only a question from Mayson would draw either man out of their private discussion.

Grand Carrington had many questions for the freedom fighters. She asked about prisoners, about their rights and how they were treated. Then she asked about the Otomi fighters' wishes—their requests and the hoped-for outcome after all fighting was finished.

"We wish for the same freedoms and rights your people hold. We do not wish to own any man, woman, or child, but to live free from ownership, to choose our own destiny. To have power over where we live and what we do with our lives," Mayson told Carrington.

"But what of the duties?" Carrington asked as she sat forward in her chair. "Who will tend your homes? Grow your food?"

Mayson smiled at these questions and raised his hands out to her. "What I cannot do, I will pay for. If one holds a special trade, then that person should be paid for it. This payment will allow that person to subsidize his life where he cannot provide for himself."

"What of those who have no trades?" Carrington's face was sober, and Svlain wondered if she talked about herself or those hidden in the palace far above.

"My trade is not physical," Mayson said as his hands landed on the table in between them. "I am a collaborator." When Grand Carrington's head tilted in question, he continued, "I plan, I propose plans that might aid someone in obtaining land, obtaining goods such as food or supplies." He studied the giantess and finally said with a smile, "I talk for my living. I ensure two people gain what they want out of a business transaction. I cannot wield hoe or hammer, but I can and always have provided for myself and my family. Even those who cannot build or grow have means. But this is where a government can aid all, Nephilim and Gi Jón alike."

Svlain's mind started to wander. The warmth of the room and the feel of Zain's hand in hers lulled her to sleep.

When she awoke, the room was empty except for Zain, who slept in his chair next to her. Their hands were still linked.

Outside the window and open door, she noticed the sunlight was making the sky pink. Day was rising, and she wondered what it would bring. She hoped it included more reunions with her other friends. Turning towards Zain, she smiled when his eyes opened and he looked back at her.

"The day awakes and so do you," she said with a smile.

"Have you slept well?" he asked and, for the first time, Svlain noticed the new scars on his neck and arms.

"What happened to you down in the Kylix?" she asked as her fingers traced one nasty scar on his arm.

"Not as much as to you." He stood to stretch. She saw him wince when he moved his left leg, but he easily turned to help her stand. "Let us find some food first, then we can share stories."

His smile disarmed her, and they moved out of the room to find the others. Seth was the first one they ran into, and he quickly led them to a home where a meal was waiting,

"We eat under the deck. Here, let me show you," Seth stated.

After filling their plates, they followed him down some wooden steps. They saw the others from Genoa, including Colab and Maraneal. They sat down next to Toku, who then provided their tale of the ant's home and healing. Once their story was finished, Zain quickly asked about the battle with Leewana.

"We saw her in the Kylix, but it was not explained to us

how you managed to change her back," Toku said with a shake of his head. "I would have paid dearly to see Tresstéanna standing up to the snake."

"Scared ten years off my life," Captain Ray said as he joined the group.

Next it was Svlain's turn to tell her story of the great battle with the monstrous children of Dreail. She told them of the vast city of Kós Kóvar and the city's council. Of how she had been imprisoned and then freed. About her time in the oasis and how Colab the Meshi brought the Ili Yeathía to her. This stone had been the final key to overthrowing the creatures.

Colab then spoke only briefly of his struggles with the Scarent, Biard the Wright. Everyone gathered knew of his loss and the pain in losing Meshi. The Scarent snake had been their friend too, but the boy kept his tale short. Svlain ended the story with Sash's sacrifice.

Faces turned sober as everyone around her thought of the monsters. She too worried about their return to the Kylix, of how they would have to return to do battle with these monsters to overcome their parent, Dreail.

"We need the rest of our friends, and the globe, before we start that battle," Captain Ray said finally as every eye turned to him. He gave a nod and stood with a smile. "Today, we have other battles to worry about."

Ray led them to the same home they had been in the night before. Mayson and the other Otomi fighters were now there.

"The Grand lady still rests," Mayson said in response to Svlain's question about Carrington as he patted her arm. "She is well and will be guided here when she wakes."

"We have other pressing matters," Cerq said to the group as he stood over a roughly drawn map of the forest. "A band of giants broke through our defenses late last night."

"The bridge was severed," Mayson said as everyone gasped in shock. "Our men cut the ropes when several palace guards rushed the river."

SHIARRA AWOKE from her short sleep in pain. She had been able to use her magic last night to stop the bleeding, but sometime in her sleep it had started again.

Her night's makeshift bed had been a pile of ferns, which had kept her from lying on the hard ground and had also kept her hidden. She had found her hiding place only after the horrific battle she had witnessed in the darkened forest where giants dwelled.

As she lay there in pain, her mind quickly went back to last night's fighting.

With the red magic licking her fingertips, she squinted out into the black of the forest. Sounds now surrounded them, metal clashing and grunts in the darkness.

Fear rose in her as she remembered her magic was ineffective against the giants. Their armor and skin made any of her flashes useless. It was this realization that saved her.

She changed her red defensive magic to the green elemental magic. Calling forth the air elements had been instinctive when an arrow flew out of the darkness right at her. Using her magic, she blew the sharp point upwards where it hit a nearby tree. Two more came at her quickly.

She heard Mayvers and his men around her, fighting to shield themselves from the arrows as more came at the group from all sides. One arrow pierced Mayvers's lower leg. He quickly cut the wood shaft that was protruding out of his armor and moved with his men into the defensive circle again.

"Hold your ground!" he shouted as the first of the attackers came running out of the forest.

Shiarra was worried those hidden in the trees were her friends, but quickly realized none of her fellow mainlanders would aim an arrow at her. All hopes of finding her friends at the other end of this attack fled as both giants and loyalists came running at them.

"Fools! We are the palace guard!" Mayvers shouted as two attackers came at him. One had a large ax while the second held a wicked-looking long hoe.

"You are the fools. Where has the palace been these past days?" one man shouted as hate and anger filled his face.

Shiarra saw no insignia of the palace on any of the attacker's clothing. The group wore work clothing. Farmers and builders slashed at the trained military men as if their lives depended upon each stroke.

Using her magic, she made dirt fly up at any attacker who came at her. But she quickly realized there were too many of them as more came racing out of the trees. Farmers, workers, and even women raced out. Each held shovels or picks or, in one woman's case, a large frying pan.

"We no longer serve the palace!" one woman screamed as she tried to bash in the skull of one of Mayvers's men.

Shiarra didn't want to harm anyone fighting for their freedom. She was confused as to why these attackers were unorganized and using makeshift weapons, but she still thought they might be with the Otomi fighters. Still, she blew a dust storm at any who drew near her, forcing them to shield their eyes.

"I seek the Otomi fighters!" she shouted as one attacker drew near her. "Please, they are my friends," she pleaded. The man sneered.

"You will find no friend here, slave," he hissed. "We answer to no Grand nor Latria either."

He raised a large club above his head as realization sunk in for her. These were not Otomi fighters but people still fighting for their own freedom. These were the oppressed Nephilim, peasants who were forced to serve the great palace using the sweat of their backs. Laborers who spent their lives out in the hot forest and farms, working to build, grow, and serve those who sat high in the palace.

These were the people who Grand Cline had abandoned days ago when the first of the fighting had started. Renegades of the Nephilim people who no longer wished to serve the spoiled giants who were nestled up in their safe home, leaders who didn't care if these servants of the palace died while fighting a battle.

Shiarra would have taken hope from finding these renegades, except the giant's words indicated they did not wish to free the smaller Gi Jón, which meant she would not find safety with these people, only further imprisonment.

Sending a big wave of air, she tried to blast the man off his feet, but she forgot the giants weighed more than men her size. This misjudgment meant that his club grazed her right shoulder, but at least it missed her head.

Pain bloomed from her shoulder down into her arm as she ducked away from the giant. Using her magic as she turned, she scooped up a pile of dirt and blasted it into the man's face. She heard him scream once as she ducked behind a nearby tree and away from her attacker.

An arrow blasted the trunk inches from her skull, and she blew her magic out again, using only her left hand. By this time, her right arm had gone completely numb. She tried to flex her fingers and found she could still move them, but the pain was intense. She didn't think the arm was broken, but she worried the shoulder had been dislocated. She used her healing magic, sending the yellow warmth into her arm while keeping her eyes on the battle just beyond her tree.

Mayvers was still fighting the first two giants. The second no longer had his long hoe but swung a branch instead at the palace guard's head. One attacker was lying dead on the ground near where she knelt, while two more giants fought beyond the body. Only the uniforms kept her straight as to who was friend and who was foe. The uniformed men had weapons, but one of the attackers had sliced a guard down and now was brandishing the fallen man's sword.

She sent a pile of dried leaves into the face of one of Mayvers's attackers when feeling in her right arm came back. Raising both arms, she boldly walked away from the tree and slowly made her way to Mayvers's side.

"We cannot stay here!" she hissed, frustrated at how little her magic affected the giants. Even the dirt and other elements she blasted at the attackers had little impact.

"Make for the river," he yelled as he swiped his sword at the ax-wielding giant. "To your left!" he guided as his weapon struck his attacker on the neck.

Shiarra didn't wait to see the blood pour from the injury but turned on her heels and ran. She ducked and swerved around weapons aimed at her, using her magic to speed her movements as she fled.

She didn't feel like a coward for racing away from the fight. Her mind had already rationalized that this was not her fight, these were not her people. These creatures had forced slavery on the weaker, smaller humans, and, it appeared, on their own people, as well. No, this was not her fight. After all, she was a small woman lost inside a giant's land. And she was in danger.

She felt the sting of the arrow as it pierced her thigh just below her hip. Her steps faltered and she sprawled on the ground.

Spitting dirt and mud from her mouth, she held in the scream as she rolled over to blast her attackers. Finding no one near, she looked down at the arrow protruding from her leg. The tip had punched right through and protruded out the back of her leg. Its wicked metal tip glistened with her blood.

Knowing what she must do, she sent magic towards the pain

and numbed her leg. Then she grabbed the arrow's head and snapped it between her hands. The wood was strong, but after the second attempt it crackled. Then she used her magic to blast it apart between her fingers.

Next, she grabbed the shaft that was sticking out the back of her leg and gave a hard tug. She couldn't feel the pain, but the blood streaming from her leg made her light-headed. Quickly, before she could lose consciousness, she sent heat into the wound and seared it shut, slowing the blood loss.

Knowing she could not run any further now that her leg was injured, she listened to the fighting and realized the sounds had grown faint. Not sure if the struggle was ending or drawing away from her, she looked about in the darkness for a hiding place.

The ferns were everywhere and after grabbing the broken arrow and covering the blood with fallen leaves, she crawled over to her new hiding place and fell asleep.

Now, as daylight streamed through the foliage, she feared she would be discovered. She listened for sounds but heard nothing. Taking a chance, she peeked out of her hiding place.

"This will not do," came a voice alarmingly close to her.

She hated to admit it, but she was sure she squealed upon hearing the voice. A small chuckle followed, and she realized she knew the speaker.

"Gado?" she asked. She peeked from her ferns, looking for the odd lizard from the Kylix.

"At your service," Gado said as he materialized inches from her hiding place.

9

MOVE ASIDE

The Régorge Palace was abuzz with activity as the captured infiltrators, along with the two accomplices, were led up the many halls of the Latria quarters. Their final destination was the Grands' throne room, yet the group hadn't gotten far when they found the halls full of curious Latria. It appeared that word of their presence had spread quickly.

Numerous Latria moved up and down the halls, either serving the giants or completing regular duties, which included maintenance of the building itself. Some held trays, others carried brooms or dusting fans as they moved past the large group, which was currently marching toward the stairs that led to the giants' domains.

Whispered speculation floated in the air behind the group as they passed. Tresstéanna thought it was as if all the individual rooms had emptied and their occupants had spilled out into the hallway just to witness the march of the captives who had been found in the very depths of the fortress.

Several eyes held speculation, no doubt wondering how so many Gi Jón had done the impossible and infiltrated the castle. Some cast their eyes downward, either in shame or fear that they too would be bound and marched to the unknown. Others looked on with a gleam of hope behind their eyes, as if they too sought what these prisoners had attempted to gain—freedom.

Tresstéanna walked with her head high as the chains rattled on her arms and legs. She and Wizard Leian each had a guard on either side, while her friends, which now included Amándo and his sister, Madera, were chained together and made to march behind her. She knew the extra guards were given to the gifted and marveled at the assumption that none of her friends held magic as well.

Head guard Weston led the procession with Paren close on his heels. No one noticed Belent's absence, which she was thankful for. Paren had a smug look on her sour face, while Weston's face still remained sober.

As she walked, Tresstéanna's fear ate away inside her. She struggled internally as her feet continued. Her fear wasn't for her, but for her friends. It gnawed at her and whispered horrors that might befall them. Would Grand Cline have them killed? Would they be thrown into dark cells and forgotten for years?

She cast a quick glance backwards and saw anger grow on Kriston's face. His strong jaw was set, and he flexed his arms, which were shackled before him, to test the strength of the chains.

Col's dark face mirrored that of Kriston's, but it was the wizard's fingers that flexed, and she knew he yearned to zap their captors with his magic.

She took comfort that one of the guards carried the Greilk box, which held the Globe of Corpuscle and Adulario's blue eye. But she noticed that Stria, Kip, Farin, and Hilar looked as if they yearned to struggle against their chains and race back to the room where the glides still hid.

The dragon warriors had always known freedom, and to be chained inside a giant's fortress without a fight was mind boggling.

Part of her wished to race to the glides as well, to use her magic and force their way to freedom. This fighting urge was so ingrained inside her that she had to bite the side of her cheek to keep from following these urges.

Yet, if they were to succeed in their mission, they had to gain access to the Pagilda mirror and then find the Orwic flower hidden within. Then there was the message about a new powerful foe, an enemy they had to dispatch within the mirror itself.

Word within the palace seemed to have spread, because before they had reached the hall leading directly into the Grands' throne room, they found the path blocked. Men and women of both sizes stood within the hall waiting, watching. When Weston drew close to the first Nephilim, he found his way barred and looked up into the dark face of a large rather fat giant.

"Step aside, counselor Radif," Weston demanded with a slight bow of his head. "The Grand must deal with this."

"Is it true you found them in the Latria chambers?" Radif demanded, neither moving nor acknowledging the prisoners yet. His red face spoke of heavy drinking while his waistline spoke of frequent meals, possibly including many sweets.

"Grand Cline is waiting," Weston replied and asked once more for the giant to step aside.

"We have a right to know!" Radif demanded. "If we have been overrun by the Otomi fighters, we all need to know!"

"I heard there was a breach in the lower levels, that at this very moment there is fighting going on below us!" one Nephilim woman shrieked as others shot questions at the small guard about rumors they too had heard.

"These are the only that were found!" Weston said loudly,

causing every voice to quiet as he addressed the hallway's inhabitants. "I am expected in the Grand's presence. I am sure he will address your concerns once all has been made clear."

The way was reluctantly cleared, and the large doors were opened to reveal Prime Magal standing a few feet inside the door. His Nephilim guards prevented anyone from entering, but the crowd was persistent and after much debate with counselor Radif, the Prime had to concede to the crowd's entrance.

Small and large men and women flooded into the throne room as the prisoners were led to the dais. All moved quietly to find a good place to see and hear the proceedings. Tresstéanna thought the hush in the room almost deafening.

Grand Cline stood waiting for them on his stage, his face set in anger as his eyes took in the large group. Tresstéanna felt the heat of his anger when his eyes finally landed on her.

"What have you done?" he demanded, the challenging words spat out as if she had betrayed him.

Knowing their fate rested as if it perched on the edge of a fine sword, she squared her shoulders and took a deep breath.

"My people have come to save me from your prison," she stated, the authority of her royal upbringing ringing from her every word, along with a little of her magic.

She knew what she said here would be judged not only by the leader of these people, but also by the crowd encircling them. Despite Cline feeling that he was an all-powerful ruler, he still answered to his subjects, much like she did in Genoa to her people.

"Since you imprisoned me, my kin have fought day and night to free me from your fortress. They have aided the Otomi fighters in attacking your men, striking at your supply lines, and freeing the Latria, all while trying to gain my freedom." She knew her magic would work on the Latria, but she feared some of the magic she'd woven into her words might not work on the larger Nephilim. Using all her strength, she pushed harder, spinning her importance and urgency for freedom like a mist upon the crowd. Using her feelings and pressing them against the will of those gathered around her.

"The Otomi fighters!" Gorphen said as he took a step towards her. "What of my daughter? Have they seen her inside the forest? Do they hold her captive?"

"They probably killed her," Grand Cline spat with disgust. His anger kept Tresstéanna's magic from infecting him. "Latria have no honor and no freedom, they never have!"

"No, she cannot be dead." Gorphen shook his head at Cline's words.

Glancing around, Tresstéanna noticed that several giants shook their head at Cline's words regarding the slaves. She understood that the debate about slavery ran deep within the Nephilim ranks.

"I am not Latria!" she hissed and took a step forward. "I am Tresstéanna Rose Reginald, queen of Valorna, the majestic city nestled on the shores of the golden Enry, which lays in the heart of Genoa!" Her words vibrated against the walls as several Latria shrank from her magic-infused words. "I and my people are not yours, and neither are any of these Latria!"

Out of the corner of her eyes she saw several gathered around nod their heads in agreement, while others raised their fists in support.

"Freedom will be ours again with or without your approval." She turned away from Grand Cline's angry face to study the gathered crowd. "Slavery is an abomination and will end now!" Again, several within the crowd nodded and one or two shouted in agreement. "If freedom is not given, it must be taken!"

The noise from the crowd was now deafening. As she looked around, she saw several Nephilim shrink from the room. Some disappeared out the main door while others vanished into smaller doorways. Some, however, remained rooted in their spots as if wanting to witness the outcome.

"We are not yours to possess. We demand rights to live our own lives just like you!" Tresstéanna continued. "Where I come from, all are free!"

"You are not from here?" It was Maven Gorphen who spoke as he drew close to where Grand Cline stood. There was speculation on his face, and his dark eyes held questions. He rubbed his chin as he stopped near the Grand.

"I am from Genoa!" Tresstéanna said boldly. "The goddess sent me and my friends on a quest, one that was interrupted when I was captured and then imprisoned by you."

"Genoa?" Gorphen said as he stepped off the podium towards her, but his questions were immediately interrupted by Grand Cline.

"You and your kind have started this rebellion; you are the reason my wife is missing!" Cline's hateful face turned even redder. "You are the reason for all this mess!"

"No," Tresstéanna replied with a small shake of her head. "No, Grand Cline, you have brought all this torment upon yourselves."

"No more!" Cline shouted and pointed a large finger at her. "Your services are no longer required. Take them Maven, do what you will with the gifted." Do what you want with all of them." With this, Cline turned his back on the crowd.

With his dismissal, those who still gathered grew angry. Some shouted demands to free the slaves, while others shouted insults at those in the chains. Several voices shouted louder, as if trying to be heard, while others started chanting the single word, freedom!

As the guards tugged on her chains, chaos finally erupted around them as the Latria and the Nephilim started fighting within the walls of the Régorge Palace.

SHIARRA WAS RELIEVED to see Gado the lizard sitting a few feet from her hiding place. She'd never expected to see the little lizard outside of the dark Kylix cave, let alone in the forest. She marveled at his resourcefulness at having found her as she looked at him.

"Have you seen anyone else?" Shiarra asked, and quickly looked around, hoping for her missing friends to be only steps away from the lizard.

"You are all I have tracked so far," Gado said as he turned his odd head around, each eye facing a different direction as his scaly skin shone in the morning's light.

"Gado, do you know where we are?" she asked as she slowly crawled out of the large ferns that had hidden her from the fighting the night before.

As she wiped dirt and leaves from her skirt, she hoped he could help her navigate the vast forest they currently stood in. Maybe he could help her reunite with Kriston and the other dragon warriors who were with the Otomi fighters. She didn't know where Kriston or the others might be, but she had seen the lizard guide them in the Kylix. He might know this world.

"Do you know where the others are?" she simplified after several seconds of silence from the lizard.

"I know enough. The river is several yards to your right, the palace sits high in the rocks behind you, and both are unobtainable," Gado said with a flick of his tongue. "Several of your friends are in the palace and some have traveled towards the river. But both directions are now dangerous and should not be attempted."

"I have to try; I need to rejoin my friends," Shiarra said with a shake of her head.

"No, our path in either direction would be unproductive." The lizard's words frustrated her, and she leaned down to get a better look at him. Her injured leg gave her a little trouble.

"What do you suggest?" she asked as his scales shimmered again in the light.

"We will return to the Kylix," Gado said with authority. "Leewana awaits us."

Shiarra felt torn by this news. After all, she knew the dangers of the palace. If she returned to the palace, she would be reunited with her friends and Leian but would lose her freedom.

She also had seen the dangers the forest could hold. She now knew giants with no restrictions dwelled here in the trees. Both thoughts had her hesitating as Gado turned to leave.

Her eyes moved upwards to where she thought the palace might be, and her thoughts turned to Leian once again. Only the thick branches could be seen from where she stood. Little light filtered down to the forest floor. She felt a sense of guilt standing there as thoughts of following Gado filled her. The Kylix was no safer than the other two options, but Leewana was there and it was familiar ground for her. But the cave now held none of her friends.

"Are you coming?" Gado's question had Shiarra turning to look at the lizard.

"Gado, what of my friends?" she asked, casting another look backwards.

"We will get to them later. First we must deal with what happens in the Kylix." These words had Shiarra quickly turning back to him.

"What is happening in the cave?" She rushed over to where Gado was, careful of her injury. She knelt to where he sat in the dirt.

"Much," Gado replied with a shake of his head. "Many giants have fled into the caves, and the monsters amass. They have tried to climb out of the water, but the giants fight them with great skill."

Shiarra's focus blurred from the massive forest they stood within. It spun quickly down underground to the cave called the Kylix. In her mind's eye, she once again saw the dark dirt and glowing walls of the cave. She remembered the battle with the giants that had resulted in her capture. But she had no knowledge of monsters.

"Monsters?" she asked and her mind came up with the large ants and spiders they had encountered before in the dark cavern.

"Dreail's children," Gado replied as his eyes turned to her. "Huge creatures the Protector has spawned. They slither and crawl out of the waters of the massive lake down in the cavern. They attack the giants' village down in the cave nightly. So far, Leewana has aided in keeping them from overtaking the giants, however the battles are horrific, and help is needed."

"You want to take me there? Without my friends?" Shiarra asked. Fear caused her voice to rise an octave in a high squeak.

"Leewana grows concerned," Gado said, "but she still keeps Dreail's monsters imprisoned within the waters, for now."

"Gado, I cannot fight monsters!" She dropped to the ground next to the little lizard, suddenly exhausted. Last night's sleep ripped away from her, and her injured leg ached as the lizard's words sank in, and her situation finally became clear to her.

She was a wizard, dropped into a vast new world where her magic was useless against the giants that dwelled there. She was alone, whisked away from her friends, who were still imprisoned inside the giants' palace or across a river with a war between her and them. Utterly alone in a strange world.

Despair filled her until she remembered that not too long ago her friend Anna had been in the same situation. Anna had come from an entirely different planet, one that did not even hold magic.

Her thoughts turned from her situation to the one Anna had been in, then it moved to their first meeting. They had been in Tharian, the wizard's village, then. She remembered she had rushed into the training building upon hearing that her mentor, Wizard Leian, had returned.

She felt her cheeks turn pink as she remembered how shy she had been about her feelings for Leian. She had been so focused on Leian that she had first failed to see Anna in the room.

Anna had seemed confident, yet she had been in a strange magical world. She had learned about her past, about magic, and about her situation. A situation that predicted her melting with two other women, Té and Tress, both so different from Anna. One was a warrior who rode on the back of a golden dragon and fought like a she-cat. The other was a delicate queen who ruled Genoa with grace and an underlying knowledge that spies lived within her home.

Despite Anna being in a different land, the woman had only shown curiosity, no fear or panic, much like Shiarra felt now. The courage Anna had shown during their travels those first days in Genoa now had some bravery building inside Shiarra.

"Courage in the face of danger," she mumbled. She stood once more, then turned to Gado. The lizard had his head tilted as he studied her with his odd eyes.

"Well, I cannot fight giants, but I might be of some help against monsters," she said with a smile as she lifted her head gallantly.

AVA FELT the soft sands shift into solid ground beneath her. Stones and packed ground supplied enough hold for prickly bushes and hard grasses to grow.

As the Húriya army moved out of the Rájpú Desert and into the Parós Plains, she felt the night's march catch up to her. Exhaustion threatened to overtake her with each step.

After their near miss encounter with the Scarent Biard the Wright, the army had quickened their march at Rastel's insistence. The ambassador to Genoa felt a great urgency, which he relayed to Ava and the army. He did not say why speed was needed, only that it was.

The men under her command walked the night through the desert and then moved beyond. When the sun arose in the sky before them, it found weary but determined travelers.

Yet the army of over two thousand still moved more slowly than she had hoped. Supply carts that were built to glide across soft sand had to be adjusted for hard rocky soil. Wheels replaced the sleds, which took time. Dark Gauras were still worn by most, and the long cloaks snagged on sharp thorns. Soon, most of the men had their cloaks off, rolled into their packs, and their pant legs tucked into their high boots.

"Rest is close at hand," Rastel said close to Ava as she shielded her eyes from the rising sun. "When you find the first shade, take it. I will go ahead and gather those who hold true to our mother's ways."

Shade? Ava thought as she studied the rolling plains before her. The odd dead grasses and thorny low bushes offered nothing close to shade in the morning light. Light that she knew too well would blast down upon the army with unforgiving heat.

It took several more hours before they found a large, long, and deep crack in the ground that offered the much-needed rest and shade. The entire army fit inside the crevice with room to spare. Soon men were asleep against the cool rocks or dirt.

Several guards were posted, and Ava too found comfort in the little shade provided. Using her rolled up Gaura as a pillow, she dropped off to sleep. When she awoke, it was well past midday, and the sun was moving towards the eastern horizon in its lazy path.

"My Zaeim, Rastel has yet to return," Pothel said as he handed her a full water skin.

"No matter," she replied as she stood and dusted off her long black cloak. "We continue to the forest."

"Our scouts say we are close to where the forest starts," Pothel informed her. "They have followed the tracks of the Scarent but, luckily, did not see the creature."

"Very well. Any Mellifera sightings?" Ava asked as she turned to study the sky around her.

"None," Pothel said as he too turned to look at the blue

sky. "But we have been well hidden in our shade. Maybe they are looking for us far to the south?"

"Very well," Ava replied and handed back the water skin. "Where is Commander Switz?"

"Here," Commander Switz replied as he came up to her from behind. "Our men are ready; they have finished their meals and await orders."

"You let me sleep?" Ava asked Pothel, who turned a little red when he nodded. "Very well, I can eat while I walk."

The scouts were correct. Before the heat of the day lessened, they noticed the first of the massive Kelan trees of the Median Forest. At first the trees, which were small and bent in odd shapes that spoke of high winds or drought, were sparse. Then the underbrush grew greener and the trees themselves taller with thick trunks. When the trees grew closer together, Switz stopped the army and consulted the maps.

"We are too far west," Switz said as he pointed at a spot on the map. "We should have hit the end of the river and turned left to reach the northern side of the Tabescent. Instead we will reach the southern banks with no means to cross the river, except by the giants' bridge, which lays deep within the forest. A forest they control."

"If the bridge still stands," Ava speculated as she leaned over the map to get a better look.

"It does not," one of Switz's scouts said as he ran up to them. "The path to our right is blocked and fighting is taking place far inside the forest, near the water."

Ava quickly studied the dense forest, as if trying to see what lay beyond the large trunks. But since she couldn't even hear any fighting, she quickly turned to look at the scout.

"Fighting between the Otomi and Nephilim?" she asked, concerned their forces were too late to make a difference in the war.

"No, only giants struggle that way. I saw no Gi Jón," the scout said with a shake of his dark head.

"We need a Mellifera to scout out what is going on," she said with frustration.

A shout rang out from the rear ranks of the army. Thinking they were under attack, she turned quickly from the map. Pothel and Commander Switz both pulled swords from their belts as more voices rang out.

"Rastel comes!" Ava heard one of the captains say.

"Where?" she hollered. She placed a hand on both Commander Switz's arm and Pothel's so they would lower their blades.

As she rushed through the ranks of the Kós Kóvar army, her eyes scanned the open fields. She knew she couldn't see Rastel, but she smiled when she noticed what the ambassador had brought.

Behind the desert army stood a new one. This army held twice as many men but also included women and children. Most wore work clothing instead of uniforms. Some carried weapons, while others carried bags or pulled carts behind them.

Shouts of joy rang out from the newcomers as they drew near the impressive army of the desert people. Women wept with joy, and babies wailed at the commotion. As Ava drew near the edge of the Húriya army, she noticed hope in every face that approached them.

"Zaeim, these are the lost," Pothel said from beside her.

She didn't need his words to know that those who approached were Latria who had been taken from Kós Kóvar and their descendants.

"So many," she whispered as tears trailed down her face.

"My lady, these are Húriya. They have been held against their will and wish to join you," Rastel's voice echoed near her. "Will you accept them?"

"Yes, these are my people too." She reached up to scrub the tears from her face.

The approaching Latria paused as they drew near. The men at the front looked similar to those who currently were behind her in the Kós Kóvar army. Women came next, and Ava noticed similar faces to those she had left. These were her kin, people who had been ripped from their homes and family. People who had flourished even while under oppression.

Hundreds of faces looked at her as she stood before the Kós Kóvar army, her dark cloak thrown back, her eyes painted black, and tear tracks still fresh on her cheeks. The faces were filled with questions and hope. The men and woman who stood yards before her studied her, waiting.

Waiting for freedom.

"Húriya people, we have come for you!" she shouted as cheers rose from those before and behind her.

BELENT FELT Tresstéanna's magic flow through the air as she spoke. Pride and respect filled him as he watched his queen influence the large crowd gathered in the throne room.

His sorcerer's magic kept him hidden from all eyes, yet he soon found his path blocked. Despite his body being invisible, it was still physical. If he wasn't careful, he might collide with those who were gathered. If he bumped into a giant or a Gi Jón, his deception would be discovered.

Keeping to the walls of the room, he'd seen smaller arguments break out long before the actual fighting started. Several Latria had gained the upper palace floors quickly upon hearing that some Otomi fighters had gained access to the palace. These slaves appeared to have hoped for their own rescue, either by family members or loved ones.

Most were women who had been sold into work for the palace kitchens, but there were a few men. These men were strong and worked manual labor that resulted in strong backs and hard muscles. Some were even guards who served under Weston. Belent heard their arguments with the surrounding Nephilim, which had resulted from Tresstéanna's convictions and words. He heard several Nephilim agree with his queen's words and they moved closer to the smaller Gi Jón, as if seeking to shelter their smaller friends.

Most Nephilim, however, remained rooted in their spots as if made of stone. Anger covered their faces as their jewels glittered in the room's lights. They shook their hands at Tresstéanna's words or nodded when Grand Cline spoke.

Tresstéanna's magic continued flowing with each of her words. But Belent saw hate grow on Grand Cline's face as she spoke. He felt that, in that instant, the man didn't really care that his wife and unborn child were missing. His anger wasn't for their loss, but for the inconvenience this rebellion was causing him.

Belent would give anything to have his wife and child back. If they were only yards from him, down in a forest filled with enemies, he would be running for the door, not standing here speaking of slavery. But his family was not down in the forest, or even back in Genoa. His family had been taken from him by the evil King Gillard, Kriston's brother. They had been killed and, hopefully, had traveled beyond this world to the next.

If Grand Carrington were to walk back into the room, safe and unharmed, Belent doubted Cline would even notice. So great was the man's anger that he missed the discord within his own throne room. Belent saw it, though. He also noticed several giants leave the room while the others, who remained, started shouting.

The physical fighting started when Prime Magal's men grabbed the chains that bound Tresstéanna. It was more than shoving and pushing now. Belent heard the crashing of metal on metal as swords met each other in anger.

He heard a woman scream and turned his eyes back to where his queen and friends had been. They were all crouched on the ground as if they had been swept off their feet with one swift blow. In fact, they had been knocked down, and the giant who had grabbed Tresstéanna's chains had been struck down. The man lay flat on his back, dead, as two huge freedom fighters stood over his body.

Several Latria men stood around the two, each with sharp wooden sticks or short knives as weapons. Their faces were set in determination as they looked out at the growing fighting. A third Latria man approached and tried to pick up a fallen giant's sword as he rushed forward. The sword must have been too heavy for him, so he moved to grab a nearby chair. The two freedom fighter giants held their large swords protectively in front of the smaller men, while several Latria women rushed forward to aid the fallen.

As he tried to move through the room towards his friends, he saw one woman hit a giant with her frying pan. She gave a mighty whack to the guard's shin, and the giant doubled over in pain while another woman jumped on his back with her own pan. When a swift hit to the head resulted in his unconsciousness, the women moved off as a team to replicate the move on another. The sound of heads being smacked by frying skillets had a smile forming on his lips.

CRACK!

"Freedom for the Latria!" one giant shouted as four more rushed forward to join the freedom fighters. Weapons were raised, swords and pans alike, as the odd fighting continued around him. Belent stopped and gazed on in amazement.

He noticed an arrow fly at the nearest freedom fighter, but it hit the man's armor and dropped to the ground in shards, harmless. Several of the palace guards rushed forward, their swords swung high as they took one of the rebel giants down. This action had more Latria pouring into the room. Odd weapons such as brooms and even crockery blasted at the oppressors.

Belent watched as Weston and twenty of his men turned and faced the onslaught of guards. The small loyalist guard had a smile on his face as he turned towards the approaching giant force.

"Freedom or death!" Weston shouted as he and his men raced to meet the palace giants.

Dishes and vases flew through the air as the noise of breaking cutlery mixed with the screams of pain. A well-aimed vase hit the forehead of one of the palace guards near Belent's hiding place. The giant toppled close to Belent, and he felt the floor shake. He finally sprang into action.

Time to go, Belent thought, and he raced towards his friends. He dropped his invisible magic as he ran and started to blast the room with bright red lights. He didn't aim for any one person but wanted to add to the chaos of the fighting, hoping to draw attention away from himself.

He had to move around several skirmishes as he raced to where he had last seen Tresstéanna. The Latria outnumbered the giant guards, but with the size of the giants, the battle was intense. He thought that the smaller Gi Jón would surely lose, except there were several Nephilim who stood with them, battling their own to ensure freedom for all. This might even the fighting field and, if Belent and his friends helped, the Latria might win.

Belent slipped in some blood that was pooled on the

ground as he neared Tresstéanna and the others. Kriston held a large sword in his hands. It appeared to be two sizes too big for him to wield. His large arms strained to keep it pointed out at the fighting while Col and Leian used their magic to blast any who neared.

The other dragon warriors were using their chains to whip out at any attackers. Several Latria stood guard, using sticks or pottery on any who wished harm for those who were chained.

"Hurry, this way," Belent said. He pointed to one of the side doors he had seen many of the Latria escape or appear from.

"The chains!" Col shouted and turned his magic upon the iron.

Belent also blasted his magic at the iron, and soon the chains were pooled at their feet. Another scream rent the air as Kriston flung the useless sword away and charged a nearing attacker.

When the prince rammed his head into the giant's stomach, Belent sent his own magic at the man's head. Either the momentum of Kriston's blow or the blast of Belent's magic did the trick. The large giant fell backwards, taking Kriston with him.

"Kriston!" Tresstéanna screamed and rushed forward just as the prince reappeared, climbing over the unconscious giant's body as if it were a boulder.

"Quickly, over here!" A loud shout had Belent turning. He saw Weston and several more of the Latria guards standing near the very doorway he had pointed to previously.

"Hurry!" Belent shouted, sending his magic out at two approaching guards.

He followed behind his friends as they fled through the chaos that now filled the once quiet throne room of the Régorge Palace.

BIARD HEARD the cheer rise into the air from far behind him. Hate filled him upon hearing the joyful voices as his frustration built.

He could smell the thief, taste the very air he had passed through. In his mind he registered the difference in the smell, but so great was his anger, that he no longer cared.

The forest would not stop him from seeking his revenge. His long legs ate up the distance, even in this jungle. Underbrush and large tree trunks continued to block his way, forcing him to zigzag around obstacles.

Biard could all but taste the revenge he craved. The act started to take a solid form inside his mind. It filled his vision as his thoughts turned to how sweet it would feel to crush the life of the Scarent. To see both snake and host die.

He no longer cared who got in his way, giant or animal. They all burned before him as he continued to follow the faint trail. He had accidently happened into a camp of giants settled inside a large glade in the jungle before he registered danger. Annoyance filled him as they started to attack.

Red and green blasts of magic flared from his hands as his eyes sought his prey. His anger sparked brighter at not finding the Scarent hidden with the giants.

Spinning in fast circles, he quickly attacked. He killed most of the Nephilim before they could even draw their weapons. But several got past their fallen comrades and attacked him with large swords or arrows. One hard blast from his magic had their bodies flying away from him. The smell of burned flesh filled his nostrils as he moved to leave the glade.

He could still hear the screams of the dying, and he smiled wickedly as he neared the vast river. Finding no bridge across the dangerous Tabescent River raised his annoyance. He marched up and down the wide shore and saw no way across the Degurt-filled waters.

Biard the Wright suddenly realized his mistake. He had entered the forest on the wrong side of the water.

Birds abandoned their nests and small creatures scurried from the area as he let out a loud scream in fury. The yell echoed through the forest like a boom of thunder for all to hear.

CRAZY PLANS

Svlain held Zain's hand as they stood in the tall tree's shade and looked out at the vast river. Grand Carrington stood feet from them, her head covered by her cloak as the hot sun filtered through the leaves.

Even this early in the day the heat stole your breath. It sucked all moisture from your body and replaced it with salty sweat that stuck to your skin and dripped into your eyes.

Their expedition to the river confirmed their fears—the rope bridge had been severed. But it had been cut before and would be rehung again. Their biggest fear was what appeared to lie on the other side of the Tabescent River. Its raging waters roared loudly, drowning out all forest noise, including sounds from men.

Svlain shielded her eyes as she tried to focus on the vision that moved across the waters. Mayson and his men had agreed to accompany them to the water's edge, but insisted they remain hidden.

"Even from this distance, a well-aimed arrow can injure,"

Mayson said as his dark eyes studied the forest far across the water.

"Where did they come from?" Colab asked as he drew close to the edge of the tree's dark shade.

"All sentries retreated to our side of the river during the battles last night. The fighting was so intense that we lost thirty men before we cut the bridge," Cerg said with a shake of his head. When a runner came up to him, he turned his back on the small group and had a fast yet quiet argument with the lad. When finished, he turned back to talk to Mayson and the others. "Even more approach from the east."

"More?" Svlain asked as she squeezed Zain's hand for comfort.

"This new group holds giants."

Cerg's words had Svlain realizing her mistake. She had immediately assumed the army across the river held enemies. Yet when she glanced across the water, she noticed only smaller humans, no giants.

This realization had her heart leaping into her throat. What if? What if this was Ava and the army from Kós Kóvar?

"Mayson, have all the Mellifera flyers left?" She shielded her eyes from the bright sun as she stepped out of the safety of the shade and into the bright rays. Zain tried to pull her back, but she shook her head and turned to look once more.

"There!" Her shout had several men stepping deeper into the trees while Zain gave her a hard tug. As she landed on the ground with Zain's body protectively covering her, she gave a small squeal.

"Let me up!" she urged. She pushed his large shoulders, with no results. "She may move away if she does not know I am here."

Her words did what her attempts to regain her feet could not. Zain stopped trying to protect her and looked down at her worried face.

"She?"

"Ava!" she shouted and scampered out from under Zain's body. She boldly stepped into the sun and waved her left arm and pointed with her right. "See! There she is. The figure in the black cloak!" Svlain shouted as a small figure from across the river mirrored her movements by waving her arms.

What came next seemed to take forever. With the appearance of Ava, the Zaeim from Kós Kóvar, along with the vast army, plans to hoist the replacement rope bridge started immediately. But since this plan involved pullies and very large crossbows, this took some time. They were able to use the Mellifera riders to fly the ropes across the water, but even with their aid, it took time.

Before midday the work had to stop due to the intense heat. Svlain felt saddened to see the army, which was settled across the river, disappear into the forest shade. The bees settled down along the river's shore, finding shade where they could.

Zain insisted Grand Carrington use this time to rest and ensured she drank lots of water. She and Svlain found a nearby abandoned home to rest in. Even inside the home's protective walls, the heat was almost unbearable.

Svlain helped Carrington remove her long dress, and the two women lay around in their undergarments, fanning themselves. Maraneal joined them, and the desert woman gave them a root to chew that helped lower their body temperatures.

"The Knoda root is usually sipped in water, but during intense heat, it is best chewed raw," Maraneal said with a small smile.

"I have never heard of this root," Carrington said with amazement as she took another bite of the pale pink root, which looked so small in her hands.

"It only grows in the sandy desert," Maraneal said with a small lift of her shoulders.

After the heat of the day lessened, the work to replace the bridge resumed. Both sides of the river were now filled with many people as they waited for the joining with the resistance army. Several had never seen the large bees and shouted and pointed when one flew close to them.

It appeared word of the Húriya army's arrival had spread quickly in the ranks of the freedom fighters. All soon gathered, anxious to see the people from across the desert. Soon men and women lined the river's edge and both Gi Jón and Nephilim children alike ran around. All kept in the shade while they waited in the hopes of catching a glimpse of the army that had come to aid in the fighting.

Svlain saw Ava and her man Pothel giving directions while they attempted to aid in the hanging of the new rope bridge. Svlain realized that the army across the river had doubled in size since she had first seen them. She counted twenty Mellifera riders and wished one would come to pick her up and bring her across the water to her friend Ava, but she had to practice patience until the bridge was finished.

When giants were spotted joining the forces across the river, Mayson told her he recognized one as a farmer who was sympathetic to their plight. She counted over fifty giants, including young children, who were smaller than their parents but still larger than the tallest of Gi Jón.

"These must be people from the plains, farmers who work in the fields that feed our land," Cerg said when Colab asked. "Far to the south there are great farm fields."

"Yes, we—I mean, I—noticed them on my travels when I first arrived here," Colab said as he absently rubbed a hand over his neck where once had laid the Scarent snake Meshi. Svlain felt sympathy for the boy who had already lost so much. When Maraneal's hand reached up and took Colab's wandering hand, Svlain hid her smile by looking back out at the progress of the bridge.

When the last rope was tied and the bridge had been tested for strength, Svlain and her friends moved across to be the first to welcome the growing army. Ava was there to greet her and make introductions between Mayson and Commander Switz.

Svlain was shocked and pleased when Rastel made his presence known. She found it comforting that Genoa's ambassador was present. Colab expressed his relief that the invisible creature had survived his battle against Biard the Wright and, after locating the tall creature, threw his small human arms around the ambassador in a hug.

The leaders of the Húriya army—which included Commander Switz, Ava the Zaeim, and her man Pothel—met with the Otomi fighters' leader, Mayson. Svlain and Zain joined the meeting along with Colab and Rastel. Grand Carrington too was present at this meeting, which was held in the shade of the largest nearby tree.

Plans were quickly discussed between this odd collection of Gi Jón, Húriya, and Nephilim. Grand Carrington urged them to limit the fighting in the hopes of preventing the death of many. She talked about trying a peaceful march upon the palace, one where she led the procession and demanded the palace guards lay down their weapons.

"If we gain the bridge to the palace, the rest should be easy," Carrington explained, her large hands nestled in her lap as she faced the leaders of the army who were there in the forest to lay siege to her home. "The bridge is the only way in and out. We can demand my husband relinquish the Latria who remain within the walls. Once that is done, we will then begin talks to ensure peace will continue in Midzark."

"My lady, you hold much hope that your husband will value your return," Commander Switz said boldly with a shake of his head. "We must have another plan set if your idea fails."

"I know my husband; I also know my father would not allow Cline to abandon me," Carrington said, but Svlain noticed doubt in the woman's eyes. When she finally saw courage bloom in Carrington's eyes as well, she smiled.

As a strong wind blew across Svlain's face, her eyes went wide with shock as her magic took ahold of her.

Buzzing filled the air as the trees that surrounded her shook with fire.

Turning, Svlain watched as a massive tree arched across her vision and fell towards the river. Screams rose above the relentless buzzing as men and women fled the fires.

"Hurry, he comes for you!" Mayson shouted from beside her.

When she turned to look, Svlain noticed the leader of the freedom fighters had been blown backwards. His body burned and smoked, and he was dead before he landed on the grass several feet away.

Colab raced into her vision, his hands raised as his magic blasted into the burning forest yards from them. Hate and anguish filled the young prince's face as he raced forward.

"You killed me!" Colab shouted as he blasted his magic into the approaching figure.

"Come at me, thief!" Biard the Wright hissed as he sent his killing magic into the body of Colab.

GRAND CLINE DIDN'T KNOW it, but he had lost any control he'd ever had over the Régorge Palace long before Tresstéanna's magical words reached the ears of those gathered inside the throne room.

In fact, by the time Kriston and the dragon warriors had reached the palace, discord had reached an all-time high. This discord traveled not only amongst the Latria who were enslaved inside the royal walls, but also the giants who felt too much control sat with their leader.

The kitchen area was where the flames of freedom had ignited, spreading out from the cooks to the scullery maids with the help of Madera, Amándo's sister. Those who whispered of freedom had to be cautious; the loyalists were everywhere. But since most of those devoted to the Nephilim and their way of enslaving others were wealthy and had servants of their own, it was easy to avoid mention of discord to them. Most loyalist were like Káric, the man who had been a trapper of magical creatures. Káric had his private rooms and kept to his plush apartments down in the Latria quarters like so many of the other loyalists.

So great was the turmoil that by the time the great throne room had been filled, the flames of freedom had grown far beyond control. Grand Cline and his Prime Magal, along with their guards, were useless to contain the outbreak. Even as Cline issued his orders for the Maven to take the intruders, the slaves were starting their attacks.

But these attacks hadn't started inside the throne room like Tresstéanna and her friends had believed. In fact, once the Prime and his guards had entered the room, the kitchens had emptied of slaves.

The first act of the freedom fighters had been to secure their own area. Large wooden brooms and mops had been used to overthrow the Gi Jón–sized guards who were still loyal to the giants. Then, once subdued, they were imprisoned inside the plush rooms along with all the other loyalists.

As the slaves moved to clean the bottom two floors of the palace, they found it quite easy to defeat their opponents, but they knew the hard part was yet to come. They still had to climb the stairs and master the top four floors, where the giants dwelled.

Tresstéanna and her group had fled the battles inside the throne room by the time the lower levels had emptied, and the fighting spread to the palace's hallways.

Kriston had replaced the large sword with a smaller one from Weston's men. Stria and Kip had long wooden sticks and were using them to clear the path as the band raced through the hallways. When Weston moved away from the large stairs, Tresstéanna gave a shout.

"No!" she hollered and pointed to the stairs leading to the Maven's quarters, "We need to gain access to the Maven's rooms!" She raced over to the guard who still carried the Greilk box and smiled when he handed it to her without having to ask. "Thank you."

"Does it really hold our mother?" he asked as wonder filled his dark eyes.

"Yes, and my mission requires that I gain access to the Maven's mirror." Fear filled her with these words, but her determination grew when the guard gave a small bow of his head.

"This way, quickly. The fighting is contained down here for the moment," Weston stated. "You, go ahead and help out where you can. Keep these stairs clear!" he ordered two more who were quickly joined by three loyal giants.

Tresstéanna and her friends followed Weston up the Latria's smaller steps next to the giant stairs. Kriston kept to her side as they raced.

"What is your plan?" he asked, his handsome face set with determination.

"Get the flower and find the new danger the book spoke of," she replied as Belent joined them at the landing.

"The new enemy draws close, but we have some time yet," the sorcerer said as he closed the book and led the way towards the Maven's rooms.

They met no resistance. Tresstéanna was grateful for this, but she feared their luck would not hold much longer. Sounds of the battles far below could be heard even this high in the palace.

She rushed to the large door, and Kriston and Weston pushed against it but found it locked.

"It is barred!" Weston said with anguish as Amándo rushed up.

"No, just the large door. I hold the key to my door." The lad slid a small silver key into a hidden lock at the door's center. When a smaller concealed door slid open, they all rushed inside.

Tresstéanna's eyes fell on the mirror as sweat beaded down her back. Fear and memories came to her. Thoughts of the grey mist and being torn apart over and over again almost overwhelmed her.

"Hold my hand," Kriston demanded as he tugged her towards the mirror.

When she remained rooted, Belent walked forward and took the Greilk box from her and handed it to Farin.

"Let me." Belent took Tresstéanna's hand from Kriston. "Magic might be needed."

Fear still filled her, but the courage of her friends eased her worry as the mirror loomed closer. Her heartbeat threatened to overwhelm her ears as silence filled the room beyond.

The golden frame of the mirror mocked her as the grey of the shiny surface refused to throw back her own reflection.

She could feel her body revolt from what was hidden inside the mist.

"I do not think we need to enter it," Belent whispered next to her. "Just reach in. I will hold your hand to prevent any slippage."

Hearing his words gave her hope, and she spared him a glance before closing the remaining distance. Belent held her left hand while she reached up with her right, her fingers white against the dark swirling mists inside the mirror.

Taking a deep breath, she cast a glance back and noticed her friends. Kriston was close, just a step behind Belent, his face filled with worry as his eyes remained on her. She gave him a small smile then glanced at her other friends.

They all stood around the room, frozen, as if to move would break the spell and put her in harm's way. After taking another breath, she plunged her right arm into the mirror, all the way up to her elbow.

The cold was intense, it felt like her arm had been frozen. Pain shot up through her fingers and almost sucked the breath from her.

She didn't realize she was screaming until Belent tugged her backwards, away from the mirror. She landed on the floor and cradled her right arm as if it were shattered.

Her arm and hand were whole. Kriston quickly picked her up, anger and a mixture of fear in his eyes.

"What in the king's name!" he hissed as she wiggled her fingers.

"I'm ok," she insisted and made a quick fist as she looked at her hand.

"Where is the flower?" Belent asked as the others surrounded her.

"I forgot." She looked at him. "I forgot about the flower; I was so worried about the mirror that I forgot why I stuck my hand in."

"Let me try," Belent said, but he stopped when she shook her head.

"No, I must do it." She brushed Kriston back a step and once again grabbed Belent's hand. "I won't forget now."

Steeling her thoughts from the pain she knew would come, she sucked in a breath and held it as she plunged her hand back into the mirror.

The pain was instantaneous, but she focused her attention instead on the image of the purple flower. So hard was her focus that the pain subsided briefly. She had felt her arm shatter and reform, but this time it felt like there was something inside her hand when it became whole again.

"Now!" she hissed and once again Belent yanked her away from the mirror.

This time, when she fell to the floor, she was cradling the small Orwic flower planted inside a clay pot. As she hit the ground, she heard a yell behind her and turned her head in time to see Maven Gorphen push Farin to the ground and wrestle the Greilk box from the cave expert's hands.

"You brought this upon yourselves!" Gorphen shouted as he fled. "Carrington, my daughter, my only joy!"

"Stop him!" Weston shouted as the giant disappeared through the opened door, carrying the magical box that held the Globe of Corpuscle, Genoa.

As SHIARRA and the lizard Gado raced to reach the high opening to the Krack, she stopped once again to catch her breath. Sweat ran down her face and made her long hair stick to her neck in coils. She had tied the long dark hair back with a strand of her ripped dress, but still small wisps fell around her face and neck.

The climb up to the cave's entrance had been hard and steep and didn't help her injured leg, but magic kept the wound from stopping her. Most of the injury had been healed through her magic before they'd started. She found she only needed to stop twice to push her healing magic more so she could continue her climb.

She had been unconscious when she had been captured and taken out of the cave and now found the height quite intimidating. The path was wide and there were tracks from carts and footprints in the dust from many giants traveling before her. But the edge always seemed to be too close, and the drop-off too great.

Several times she found herself stopped and clinging to the inside cliff face, as if she feared the fall. Gado had talked calmly to her and coaxed her into moving again. But the higher they got, the more frequent the stops had been.

Shiarra tried to distract her mind from the vision of their height by worrying about her friends. Sometimes this worked and her feet would move forward while her mind was engrossed in her concerns.

She would think of Leian. His acts of bravery would make her feel embarrassed by her current fear, and she would square her shoulders and march forward. Until the next switchback. Then her vertigo would take over once again.

The struggles inside Shiarra confused the lizard, but Gado did not show his frustrations. Only once or twice did the lizard shake his head at the woman. But the urgency to return to his home helped him keep his patience with her.

Now, standing at the precipice of the dark cave's mouth, Shiarra did the unthinkable. She looked down at the land far below them.

The Hessite cliffs rose behind her. Even at this great

height, she was amazed that they had yet to scale halfway up the massive cliff. The waterfall was to her right. The sound of the water crashing to the rocks far below was low, but she could still hear it.

Her eyes ran down the ribbon of water and landed on the Régorge Palace. It looked so much smaller than she knew it to be. The brightly painted trimming was dulled at this distance, and part of the palace was hidden from her vision by the center tower.

Her eyes swept over the bridge and landed on the forest far below. She could only see the treetops from this angle, and her eyes quickly moved past the forest to the plains beyond. They seemed so vast and empty until she spotted the golden sands of the desert beyond. Then the plains shrank in size compared to the rolling sand dunes.

Turning to enter the cave, she was momentarily distracted by the farmlands far to the south. Here she saw movement for the first time.

The land had been divided into vast squares. Rows upon rows of growing plants made a patchwork on the ground. It wasn't the farmland that drew her attention but the massive road that split the land in two.

Squinting, she looked closer and found that the road was filled with people. She took a small step towards the edge to get a better look when Gado finally spoke up.

"Those who were enslaved march to the palace," Gado said from his perch next to the cliff's drop-off. "Before the sun sets, the palace will be surrounded."

"But my friends are in there," she finally said when the lizard's words sank in. "I have to…"

She was several steps back down the path when Gado blocked her pathway.

"No, my lady, Leewana needs you," Gado insisted as his

golden eyes flashed at her. "Your friends will join us after this land settles its disputes. You are needed now."

Torn, Shiarra took several minutes to study the approaching army. It was vast and filled the whole of the road. But as she looked closer, she noticed not all were fighters. She saw carts filled with household goods and animals being led behind and even small children racing next to the carts and wagons.

"The Gi Jón are done with their hard work. Most will go back to their homes, but others will travel the great sand and join their forgotten families in the vast city of Kós Kóvar," Gado said with a tilt of his odd head. "I went there once; it is not to my liking. But the humans are happy there."

"Gado, I am done with this land. I wish to never set foot here again. But my friends, will they really join us in the Kylix?" she asked as she knelt before the little lizard.

"We must wait and find out." Gado turned and disappeared into the darkness of the Krack, the tunnel that led down into the rocks and joined with the Kylix.

Standing, Shiarra took one last look at the land far below her and then followed the lizard into the darkness. The Krack was long and dark. Shiarra used her magic to create one of Leian's electrical balls to give her light. The orb floated feet in front of her as she moved down the cave.

The odd lights the giants used were dark, and this gave her some pause until Gado explained that the giants were using the power to fight the monsters far below.

"They pull their resources to fight the children of Dreail. Even the walls of their village have been fortified."

"Village?" Shiarra asked as she remembered the one vision she had seen of the small town deep down in the Kylix. Belent had been held captive there for a time. "I forgot about the village. Are there many giants that live there?"

"Many. They use the caves to beat the heat of Midzark.

They also live down there to lessen the hold the Grands have over them."

"Outcasts?" she asked, a part of her hoping the village was filled with mercenaries and thugs. This way she did not feel so bad if the monsters destroyed all who lived there.

"No. More like a refuge."

Shiarra kept her eyes open as they descended into the dark cave, but her mind wandered back to the sight of the village. It had been a brief look and one done so long ago that what came to her mind was a rather dirty vision of a city on the edge of a vast underground lake, much like Byways sat on the edge of the vast ocean in her land.

But where Byways had flowers and colorful fields with painted homes, this undergrown town had dusty homes made out of rocks and wooden planks.

"You said the giants are capable of fighting these monsters. How so?" she asked as the heat from Midzark finally lessened, and she found her arms and neck cold with chill as they traveled further underground.

"The monsters are easily killed; giants can smash them with clubs and cut them with their large swords. But there are many and the attacks are sporadic," Gado informed her.

"If these giants are here to escape from the Grands' tyranny, will they aid us in our quest?" Shiarra asked as she rubbed her arms to keep them warm.

When Gado stepped out of the Krack and into the vast cavern of the Kylix, he stopped and turned to study her.

"That is for you to discover," Leewana said as she flew out of the darkness and landed on the dirt floor feet from where Gado sat.

Shiarra bowed when she approached the Protector and then smiled up at the beautiful creature Genoa had created. Leewana was one of three Protectors that Genoa had created upon her arrival. When Genoa had fallen out of the heavens and settled on this planet, she had then created all life using the tools her father had given her.

The life had spilled from Genoa and spread out into the land. But the goddess had needed protection from evil from other planets and had created the three Protectors.

Adulario was created from rocks, soil, and gems. They had met this first Protector, who had been changed by an evil wizard into a vast wall of mist. Tresstéanna had tricked the creature and then changed Adulario back to his former glory by placing the Globe of Corpuscle into a chest piece.

Now Adulario was a massive stone creature with an ivy robe and gems for a crown. He had provided one of his magical eyes to Tresstéanna to help her find the other two Protectors.

The eye had aided them in locating Leewana, the second Protector, who had been transformed into a large ribbon snake. But once again Tresstéanna had tricked the monster and transformed Leewana back into the beautiful creature that settled before Shiarra.

Four large blue transparent wings beat at the air and green and blue scales covered her body. Leewana had a beautiful tail and a rather feminine head with blue eyes and two long horns with a single blue gem resting between them. Shiarra thought the Protector was the most beautiful creature she had ever seen and was joyful to see her again.

"Leewana," Shiarra said as she stood before the large creature. "How can I help?"

"Wizard, there is much to do," the Protector said as her wings continued to beat the air around them. "Come, we fly to the giants."

THE MARCH of the Otomi fighters through the Median Forest was fast and a bit chaotic. Once Svlain had provided her vision's details to Mayson and Commander Switz, their action was immediate.

"We have seen this foe before," Ava told them as her dark eyes turned to look back at the flowing waters of the Tabescent River. "We should cross the bridge and cut the ropes."

"No, you are needed at the palace." Rastel's statement had all eyes turning towards where his voice sounded, only feet from where Svlain stood.

"The palace." Grand Carrington said with hesitation in her voice. "What can I accomplish by returning?"

"There are many truths in Svlain's vision," Rastel replied. "One is that this creature is close. The other is that if you stay here, he will arrive and kill you all."

Svlain noticed fear and uncertainty in the eyes of the friends who surrounded her and spoke her own concerns. "My friends are in the palace; do we go to aid them?"

"What have you seen?" Colab asked as he studied the spot where the invisible creature's voice sounded.

"Tonight will be your last in this land," Rastel said as Svlain turned her eyes upwards to where the shining windows of the palace were barely visible through the canopy of the trees.

"You mean…" Zain started his question but Svlain interrupted him.

"Our path will lead away from Midzark and back to our original quest." She smiled as her milky eyes turned green once again. "But haste is now needed!"

Svlain's words were no sooner spoken in agreement with Genoa's ambassador when Commander Switz and Mayson were calling out orders to their men. Those who would not or could not fight were sent back across the river to the northern shores. Families with small children, the elderly, and the injured were directed to find shelter in the homes on the northern side.

"Use the homes there. If we fail, head out of the forest and across the desert. Seek refuge in Kós Kóvar," Ava instructed. "The Húriya will welcome all."

"Cut the bridge when all are across safely," Mayson demanded as he pushed his little brother, Max, towards the bridge.

"No!" the young boy hissed at his brother. "I stay with you."

"No, you will lead these people to safety," Mayson insisted as he shook his head.

"If Kiev goes, I get to go too!" Max said as he crossed his arms and planted his feet in defiance.

"I do not care what the blasted goblin does. He is not my charge! You will do as I tell you!" Mayson scolded, his dark face angry. Two red patches appeared on his cheeks.

"When have I ever done as you tell me?" Max demanded. "I go to fight, just like all the other boys my age."

"Let the lad come," Cerg insisted as he placed a hand on Mayson's arm. "You were fighting for freedom at his age. Let him see the end of this, whatever that maybe."

"I will watch and protect," Kiev insisted as he stood next to his friend. "I will keep safe."

Mayson turned his angry eyes upon the goblin. He must have seen his own worry in the strange eyes because after a moment of silence, he nodded.

"Come, I will lead the way," Grand Carrington instructed as she pulled her dark cloak close. "My destiny awaits."

Svlain walked next to the giantess for a time but soon found she fell behind as she tired of the pace and heat. As the sun lowered out in the east and the heat inside the forest dipped, her mind started wandering.

As sweat dripped down into her eyes, she thought of the last vision she'd had. It showed her stepping down into the caves. The darkness appeared to absorb her and her friends, who had been walking behind her. One by one they had been swallowed by the cave's darkness.

A shiver ran through her as Zain stepped closer to her on the path. When he reached for her hand, she squeezed it hard.

"Tell me what you saw," he demanded. She took comfort in his presence as she tried to formulate the words to describe her vision.

"We leave Midzark as the sun rises tomorrow," she said. She paused as she swatted at a biting bug on her neck. "We, all of us, will walk freely into the cave once again, much like we did at the beginning."

She thought of the Kylix, its dark walls and dank smell of dirt and moisture. Of the creatures they had already battled under the ground, and of the creatures they had yet to fight.

So much time had been spent under the ground on their trek to the cradle. Yet they still had battles to fight, monsters to eliminate, and one of Genoa's Protectors to change.

After a long moment of silence, Zain spoke, "And?"

"And the darkness of the cave reached out to welcome us," she said, turning her eyes towards his. "A blackness so dark that light cannot penetrate will reach out to greet us."

BRIDGES

Grand Carrington felt nervous as she walked inside the Median Forest, a forest she had seen since her childhood but had never set foot in until recently.

Upon her first steps inside the forest, she had found her courage grow. Her rebellious act of leaving the safety of the palace had been justified. She feared for her and her child's future. But it had been more than that. She had feared for the future of Midzark too.

The vision she had been shown by the gifted Tresstéanna had sparked a flame inside her. That flame had burned brighter each day after the vision. It spoke of the injustice the Gi Jón had endured, yet it also spoke of the prejudice her own people had experienced too.

As a third cousin to the Grand's family, she had grown up within the palace, raised by her father, who held a high position within the courts, brought up with privileges that many were denied.

She had never wanted for anything. She had no job because no vocation was required of her. Yet through her father's ambitions, she had lied and hid secrets that allowed her to gain the marriage with the Grand himself.

Of course, her father had cleared the way for her. This dark secret had eaten away inside her for a time and even now she still felt her heart skip a beat when she thought of Cline's prior wives.

As she walked, she placed a hand over her unborn child and continued to think about what she had seen inside the forest. She had been shocked to see that darkness had lived so close to her perfect world. It had been hidden by the canopy of the trees, yet now that she walked amongst their trunks, she saw it clearly.

Here, within the forest, slavery did not hide inside well-dressed servants who smiled and appeared eager to serve. Even the giants who dwelled here showed signs of oppression.

Homes were small and ill built, and many were shared by large families. The sick and elderly were everywhere, and children ran barefoot throughout the forest. Many played where battles had already taken place.

Gardens lay in waste near broken homes, while the survivors tried to salvage their belongings. New graves were visible, yet the faces that surrounded her looked at her with hope, not hate.

She had seen much, even before her meeting with the Otomi fighters. She had seen that no palace guards patrolled the forest. Scavengers had pilfered and looted the homes along the main pathways while others had been left empty or burned.

She had been concerned that her choice to seek out the leader of the Otomi fighters was a bad idea, until she had run into a Nephilim family just inside the forest. Two women and four children had been hiding inside one home when Carrington had heard a baby cry, giving away their hiding place. It had taken some time, but she had coaxed them out with a smile and soft words. All six had been covered in dirt and sweat. Two small bags had been tied around the women's backs, and one carried a covered basket filled with food.

Carrington had kept her face hidden, and she was pleased that the cloak hid her royal dress. But her shock had been immediate upon hearing their story. Bandy, the oldest woman, had told Carrington of their misfortunes.

"They ransacked our home and garden two nights ago," Bandy told her. "They grabbed my man and oldest boy, insisting they go fight."

"But why did they destroy your home?" Carrington had asked.

"To ensure we did not hide any slaves. Luckily, we had sent our Latria away last week. I heard that the army was killing any they found within the homes."

This news shocked Carrington. She had asked about the fighting, but the two women only knew what had befallen them. They had been urged by the Latria over a week ago to join the Nephilim on the northern shore of the river. They had been told it was safer there, but Bandy's husband worked in the southern farm fields and had to maintain his job to ensure the family's welfare.

"We stayed because Twandall was told if he left, his job would be lost to Latria. But all the Latria had already fled," Bandy said with tears in her eyes.

"What will you do now?" Carrington had asked, saddened and sickened by all she had heard.

"We go to my sister's. She lives deep in the eastern woods. She and her Latria are safe there. The Otomi fighters have a hidden post there," Bandy replied, a small smile forming on her dirty lips. "The Otomi will keep us safe."

Carrington remembered being shocked at this last statement, but after her meeting with Mayson, she discovered the truth no longer shocked her, it just saddened her.

The palace was no longer protecting its people within the forest, if it ever had. Maybe the palace had never been kind to those outside the Régorge Palace. She had never given thought to those who lived down below her splendid home, and this thought caused her stomach to sink even further.

"How could I have been so blind? So selfish and self-absorbed? How could I not see what was in front of my eyes?" she hissed to herself, not expecting an answer. She reeled and almost lost her balance when an answer did come. It came out of the empty space next to her.

"You allowed wealth to blind you," Rastel said from beside her, his voice deep but gentle. "But you are no longer fooled by items that shine."

"R-Rastel?" Carrington cleared her throat.

"My lady, I have tried for many generations to gain council within the palace. You are the first I have had the pleasure to speak with."

Generations? The ambassador to the goddess Genoa had been turned away by the Grands? She had never even heard of Rastel, not even rumors of this creature and his power. Even her father, whose job it was to search out and study the gifted, had never mentioned a creature with the power of invisibility. Had she been so sheltered that these rumors hadn't reached her ears? Had her father and husband hidden these truths from her? If so, why?

Did they not value her opinion regarding these magics? Did they keep more secrets from her? She knew her father kept many truths from her, mostly, she had thought, about how he had secured her place on the throne, but now she wondered.

And what of her husband? She was his third wife. Were there darker secrets he kept too? These thoughts stirred inside her head before she remembered how quickly and how eagerly Cline had replaced his dead second wife with her. They had been wed two nights after the woman's funeral, something that now weighed on Carrington's mind.

Would he replace her as quickly? Even now, did he have someone keeping him company at night? What value did she really hold in Cline's heart?

"I do not know what good it will do you," Carrington finally said, looking quickly over her shoulder. "They are right, my husband may not be pleased to see me returned," Carrington said truthfully, for the first time speaking her own fears of Cline's feelings towards her.

"Then it is up to you and me to show the palace your worth," Rastel said, and Carrington swore she heard a smile behind his words.

ANY CREATURE close to Biard the Wright was quickly blasted by his killing magic, magic so black and hot that even the bones of the creatures could not withstand the hatred the Scarent blasted at them.

The hated river had caused his anguish to increase beyond control. As he stomped through the thick, dense underbrush, thoughts of turning the whole forest into ash caused a small amount of joy to rush into him. But then his enemy might escape from him in a quick death. This thought alone kept him from lighting the fire.

He had marched for hours through the trees, keeping the water in sight on his trek east. He knew the waters thinned and finally ended out in the desert. This was his path—get to a spot that he could safely navigate across the waters. Though the Degurts were no match for him, their numbers were many. And since they lived in the waters and were diffi-cult to spot when you were swimming, it was best to avoid them all together. Their long bodies allowed them to swim faster than even Biard could with his Scarent enhanced body. The thought of the Degurts' teeth alone had Biard walking along the river's edge instead of wading into the water.

As he neared a small branch of the river, he turned to study his surroundings. The Tabescent flowed into several small fingers, which fed the vast forest. Trees lined these outflows as the underbrush kept the forest floor hidden from his sight. Turning his eyes, he spotted the vast palace high at the river's start. The falls fell both above the palace and below, keeping this forest alive.

He had no quibble with the giants. They kept to their lands and away from Biard's home. He even doubted they knew of his existence, something Biard much preferred.

As his eyes tracked down to the waters behind him, a hiss sounded in his throat. A bridge! There, near where he had hunted and tracked his prey, now lay a new bridge.

"What trick is this?" Biard hissed as he took a quick step back.

Anger, already clouding his judgment, filled him afresh as he realized his own mistake.

Those he'd hunted must have laid a new bridge while he was wasting time trekking through the forest trying to find a safe path across the waters.

Balling his large fists, he growled once and started running back the same path he had just traveled.

He would catch up to his prey before the night was over if it killed him. One thing Biard was sure of was that Colab the Meshi would not live through the night.

TRESSTÉANNA FELT her world move in slow motion as she and Belent tried to detangle themselves to start pursuit of the giant. As she gained her feet, she watched in horror as Kriston disappeared out the doorway. He was followed by Col and then Leian, who were blasting magic down the hallway already.

"Get him!" Kip yelled as Stria and Farin disappeared next through the doorway.

"Do you have it?" Belent shouted at her and grabbed her arm before she too could give chase.

"We have to follow him!" she yelled.

"NO!" Belent said, and turned to her. "Think! You know where he will end up. That is where we must go!"

Turning, Tresstéanna realized that Belent was the only one not panicked by the Maven's actions. "You knew," she said as she cradled the small plant in her arms. "You knew he would gain the box."

Belent nodded his head, and his eyes turned sad. "Your vision said as much, and the book told me."

"Why, why did you let it happen?" she asked with accusation in her voice. "You could have prevented it."

He shook his head and looked down at the plant she held in her arms like a child. "No, the pathways are set regarding that. Gorphen was destined to gain the box, just like he must try to destroy the orb. What path he chooses now will either save this world or destroy it."

"What do you know?" she asked as the sounds of her friends giving chase could still be heard from the doorway.

"My ways as a sorcerer are many and should not be questioned by you, even as my queen. But know this, I will never place you or any of your loved ones in harm. Nor will I allow Genoa to be harmed herself. But the pathway will now lead us to the top tower where we will find Gorphen," Belent said, and Tresstéanna noticed a change in her friend.

No longer was Belent a scarecrow of a man. Yes, he was still thin and unkempt. His hair had grown long from their time in Midzark, but he brushed it back now and tied it, like Kriston did, at the base of his neck.

His overall appearance was the same, but Belent's eyes were now different. His trials from before Anna had met him had caused a sadness to settle inside the man, but his discovery of his magic had lit a new spark in his brown eyes. Now, the brown orbs held something else. Mystery.

If there was something Tresstéanna knew, it was that magic had many layers. As Anna, she had seen countless movies where wise wizards guided the lost or unfocused. As Té, she had been guided by her own wizard. And as Tress, the queen of Valorna, she had been raised by her trusted guide, Wizard Cenzic. Cenzic had been more father than anything to her, but she had trusted him and his guidance. He had used his magic and knowledge to keep her safe for years.

Now she knew she needed to believe in Belent as a sorcerer, one who held more magic and wisdom than even a wizard.

"My friend, I will trust you," Tresstéanna said with a slight bow of her head. "Come, show me the way."

When they ran out of the Maven's private rooms, they were met with chaos. The revolt between the slaves and the Nephilim had reached the upper rooms of the palace. Kriston and the others were trying to breach the large steps at the end of the hallway, but their path was blocked by six giants.

Kriston was dueling one while the two wizards were blasting their magic at another. Stria and Hilar were using a large staff against a giant man, while three freedom fighters were trying to ward off the others. Kip jumped on the back of the nearest giant as Belent tugged on her sleeve.

"This way," he shouted.

She found it hard to race away from her friends, who were fighting for their lives. As they ran in the opposite direction from the fighting, she glanced backwards in time to see Kriston slash a large gash in the giant's leg. As it toppled behind him, he turned, and his eyes met with hers.

In the brief second of eye contact they had, she saw confusion and then understanding pass behind his eyes. When he gave her a quick nod, she turned and quickly raced behind Belent with a new determination.

One thing else she knew, besides that she could trust in Belent's guidance, was that Kriston could take care of himself. She knew he and her friends would fight with all their might.

"This way!" Belent hissed as he flung open a small door. She guessed it was a Latria hidden passage used by the slaves to gain access to the upper floors. Once inside, she saw that her guess was right. Shelves of cleaning supplies lined one wall, and a steep circular staircase ran upwards and also down.

At first, they took the stairs upwards two at a time, but soon the height of the palace took its toll on them and they slowed their pace.

"Blasted palace," she heard Belent hiss between breaths. She smiled.

"Great views, spacious rooms, but the location leaves much to be desired," she said. She almost bumped into the back of Belent as he stopped on the step above her.

"Are you making a joke?" he asked, turning to study here.

"Alleviating the suspense," she said with a smile and laughed when Belent's laughter barked out at her. She grabbed Belent's sleeve before he could continue. "My vision showed Grand Carrington blast magic. Did your book tell you that?"

Belent tilted his head, and the smile remained on his lips. "Mystery and magic go hand in hand. Remember this." He turned to continued up the steps.

"What?" she hissed, and shook her head. "I swear if you go all mystic and cryptic on me, I will kick your ass." She made sure to lower her voice on the last part in case he took offence but smiled again as he let out another bark of laughter.

"My queen, I would like to see you try."

The circular staircase made her dizzy and when they reached the top, she found her body swayed a bit when they raced down a straight hallway. Part of her still felt she should be spinning in a clockwise pattern and had to run with her right hand on the wall to keep from falling over.

"This way, I think," Belent said, turning down a short hallway. "Hurry, the sun has already set."

She wondered why the sun's position mattered but kept quiet as they slowed their pace now.

Up on the top floor of the palace, the fighting was absent, and all lay quiet. They met no one, either giant or small. Tresstéanna felt as if the top level had been abandoned and wondered what was up here.

"Mostly the rooms of the lower level of courtiers," Belent said quietly, causing Tresstéanna to wonder if he had been thinking the same as she. "Most of them must have gone below for the trial. I came through here once when I was looking for the globe. Of course, it was filled with Latria then. I almost got stuck in a closet once when a girl heard me and thought I was a mouse."

Tresstéanna found his grin endearing and smiled until they heard a sound from one of the rooms at the end of the hall.

"There," Belent hissed as they saw Maven Gorphen's figure disappear into the doorway.

They both raced after the giant but stopped when they reached a wooden door. The door was giant sized and held no smaller opening. It appeared to be fastened by a large metal clasp halfway up. Belent tried to reach the doorknob, but to their frustration it was several feet above his reach.

"Here, climb on my back and see if you can reach it!" Belent urged as he bent lower.

After carefully setting the plant on the ground, she scrambled on his back. She had some difficulty as the man was all sharp angles and bones.

"Hold still!" she hissed as they almost toppled over backwards when she had finally scurried onto his shoulders.

"I am trying!" he said as she reached up and firmly grasped the knob. Breathing a sigh of relief, she quickly gave it a turn. As the door swung inwards, their weight was momentarily thrown off balance. She screeched when Belent's body lurched them far forward into the black opening.

With a crash and hard bang, they toppled inside the doorway and landed up against the large rise of giant-sized stairs. The first step was just inside the door, and Tresstéanna hit her left elbow hard against the wooden rung. Belent gave a hard grunt as he bounced off the stair and fell to the ground, causing her legs to get entangled with his arms once again.

"Are you okay?" she asked, and gave her elbow a rub.

"I am fine, just my pride is hurt," Belent said as he scrambled up and grabbed the Orwic plant from outside the door. "Up there," he said, and they saw a faint light from the top of the stairs.

To their dismay they noticed that the stairs were giant sized.

"Of course," Tresstéanna said with frustration at the new obstacle they were now met with.

Kriston watched Tresstéanna and Belent disappear down the long hallway.

Fear for her tried to take over him, and he fought inside to keep from giving chase behind her. Instead he turned and shouted at Kip.

"Up there!" he told the dragon warrior as the weapons expert lifted a large giant-sized knife. The knife was larger than Kriston's sword, but the muscular warrior hefted it with ease.

Kip gave a nod and slashed the sword at an approaching giant. The giant dodged the sharp blade and turned for another attack. When nothing came at him, he turned in time to see Kip disappear up the massive steps. Luckily, there were Latria-sized steps next to the giant ones, and he was able to rush up them with ease.

Kriston blocked a spear that had been thrown at him from somewhere down the hallway and shouted at Stria and Farin, who were at that end of the hall.

"Get the spears!" he shouted and turned to meet the giant that Kip had left for him.

Raising his sword, Kriston had a quick wish that it was his own. He missed his curved blade, the familiarity of it in his hands, its weight and the ease he felt when swinging it in battle.

The current sword he held was much like Kip's borrowed one. He was sure it was a pocketknife to the giants, but it fit in his hands, and he was able to slash at the approaching giant.

Ducking the massive fist aimed at his head, he swung the blade again at the giant's exposed ankles. This tactic had worked with the last giant, slashing the exposed flap between shoe and shin guard. He had one giant down on the ground behind him to prove this and hoped it would work on this new one.

The new giant had armor of silver with brass buckles that latched it to itself. Trimming of black poked out from under the metal, giving Kriston hope these were the weak points.

Turning, Kriston jumped away from the sharp stab of the man's dagger and spun in a circle as he slashed at the man's knee joint. Hearing the resulting scream from his hit, he took courage and executed a cartwheel to pick up another fallen sword. Now armed with two weapons, he turned to see the giant bent over clutching at his left knee.

Racing at him, Kriston swung the butt end of the new sword down on the man's exposed head, giving out quick praise for the giant's missing helmet. Maybe he had thought one wasn't needed or had been in too great a rush to get one on his head. Either way, the resounding *crack* had a smile forming on Kriston's face as the man tumbled to the ground. He saw the giant give one giant huff before he lay still.

Kriston climbed over the man's legs and found the hallway cleared. Four large giants lay unconscious in the long hall. Their armor and weapons littered the area, and the remaining dragon warriors searched for blades and weapons in a size they could handle.

"Where is Kip?" Wizard Col asked as Leian walked up and patted at a flame on Col's cloak.

"Set yourself on fire in your haste," Leian said with a smile.

"I sent him up after Gorphen," Kriston said as he neared the same stairs the giant had disappeared up.

"No, not that way," Col said with a shake of his head. "We are needed down below."

"I go after Tresstéanna," Kriston growled and turned back to the stairs.

"No!" Col once again demanded. "She will be safe; we need to get the mirror!" Col urged. "Time will run out and we will fail if we do not move now!"

The growl and scream that came out of Kriston had Col narrowing his eyes at him. The wizard stood his ground and crossed his massive arms, a frown on his dark face.

"Feel better?" Col finally asked in a condescending voice when the last rumble came from Kriston's throat.

Between the frustration and anger, Kriston realized that the man was laughing at him. So great was his need to race after Tresstéanna that he didn't even care he was being made to appear foolish.

"I know you love her; I too love her. But we are needed down below. Belent will take care of her." Col stepped towards Kriston, concern and understanding written on his face. "Remember the plan."

After taking a deep breath, Kriston consented and his shoulders drooped in defeat.

"Good. You three, quickly, over here. We have to find a cart or something with wheels to move the mirror," Col commanded.

"Where are we moving it?" Stria asked as Hilar and Farin started opening closed doors to search for a wagon or cart.

"I think the throne room will suit us nicely," Col said with a smile.

They found a large cart in a storage room three doors down from the Maven's rooms and lifted the mirror onto it quickly. Kriston and Hilar pushed the cart while the others ensured the way forward was clear.

"What do we do when we get to the stairs?" Stria asked halfway down the hallway. Her question had everyone scratching their heads until Leian spoke.

"We float it down them," the wizard advised, and Col laughed.

"I have not used that spell since I was a child!" Col slapped a large hand on Leian's back, which had the skinny wizard stumbling to regain his feet. "Used to use that on my school maiden. I floated the furniture around and told her it was ghosts until my mum told her I had magic." The wizard laughed again.

"What if there is still fighting down there?" Kriston grunted as they neared the head of the stairs.

"You three clear the way, we will follow," Col demanded. They watched as Stria, Farin, and Hilar disappeared.

Kriston quickly turned, his sword raised, when he heard footsteps behind them, but he lowered his weapon when Amándo and Madera came running up to them.

"Weston and the others are clearing the lower levels. Most of the loyalists have given up," Madera told them. The young girl had a large gash above her right eye, but the smile on her face told Kriston she was otherwise unharmed.

"They gave up until they know which side will win," Amándo advised. One of his eyes was swollen shut, and his left arm hung limp at his side.

Leian immediately walked over to him and started a healing spell to repair the arm while Amándo continued to provide details.

"Weston said the northern side of the palace is clear. If we need to, we can go down these steps and go to the left, not right. Most of the fighting is taking place near the Ingress Bridge now."

"We need to get into the throne room," Col stated and the boy smiled.

"Then you are in luck. Weston and his men have set up in there to aid the injured."

Getting the mirror down into the throne room was easy, but Col insisted the hallways needed to be clear of all fighting before their trap would work.

Belent had given Col some insight into what must be done before they had all rushed to the Maven's rooms. Based on his guidance, they had agreed upon a plan, one that had two parts—gain the mysterious flower from the mirror and then, using the mirror, set a trap for the unknown foe.

Tresstéanna now had the flower, so that part of the plan had succeeded. All that remained was to ensnare and vanquish the unknown enemy.

Kriston knew Col had an idea about the trap that would snare this person or creature that approached, yet he still itched to race after Tresstéanna. He knew she was somewhere far above him, racing after the Maven. He also knew that, according to her vision, the giant would—

"The tower!" he hissed to himself as he moved debris along one wall, according to Col's instructions.

"So, you finally remembered," Col chided with a shake of his head. "Yes, she has an appointment with Gorphen at the top of this blasted palace. Nothing we do can aid her, so continue to put your back into your work," Col scolded.

Col's plan was simple—using the large debris from the prior battle inside the throne room, they would create a narrow passage down the room's center.

The idea was solid, but Kriston knew it lacked something. That something was bait, yet without knowing the approaching enemy, that bait would have to be discovered later. Col speculated that they could all stand at the trap's center. He hoped this would lure the unknown into their reach, but much depended on the enemy, all of which worried Kriston as he bent down to his task.

SHIARRA FELT the cool air of the cave envelop her as Leewana flew downwards into the darkness.

The smells and feel of the cave reminded her of the days spent traveling in the Kylix. She had been with friends then and not alone with a massive Protector. Somehow, she found that even with Leewana's size and gifts, she had felt safer surrounded by those from the mainland.

She didn't doubt Leewana's powers, but the fact that her friends were missing weighed on her. Her thoughts turned to Leian, and she took a deep breath. Thoughts of Leian would have to wait. Her focus was now needed on the task at hand. She thought of this task as lights appeared far below them.

Giants. Monsters and the Protector called Dreail.

Much rested on her shoulders now, according to Leewana.

"Sway them, talk of the aid you and your friends can give them with their fight against Dreail's children," Leewana urged as they flew downwards. "They have battled these creatures for several days. Their supplies run low, and most have given up hope. They refuse to return to the surface and live under the oppression there, but their lives are dark down here."

"What can I promise? We have yet to defeat the giants. How can we promise to defeat giant monsters?" Shiarra asked as the lights grew brighter.

"One of you has already blocked Dreail from entering

Midzark. I felt the magic of my mother several days ago," Leewana replied.

"One of *us*?" Shiarra asked in surprise, realizing that her imprisonment had restricted her knowledge of the actions of all the others from Genoa. Had Col and Kriston managed to block Dreail? If so, how? And where were they now?

"I know not which one, but the Ili Yeathía stone was used. There is no escape for Dreail now. When the others come with our mother, they can change Dreail back," Leewana said, and Shiarra heard confidence in the Protector's voice.

"You know this?" Shiarra asked with doubt.

"I was returned to my original form." Leewana's voice was filled with confidence, some of which filled Shiarra with hope. "Dreail too will be returned."

Shiarra had many more questions, but the lights grew more distinguished, and she noticed that they were fires. Large wood had been stacked along the water's edge between the shore and the Nephilim's stone buildings.

As Leewana swooped out of the darkness, Shiarra heard a shout of alarm raised. Shiarra had time to see several sentries emerge out of the nearest building, carrying large swords and bows. Several arrows were pointed at the Protector as she gently set herself down beyond the fire's light.

Unsure of her actions, Shiarra remained hidden behind Leewana's back. The Protector's iridescent wings remained beating as she looked out at the approaching giants.

"Stand, I bring the one I spoke of," Leewana said calmly as if she had arrows and weapons pointed at her all the time.

"Show us," the nearest giant growled. Shiarra took several deep breaths and climbed down off Leewana's back, mindful of the flapping wings. Leewana and the giants towered over her, making her feel ridiculously small.

"I am here," she said. All the weapons were lowered and aimed at her. "I have come to aid you in this fight."

"What aid can you give?" the same giant asked, apparently the leader of the group. There was speculation and doubt on his dark face.

Shiarra noticed his armor was no longer shiny. Several straps were now tied together by string and there was a large dent above his left breast. The sword he pointed at her was clean and still looked very sharp, but the dirt that covered his form spoke of his people's struggle down here in the dark.

Holding her right hand, palm upward, she brought forth her magic. The orange orb she manifested above her hand was impressive, but useless. The giants gathered around her didn't need to know this. She kept it there, burning brighter as gasps and exclamations were spoken by the Nephilim that surrounded her.

"My friends too hold magic," Shiarra said. She hoped her next words would ring true soon. "They come from the Régorge Palace to join me soon."

"No gifted has ever left the palace," one giant from the back of the group said. Shiarra was pleased to see the arrows and swords were no longer pointed in her direction.

"I came from the palace," Shiarra said as she let her magical flame ball die back down. She closed her hand and dropped it to her side. "I was one of the gifted enslaved by the Grand and the Maven."

"How do we know you speak the truth. None of us have even set foot in the palace," another said as they drew closer to her.

"I wear the dress of a gifted in service to the Grands," came her reply.

"How did you escape?"

"I..." She wasn't sure she should tell these giants she was standing here only because the Grand's brother tried to overthrow him, but she felt Leewana's large hand rest on her shoulder and took comfort from it. "I was kidnaped by

Grand Cline's brother, Brine. Then I was rescued by the palace guards. We were attacked inside the forest, and I lost my way and found my way back here."

"Was the Grand overthrown?" one giant wanted to know.

"Who is in charge now?" another shouted, and confusion erupted around her. She held her hands out to calm the giants gathered around her.

"I do not know the answers to your questions. I know the Latria were uprising against the palace in search of their freedom, but I do not know what has happened inside the palace since the night of the Feier Celebration."

"When do the other gifted arrive?" the leader demanded, and Shiarra shook her head in reply.

"I do not know, but for now my magic is at your service." She noticed several giants nod with approval, but the leader still frowned.

"Well, we can see how you fare against the creature that walks on legs," the leader said. He turned to Leewana. "This one refuses to fight it."

"It is not my place," Leewana said, turning to Shiarra. "It used to be one of you."

MONSTERS IN MEN

Tresstéanna and Belent were covered with dirt and sweat by the time they reached the top of the massive staircase. Its rungs wound around in a rising circle much like the lower flight, but this one took twice as long to traverse.

The doorway at the top had been left open, luckily, and a breeze blew into the darkened stairway. It was a hot one, but any stirred air was welcome.

Trying to catch their breath, they both bent over with their hands on their knees and gulped in the hot night's air. She heard Belent grunt once and looked up at him. The sorcerer had dirt on his face and clothing, but his eyes were wide with fear as he looked out the doorway.

"There," he hissed, and grabbed her arm to pull her closer.

Looking through the doorway, she noticed the same details from her vision two nights before. Gorphen stood upon the opened tower as lights surrounded his form. When he turned to pull the Globe of Corpuscle from the Greilk box, she realized that tears were trailing down the giant's face.

"He really does love his daughter," she whispered to Belent as the red orb started to glow in the man's hands.

"He should not be touching Genoa," Belent hissed, and Tresstéanna had to reach out to stop him from rushing the giant in his attempt to defend the goddess.

"Come, slowly, this way," she whispered, and she crept out of the doorway to the ledge, far to the giant's right. Keeping quiet, they remained unseen in the darkness of the terrace as they neared the far edge of the tower. When Gorphen's eyes alighted on something far below, she stopped and tried to look out between the gaps in the terrace walls.

"Quickly, we have to see what happens," she said. She shoved at Belent until he was doubled over. Neither of them was tall enough to see over the terrace's half wall, so she once again scrambled onto the sorcerer's back.

The army that approached the palace's bridge was impressive. She watched both Nephilim and Gi Jón walking up the wide path on the other side of the bridge. Torches and lanterns were floating amongst the army, giving an impression of a festival instead of an invasion.

At the forefront of the army, standing tall, was Grand Carrington. Her long dark hair was unbound and falling to her slender waist. Her cloak was thrown open to show her royal dress. Carrington raised her face upward, and Tresstéanna saw movement behind the giantess. Hundreds of Gi Jón rushed up the cliff face to stand at her back. Some flew on massive bees, holding lanterns, which made the creatures look like large lightning bugs, while others carried weapons and marched along the cliffs.

She knew Gorphen only noticed the invading army. His grief was so overwhelming that Tresstéanna doubted he even spotted his daughter so boldly standing, safe and whole, at the army's front.

"Húriya and Latria," Maven Gorphen shouted as the

giant's tears fell freely from his eyes. He held the globe in both hands as if it were burning his skin. Slowly he raised the Globe of Corpuscle above his head. Hatred and pain crossed his face as he stood there.

"Father!" Carrington shouted from far below, and Tresstéanna saw her raise her arms.

Hope and joy filled the old man's face, but then his eyes grew large with shock as sparks flew from Carrington's upraised hand. Flashes of blue magic flew from the giantess's hands and raced towards the palace with a blinding speed that shook Tresstéanna from her perch on Belent's back.

The blue magic rose around the whole tower and turned night into day as Tresstéanna and Belent once again became entangled as they fell.

"What in the king's name was that?" Belent hissed as he pushed Tresstéanna's hair out of his face.

"That was my daughter!" Gorphen said as he stood above them.

Thinking they were under attack, Tresstéanna moved to start her magic but soon found herself being pulled into a standing position by the giant.

"I am sorry, I thought she was dead. My grief overtook me," Gorphen said as he pulled Belent up next.

Finding no threat from the giant, Tresstéanna lowered her hands, extinguishing her defensive magic. When Gorphen held the Globe of Corpuscle out to her, she quickly took the orb.

"Please forgive me," Gorphen said, turning to pick up the Greilk box from the floor. He quickly handed it to her. "We, we should not have imprisoned you."

Tresstéanna studied the man as the blue light faded around the tower, returning it to the darkness of the night.

"There might still be time to fix your mistake,"

Tresstéanna said with a nod of her head. "Come, let's see what your daughter has brought."

Returning down the stairs was far easier than climbing up them. Maven Gorphen carried them down the large steps and showed them the fastest way to the bridge.

There was still fighting in the main entryway, and Tresstéanna and Belent had to remain in a doorway while Gorphen boldly walked out and started shouting at the other Nephilim.

"Stop!" Gorphen shouted to no avail as the fighting continued.

Tresstéanna could hear the clashing of swords and heavy grunts. When a loud scream came from the large entryway, she stepped out of her hiding place and walked up next to the Maven.

"Here, let me." She knew it would cost her, but immediate action was needed. Placing one hand on the stone wall, she called her magic forward. "They can't fight if they can't see."

When all the flames and lights were extinguished inside the massive square, several people screamed while a single grunt could be heard far to her left.

"Blasted!' came a voice she recognized, and she turned towards where Kip's voice sounded behind her.

"Kip?" she asked but kept the light from shining inside the room.

"Here, wherever that is," Kip replied.

"Stay put. Once we have everyone's attention, I'll turn the lights back on." She shouted out to all the people gathered inside the massive entryway. "People of Midzark!" Upon hearing no reply, she continued, "I am Tresstéanna, queen of Valorna, from Genoa. Outside this palace is a vast army. They come to ensure freedom for everyone, be you giant or not. If you wish to remain free, lay down your weapons and join us."

Again, no response as her magic continued to seep the light from the large area.

"Please, the army outside is led by my daughter, Grand Carrington!" Gorphen shouted finally.

"The lady Carrington leads this army against the palace?" came a voice from the darkness.

"Does she attack her own husband?" another shouted.

"Is she overthrowing Cline?" a third voice shouted.

"Down with Cline and the tyranny of the Grands!" came another shout.

Agreements could be heard throughout the darkness, and Tresstéanna smiled when they could be heard throughout the palace.

Svlain watched the magic flow from where Grand Carrington had been and was amazed as it surrounded the tower to their left. She almost lost her footing as Zain grabbed her arm in astonishment.

"What?" he gasped as Ava rushed up to them.

"How?" Ava asked and pointed to where the giantess stood, her hands once again dark as the magic continued to encircle the tall tower.

Svlain squinted her eyes at the woman, and a small smile formed. She saw Carrington nod her head and slightly tilt it, as if she were listening to instructions.

"Who," Svlain said. She laid her left hand over Zain's, which was still on her forearm. "I think Rastel has finally found a Nephilim who will listen to his guidance."

As they watched, Carrington moved to the very edge of

the Ingress Bridge. What guards remained on their post bowed quickly and dropped their weapons. Before moving onto the wooden structure, Carrington turned and, after locating them, motioned for Svlain and Ava to join her.

"If you will, could you join me?" Carrington asked with a slight nod of her head. "I give my promise that nothing foul will befall you. You are my guests."

"As you wish," Ava said as she moved to stand beside the woman.

"If you please, I would also like Colab and Commander Switz join us?" Svlain asked as Zain moved forward.

"I too will be coming," the dragon warrior said with such authority that Carrington smiled.

"Where Svlain goes, so do you?" Carrington asked and nodded. "As you wish." Maraneal cleared her throat from beside Colab and also received a nod from Carrington. "Any more who wish to come?"

When Mayson stepped forward followed closely by Max and Kiev, once again Carrington nodded.

As Carrington led the way across the bridge, Svlain studied the massive structure before them. Lights were scattered about the huge structure, giving it the appearance of floating. Brightly colored trim edged many windows on each floor, some so large and ornate she marveled at them.

The two towers on this side rose to great heights and only the top of a center tower could be seen. Gold reflected off well-positioned lights, which gave the building a rather rich look.

The deafening noise of the waterfall grew intense as they neared the walls. Svlain wondered if it was so loud because the sound was echoing off the walls. She felt the cool air from the waterfall's mists hit her and realized why the giants had built their home so high up on the waterfall.

Her time in the forest had been short, but it had taught her that even in the dead of night the heat remained intense.

They drew close to the massive door at the bridge's end, but it remained shut. Carrington seemed unsure how to proceed as she stood tall waiting for the two doors to swing open. Several minutes later the doors did open, and Svlain found, to her delight, her lost friends.

Tresstéanna stood there with Belent. The two seemed small compared to the old giant next to them.

"Carrington!" The giant who had stood on the top of the tower rushed to give the giantess a hug.

"Father," Carrington cried.

Svlain hurried to Tresstéanna and, after giving the queen a quick bow, ran into her open arms.

"My queen!" Svlain said with tears in her eyes. "You are a wonderful sight!"

"I do not know; she looks a bit dirty to me," Zain said teasingly as he gave Tresstéanna a quick punch in the arm. It reminded Svlain that Zain and Té had grown up in the same village.

"Zain!" Tresstéanna shouted and punched him right back. "And..." Here Tresstéanna's eyes grew wide with shock as she studied the young boy behind Zain. "Calob?" she asked and squinted her eyes at him.

"No, my queen, it is I, Colab. Meshi was lost to me but, through our mother's magic, I was returned to my original form."

"Colab!" Tresstéanna said, and tears formed in the woman's eyes. "Meshi will be missed," she said as she drew the boy in for a hug. "Come, there is much to discuss, and we need to check on Kriston's progress."

"Progress?" Svlain asked as she studied the chaos behind her queen.

"We have a new enemy coming and have a trap to set," Tresstéanna said as her eyes swept behind Svlain.

Feeling her new friends draw near, Svlain turned and introduced them. Tresstéanna was happy to see Kiev and was reaching out to give the goblin a hug when Carrington's raised voice interrupted them.

"Father!" Carrington said with authority. She turned to study Tresstéanna and nodded. "Quickly, we must move the army inside the palace. The one that follows is drawing near."

"I tell you, we cannot have the army inside the walls," Gorphen insisted. He turned to study the vast army still on the other side of the bridge. "Even if Grand Cline agreed to this…"

"Cline is no longer in charge," Carrington stated with authority. "Our people have spoken and, if the goddess is willing, I am now in charge."

Svlain saw the old giant's face turn pale as he studied his daughter. "Carrington, think!" he hissed. He turned around to see that the entrance hall was full of those from the palace. All had their eyes on them as they listened quietly. "What you say will put you in danger."

Nodding, Carrington turned from her father and addressed those inside the palace.

"People of Midzark, Nephilim and Gi Jón alike. Our way of life is in danger from a new foe. Slavery has just been abolished and all are now free. But freedom is fleeting if we cannot banish this new enemy. This Biard the Wright comes from another world and holds vast powers. Powers and magic that will destroy all who dwell here unless we banish him. To do this we must trust our new friends from the mainland." Here, Carrington turned to Tresstéanna and gave her a large curtsy. "We place our lives in your capable hands, queen of Genoa."

Tresstéanna nodded and turned to study the vast room

full of giants and Gi Jón. Wounded were still sitting upon the floors or leaning against the walls, and the dead littered the area.

Tresstéanna took in their surroundings quickly and then turned back to Carrington. "We need to get the army to safety and clear out this room."

Those gathered near immediately started moving, and Tresstéanna turned and led them down a long hallway.

"We still have Grand Cline somewhere in the palace that we'll need to deal with later," Tresstéanna informed Carrington as they walked side by side before Svlain. "But for now, the trap must be set for this Beard guy."

"Biard the Wright," came Rastel's voice from beside Tresstéanna. She crouched at the unexpected voice. "My queen, I am Genoa's ambassador, here as a guide to all."

Svlain tried to hold in a giggle as Tresstéanna's eyes swiveled around trying to locate the ambassador.

"I assure you, I am quite invisible," Rastel said finally, after which Tresstéanna stood once again and shrugged her shoulders.

"Very well, what guidance do you have for us?" she asked as they began to move down the hall once again.

"Biard is very smart but his conceit is always his undoing," Rastel advised as Colab moved forward.

"His minions killed Meshi," Colab stated. "Do we know if he is alone?"

"Only the Scarent comes," Svlain said. She stopped walking and her magic took ahold of her.

She watched the large Scarent march up the cliffside, aiming for the palace.

Where the army had once stood, the cliffside was now empty and the bridge unoccupied. The massive doors to the palace were closed and locked. As the creature approached, he blew the wooden and iron doors to dust with glowing hot magic.

Biard lowered his hood and his snake-like lip twitched with hatred as he walked through the burned opening and into the wide entrance hall.

THE CREATURE who called himself Biard the Wright was angry. Fury poured off his snake's skin as his powerful legs moved him through the Median Forest and up into the cliffs as he followed the trail of the thief. Colab the Meshi had stolen from him. The Scarent, along with the goddess's ambassador, Rastel, had tricked him. This fact alone had sealed the fate of both.

Biard knew that Rastel was dead, killed when he had shattered it into pieces. This had been a personal triumph for Biard, who considered Rastel to be annoying. Biard had always been weary of the ambassador. As one of Genoa's direct creations, he held powerful magic.

But now that he was gone, Biard only had to destroy Colab the Meshi and then attempt to find the trail to the mainland. Once there, he hoped to locate the doorway to another planet, maybe one where the settled goddess was weaker than this planet's deity.

This thought had Biard pausing on the trail leading up to the vast structure above the forest. If he could gain access to another planet and gain control of its inhabitants, then he could gain much. Illusions of power and grandeur kept the Scarent sorcerer standing still for several moments, until a buzzing insect reminded him of his current mission.

"First the thief dies, then everyone else," he hissed as his strong legs marched him over the log bridge.

If Biard the Wright had thought for a moment about why the bridge was deserted, he would have paused and realized there was a trap ahead. But Rastel had been correct—Biard's conceit kept any worry of a trap far from his mind.

After blasting the doors wide, he marched into the palace's entry hall as his anger once again took ahold of him. Seeing no foe, he lifted his odd nose in the air as his snake tongue flicked out to taste the air.

"Yes, I smell you," Biard hissed. He walked down a vast hallway towards the luring odor of his enemy.

When he entered the throne room, his senses lied to him. The odor was stronger here, but his sharp eyes only noticed the rubble of a huge fight. Lamps and chairs littered one side of the room, while benches and tables mixed with odd pieces of furniture were piled on the other side. Once again lifting his face, he flicked his tongue out to feel the air.

"Yes, you are here," he hissed as his magic flowed to the tips of his fingers. "Come face me, thief! Come meet your doom!"

When Colab the Meshi stepped out from one of the rubble piles on the far side of the room, Biard blasted the image with his killing magic.

Smoke and fire scorched the image to pieces as another Colab the Meshi appeared far to the left of the first.

Confused, Biard sent another blast of magic into the second image, yet a third appeared to his right. Infuriated and frustrated, Biard sent magic into the new image as yet another appeared far to the left.

"Tricks!" Biard the Wright hissed. "You meet me with tricks." Biard blew a net of magic over the entire room as he scanned for the creature he sought.

"Ah!" he hissed, and smiled as he felt his prey yards from him. Colab the Meshi was kneeling down behind a rather large pile of odd furniture. "I found you. You will pay for stealing from me," Biard whispered as he rounded the heap of odds and ends.

There, behind the pile, crouched next to an odd frame, was Colab the Meshi. His back was turned to Biard as he sent yet another image of himself out into the vast room. Dust covered the Scarent, who knelt in the dirt while trying to hide from Biard.

Using all his magic, Biard lurched forward to grab the thief by his dusty collar, but his world fell away from around him.

Confused, he realized that his prey had disappeared. Looking down at his hand, he noticed he was surrounded by fog. Dark grey mists swirled around his outstretched arm, preventing him from moving.

"What magic is this?" Biard the Wright screamed as the Pagilda mirror shattered him to thousands of pieces, only to then rebuild him and shatter him again, over and over.

GRAND CLINE SAT in his private rooms and poured himself a glass of fine wine. The cup was made of gold and had an intricate design of bees encircled by large hoops.

As he lifted the cup to his lips, the door burst open and his Prime, Magal, entered without bid.

"What is the meaning of this?" Cline growled and turned his dark eyes on the one he entrusted his army's leadership to. "How dare you enter my rooms without my say!"

"Cline!" Magal said as he limped into the plush room. "They come for you!"

Cline studied the man, and the injuries Magal had caused

alarm to rise in him. A large gash crossed Magal's cheek. The cut had sliced off part of Magal's mustache and the tip of his nose. Blood ran from the man's right shoulder and his knee, while a rather wicked-looking knife stuck out of his left thigh.

The Prime had his sword drawn and red blood dripped from it and onto the very expensive rug on the floor. As he limped forward, Cline heard sounds from outside the hallway.

Two steps inside the door, Magal turned and quickly shut and then locked the door. When Magal leaned against the door, the Grand saw more wounds across the man's back.

"What has happened?" Grand Cline insisted as he stood. "Who did this?"

"The Latria, and several courtiers," Magal said as he moved towards the side table. After he downed a glass of ale, he swept all the contents off the top and tugged the table towards the door.

"What are you doing?" Cline demanded, still standing in the center of the room, shocked by the Prime's actions.

After the table was shoved across the doorway, Magal moved to the balcony. "Do you have an escape route?" Magal asked as he marched through the glass doors.

"Escape? And just who do you think I should flee from?" Cline sneered as he finally drank his wine and set the cup calmly down on the little table.

"Your wife!" Magal said as he came marching back through the doorway. "No exit there. How about these rooms?"

Magal couldn't have shocked Cline more with his words. His wife? Carrington? Had she been found? Cline's mind swirled with thoughts and plans upon hearing that Carrington was alive.

After several seconds of silence, as Magal searched for an

exit in the back rooms of Cline's quarters, Cline finally asked another question.

"Why would I flee from Carrington? She is *my wife*. She obeys me," Cline said with authority.

Magal laughed, and Cline grew angrier.

"Your *wife* seized the palace with an army. At this moment, she orders your guard. She has set the Latria free, and they now follow her," Magal hissed as he drew near to Cline. "Now, where is your hidden exit?"

"Free? How can she set them free? I am the ruler here, not her!" Cline growled as he crossed his arms with doubt. Maybe Magal was working too hard? Maybe the heat had finally fried the man's brain.

"Your days are numbered if you do not escape," Magal said as he stood in front of Cline. "As your friend, I came here to save you." When pounding started on the door behind him, Magal grabbed Cline's shoulders and shook him. "Please, where is your secret exit?"

"I do not have one, why would I? I am the leader here!" Cline hissed as the severity of the situation finally set in.

"They aim to kill you. There may be no gentle banishment where the desert takes you. They cry for your head!" Magal said and studied Cline.

"They dare not kill me," Cline yelled as the pounding grew louder.

"Maybe, but they will surely kill me," Magal said with a shake of his head. "My sins outweigh my armor."

With this, Magal bowed his head to Cline and ran towards the balcony windows at full speed. He flung his body over the railing and held his bloody sword cradled across his chest as he fell to his death.

TRESSTÉANNA NOTICED that the throne room was still in shambles, thanks to Kriston's trap.

The illusions of Colab the Meshi had been courtesy of Genoa's ambassador. Rastel had used his magic to cast several images of Colab the Meshi around the room in a disarray of confusion.

But it had been Colab crouching behind the last pile of rubble. Colab hadn't been in danger. It had only been his reflection inside the mirror itself that Biard the Wright had tried to accost.

The trap had utilized Biard the Wright's arrogance against himself. Believing he was far superior to Colab, he had quickly rushed forward to catch Colab when he was really rushing into the mirror itself. The mirror's surface had been disguised as the dust that surrounded Colab's false image.

Tresstéanna had been relieved when the trap worked, but this feeling was replaced quickly by shock when Rastel then took the mirror and shattered it into dust.

"There must never be any escape from this prison for Biard the Wright," Rastel had stated, and Tresstéanna had shivered with her own memories of her short time inside the horrid mirror.

When Grand Cline was captured and brought before them in the shambled throne room, she studied the former leader of Midzark closely.

Tresstéanna felt Carrington tense next to her as they stood tall at the top of the dais in the position of leader. The army of the Húriya stood to the left of Tresstéanna, while the inhabitants of the palace and those who lived inside the forest filled the right side of the large room. Nephilim and Gi

Jón alike stood side by side as they looked at their former leader.

Feeling Carrington's discomfort, Tresstéanna tugged once on the woman's dress. Sending her a smile, Tresstéanna stepped forward to address the prisoner.

"Grand Cline, you are hereby charged with crimes against humanity. These charges include enslavement, discrimination, murder, and imprisonment." Those gathered around raised their voices in agreement as Tresstéanna continued. "You have used your power for your own gain while those around you suffered. You are hereby stripped of your title and power."

The roar of approval was deafening until Carrington stepped forward and held her hands up for silence.

"People of Midzark, freedom is a right to all who live here!" Again, the noise rose as cheers and praise echoed in the palace halls. When it once again became quiet, Carrington continued. "For years we have lived a life away from our host mother, Genoa. We have enslaved her children, sought her magic, and forced oppression upon those she loves. We have turned a blind eye to our actions and closed our ears to her ambassador's guidance for the last time."

Tresstéanna watched as Cline turned his face towards his wife's. Anger and hatred filled his features as Carrington stood where he once had.

"Now our actions must reflect those of a free land. If we are to start this fresh new breath, we must cleanse this world of the hatred it has lived under for so long. Therefore, I ask you, what shall we do with the last Grand?"

Silence filled the hall at first. Tresstéanna thought it was from shock that a person in charge had actually asked for the people's opinion.

It was Paren, the loyalist who had tried so many times to turn in Tresstéanna and her friends, who spoke first.

"Banish him!" the woman screeched and soon she was joined by others.

"Banish him!"

"Banish him to the desert!"

"Let him face the heat of the sands!" another shouted and soon all within the room had sentenced the last Grand of Midzark.

When Carrington held her arms up again, the room grew quiet once more.

"Your sentence has been passed," Carrington stated. She turned to her husband. "The people of Midzark have spoken. Know this, husband. I am not the ruler here. I am the people's mouthpiece only. Know also that I once loved you. But when my eyes were opened to the evil done in this place, I saw that your ears were closed to wisdom. Go, and may the desert take your life quickly."

When Carrington was finished speaking, several guards, both Gi Jón and Nephilim, stepped forward and marched the last Grand out of the palace's throne room.

"Before the sun rises on our new world, we must aid those who have been entrusted with saving the goddess," Carrington stated after the doors had been shut behind her husband. "Without Genoa, all life in our home will diminish. I ask now that you raise your weapons one last time. Come, fight with me against the monsters down in the Krack."

Silence met this request as those gathered turned to study Tresstéanna. She stepped forward and withdrew the Globe of Corpuscle from the magical Greilk box. The orb glowed brightly as red rays of magic shot from Genoa.

"Behold, Genoa!" Tresstéanna said as several Gi Jón fell to their knees in reverence while others fell on their faces. "She was stolen years ago, and her capture changed this world you live in. She spoke to me of a Midzark where water once fell from the sky, keeping the heat at bay. Where the flowers only found in the far southern plains once bloomed on the sands of the desert. Because she was taken from her home under the Márseille Lake, your world was changed. So was my homeland." Tresstéanna turned to study those closest to her. "These are my people. We have traveled many days underground. We fought monsters and elements to find the cradle where Genoa once rested peacefully. We must return her, but first we must defeat her last Protector." Here she withdrew the eye of Adulario and asked to see Dreail. When the image of a giant shark swam from the murky blue of the large crystal, several shrank away from the dais.

"This is Dreail, who was once Genoa's Protector. Dreail was changed when Genoa was captured. To change Dreail back, we must first fight the children this creature has birthed. These, I am told, are vast in number, monsters who are swarming down in the cave you called the Krack." Turning, Tresstéanna glanced out at the two armies before her. "Together, we can hold off the monsters until I can change Dreail back."

"You?" one giant shouted and stepped forward. "What can you do? You are a tiny little thing, even for a Gi Jón."

"She has already defeated two Protectors!" Kriston growled, glaring at the giant until he stepped back into the crowd. "She alone went into the mist and changed Adulario back to his true form, a Protector made of stone who is well over thirty feet tall. See, she holds his eye, a gift he presented to her in thanks for her deed. Then she changed Leewana. She was a giant snake that flew around inside the Kylix. Tresstéanna shoved the globe right down the snake's throat and—poof—Leewana was restored too," Kriston said. Tresstéanna felt both embarrassment and pride at Kriston's words. "Then you lot imprisoned her and now look at where you are? No more slaves! She did this!" Kriston pointed a finger at her. "She can do anything! And if she says she can change this huge monster back into Dreail, then she can!"

The cheers that arose after Kriston's speech made Tresstéanna's jaw drop in astonishment.

"Well, where do we start?" Carrington asked Tresstéanna with a smile.

"I guess we need to start down a dark and cold hole," Tresstéanna said. The crowds once again picked up their weapons, this time not to be raised against each other, but to battle the large monsters under the ground.

13

FIGHTING FANTASY

*S*hiarra, along with the leader of the giants who lived inside the Kylix, crouched in their hiding spot while they waited.

Shiarra had been confused at first to find out the man's name was Stand. She had thought Leewana had been giving the giants a command to stand still and not actually calling the giant by his name. Feeling foolish after discovering it was the giant's name, and not an order, she had quickly turned to the task at hand.

If this walking monster had once been one of her friends, then she had to use all her power to try and save them. Yet she wondered how she could. She worried that any magic she attempted on this creature would result in harming the friend trapped within. She asked Stand if he could describe the creature, yet it appeared the leader hadn't actually seen it with his own eyes.

"Knoll and Stemp saw this monster. It hides and attacks with such swiftness that I have only seen its shadow," Stand provided. Two large men approached when he waved his hands.

"The men call it the Kagmar," Knoll told her. "It has claws like a creature from the sea but walks upright like you or I."

"Its head is odd, like it melted, with huge black eyes on the sides," Stemp interjected as he held his hands near his face while trying to explain.

"It cuts its victims by using the claws, but I have never seen anything so fast before," Knoll resumed. He turned to Stand. "The men say it favors the shores on the east side of the cavern. We abandoned that area after the third attack."

"It patrols far from the dam, so we have tried to leave it alone for now, but some fear our escape route will be blocked if it gets between us and the stairs to the lookout," Stand said with a grim expression on his face.

"I need a look at it," Shiarra said with more confidence than she felt. She turned to Leewana and studied the Protector. "Can you fly me over there so I can spot it?"

Leewana shook her head no. "It hides when I draw near. It may be better if Stand takes you."

Now, Shiarra and Stand, along with his men, had been hiding behind two large rocks for a long time, waiting for the creature to appear. Several times Shiarra had needed to stretch her legs to relieve cramps in her calves. Stand had provided water for her and after a while he'd even provided large square cubes of food. The cubes tasted like nuts and sugary fruit, which she found to her liking.

After a rather long, silent wait, they were made aware of the Kagmar's approach by a sudden scraping noise.

"It comes!" Knoll hissed from her left.

Shiarra slowly raised her head above the rock, but she didn't see anything at first. She could hear the scraping grow louder, but still the dark cavern remained empty.

"There," Stand hissed next to her ear, pointing far to her right.

On the water's edge, a large mound of sand grew up from

the shore. At first, she thought the creature was coming out of the water but soon amended her opinion.

"It comes from the sand," Stand voiced as they watched a large monster emerge from the wet sands. It gave one massive shake, and sand and dirt dropped from its impressive form.

Shiarra held her breath as she studied the creature. She hoped she would recognize the friend trapped within this new form but was disappointed when no name jumped into her mind.

The creature's back was facing their hiding place as it emerged. When it was finished shaking its body clean, it turned its ugly face first left then right, as if trying to find out where it was. When the lights of the giants' camp, several yards down the shoreline, reflected in its large black eyes, it gave a giant screech.

"It aims for the town," Stand said as he quickly stood. "We must cut it off!"

Before Shiarra could give chase, the giants she had traveled with had ran forward to attack the creature. Stand drew a large sword as he raced at the monster. As Shiarra watched the giants attack the massive monster known as the Kagmar, a name finally jumped into her mind.

"Sash!" she said aloud as she stood still and watched the fight several yards away.

She noticed a familiar figure in the way the monster moved and held its large claws, as if holding a sword. When it dodged to avoid one of the giant's killing blades, it slid sideways remarkably like the way she had seen Sash practice and fight many times.

When it snapped its claws and sliced a deep gouge along Stemp's back, she finally raced into action. Raising her magic, she had a red ball racing at the Kagmar's head.

"Move back!" she yelled as she sent another blast into the creature's face.

The first blast hit the monster in the head, but it hadn't even dazed or slowed it. As she ran forward, she tried another form of magic, heat instead of light. This time a scream emitted from the creature.

The black eyes turned her way as she drew near and mixed her magic with some memories. This magic was much like a favorite article, which could remind someone of the good times that surrounded that item. She used the memory of her first meeting with Sash, how he had saved her all those days ago in Pinewoods and had rescued her from the Stoles hidden inside her home village. Specifically, the Stole that had once been her mother.

Her magical blast hit the Kagmar dead center of its misshaped head, and she felt ecstatic when it took a step back from the strike. However, her smile fell away when it bared its sharp fangs at her and took a menacing step towards her. Sending anther blast of memories towards the creature, she cried out to Sash.

"Sash! It is me, Shiarra!" she screamed. She tried another memory of their time in Valorna. "Remember! Remember your oath!" she screamed as the Kagmar took another step forward, its claws snapping towards her. "Remember Tresstéanna, your queen!"

The creature stopped for a moment as its black eyes studied her. Hope once again welled inside her until the creature again ran at her.

It was feet from her when she felt large hands lifting her off the ground. Stand the giant had her thrown over his shoulder before the monster could snap her in half. As he raced towards the village, Shiarra looked up and saw the Kagmar give chase.

"Got any other magic?" Stand asked as he ran.

TRESSTÉANNA HELD the small carved unicorn knife in her hands and smiled. It, along with all their other weapons, had finally been returned to them. Most of their weapons had been closed off inside a closet on the main level of the palace. The magical items that had been stored inside the Greilk box she now carried inside her backpack.

Her magical bow, a gift from Belent, had also been returned. The carved dragon bow and arrows now rested on her back, next to her backpack. She secured her unicorn knife in the sheath on her hip and continued to smile.

She had been missing the swan bracelet and asked after it. It was found that the jewelry had been presented to Carrington. The giantess had quickly found the item in a box in her private rooms and returned it to Tresstéanna.

"I thought this was a ring, but it did not fit me, so I kept it amongst my other items. I did not know it was yours," Carrington said as she bent and tied the leather straps on Tresstéanna's wrist herself.

"If you are finished, I believe we should return to our mission," Kriston said as he returned his own sword to its leather sheath on his back.

"Most of the army has already started," Wizard Col said as he turned his dark eyes upon Tresstéanna. "The climb is steep, but our way is clear until the tunnel."

"What then?" she asked and turned eyes to Carrington.

"I have not left the palace much. My father knows more," Carrington stated as Maven Gorphen joined them.

"The small village has been cut off from the palace for

many days now. Most of the giants down there felt the Grand had failed them. I guess they were correct because no supplies or reinforcements have been sent to them."

"Reinforcements for what?" Col asked. "The Otomi fighters kept the fighting in the forest."

"Not the resistance, the monsters," Gorphen said as Svlain stepped forward.

"Dreail's creatures?" Svlain asked and when Gorphen blinked in confusion, she explained further. "Large snakes, spiders, and sea creatures?" When the giant nodded, she turned to Tresstéanna. "The Húriya people have some skill in defeating these creatures, but the numbers must be greater down in the caves than what was in Kós Kóvar."

"Either way, the cave is our path," Col said grimly as they made their way across the Ingress Bridge.

Tresstéanna had a fleeting second to cast her eyes back at the Régorge Palace. Lights flooded the building, which seemed so vast. She felt anger over her days imprisoned inside the palace, but now, she also felt relief. Relief at finally getting to leave this place, and relief that she had made a difference for those who had been trapped inside those walls a lot longer than she and her friends had. As her eyes scanned the huge building, she realized that if she hadn't been captured and forced into slavery, then all who called Midzark home would not be free now.

"Out of the darkness shines the light," she said more to herself than the others. Then she finally turned her back on the palace for the last time.

Col was correct. The steep incline up the Hessite cliffs took energy and time. Well before the sun rose on the day in Midzark, the group from Genoa was once again stepping into the Kylix's darkness.

Tresstéanna saw Svlain hesitate as the land nymph neared the cave and moved to stand next to her.

"How are you?" Tresstéanna asked as Svlain's green eyes turned to her.

"I am better now that we are all reunited," Svlain replied.

"Not all of us," Wizard Leian said gruffly as his eyes scanned the darkness before them. "If Belent's book is correct, then Shiarra is ahead, or below." With this, the skinny wizard quickly disappeared down into the darkness, determination in every step.

"I know how he feels," Zain said as he grabbed Svlain's slender arm in a protective manner before they too disappeared into the cave's entrance. Tresstéanna turned to see Kriston beside her. His dark eyes held concern as he watched her. Reaching out, she traced a finger over his chin.

"We have the flower, we have our friends, and now, we can continue with our mission." She took a deep sigh. What she didn't say now would keep him from worry, but in her mind, it hung between them like a dark cloud.

She had been shown what she needed to do when she had last talked to Genoa. The goddess had given her an insight into what must transpire down in the dark cave of the Kylix. And it frightened her.

The giants called the cave the Krack, and as they traversed into the darkness, Tresstéanna found it fit the narrow cavern. Odd lights lit the way down into the mountain, and the hot air of Midzark soon was a fleeting memory as a chill swept over those who marched into the cavern.

She was provided a coat, one that was sewn together like a patch quilt and had fur around the neckline. It kept the cave's chill at bay, and she welcomed the gift, which had been presented by one of Mayson's men. Kriston was provided a cloak. It draped from his broad shoulders and cut short of his sword belt.

The army of both the Nephilim and the Húriya marched ahead, some wearing new cloaks while others remained in their thin black cloaks. Giants led the way while the smaller desert people walked hesitantly into the unknown.

Ava kept close to Svlain and Zain, while Carrington and her father remained near Tresstéanna. Mayson and his men also kept near to those from Genoa, and Tresstéanna realized from their banter that the Otomi fighters had grown fond of her dragon warrior friends.

Seth and Mayson's young brother, Max, kept telling jokes to Kiev, no doubt trying to make the goblin laugh as they moved further down the tunnel. Colab and the pretty girl named Maraneal stayed close together, and Tresstéanna took comfort knowing that Kriston's nephew had found solace in her company after his loss of the Scarent snake, Meshi.

Rastel, the ambassador of Genoa, was nearby. She could hear him consulting Carrington as they walked. It appeared Rastel was her new guidance counselor; the giantess seemed to listen to every word the ambassador uttered to her.

"Will Genoa really change Midzark back?" Kriston asked as they walked side by side.

Smiling, Tresstéanna squeezed his hand as they continued. "Yes. Much will be different once I place the globe back in the cradle."

"You?" Kriston tugged her hand until she stopped. "No, you do nothing without me."

Cursing herself, she tried to smile up at him.

"I can see you trying to formulate a lie," he hissed, drawing her closer. His large hands squeezed her arm protectively. "We will not be separated again." The last word was more growl, reminding her that Kriston's royal magic allowed him to shift into the form of a large black wolf.

"I only know what guidance I was given. If it is possible, you will be by my side," she said, choosing her words carefully.

"What guidance?" he quickly demanded, and she shook her head.

"The flower grants the wish of the one who asks it. Two cannot ask." She once again traced a finger along his chin. "If I can ask correctly…" She stopped and shook her head. "I have an idea about that, but it might be tricky." She smiled as a new thought formulated inside her head. "But if my time on Earth showed me anything, it's how to get a happy ending."

SHIARRA WATCHED as the monster that had once been Sash drew close to the giants' village. The giant named Stand had run the entire way to the village with her over his shoulder and had beaten the monster by several seconds.

Those few seconds had been enough to raise the alarm, and Shiarra watched firsthand how these people fought off the monsters of Dreail. The wooden and stone walls were tall around the village, but still there were a few outlying buildings. Runners and sentries raised the alarm for the entire area. Even the women and children were well armed with large weapons. Usually they were placed in a large battalion and were kept well away from the walls, but there was no running and hiding for them down here in the Kylix.

By the time Stand had reached the center of the village, the monster they called the Kagmar was fighting the border patrols.

"Wait here!" Stand ordered. Her dropped her and ran back the way they had just come.

"I can help!" she shouted but the man was already gone.

"Child!" Leewana said as she quickly dropped out of the darkness above her. Shiarra squealed at the Protector's sudden appearance, and when several nearby giants turned her way, she quickly covered her mouth.

"Child! Your friends draw near!" Leewana stated and pointed far to Shiarra's left.

"Are you sure?" She had no sooner asked that she noticed fires far above. It wasn't the lookout fire she was seeing now, but hundreds of fires dropping down out of the darkness. "Lights!" she said, marveling at the number of torches quickly bobbing down off the cliff and onto the large stairs.

"They won freedom and bring two armies." Leewana's words shocked her.

"They won?" Shiarra shook her head in amazement. "Can you take me to them?"

"Climb on," the Protector replied, and Shiarra immediately scrambled onto her back. Excitement and amazement filled her as the lights continued to grow in number.

Within seconds, Leewana was flying over the vast staircase leading from the cave's floor all the way up to the cave's tall ceiling. Still the lights grew in number and, when they drifted close, Shiarra could see the stairway was filled with both giants and smaller humans. Thousands of them raced down the large stairs towards the bottom.

"I do not see my friends," she shouted as Leewana dipped closer.

"There, they are just starting their descent." The Protector pointed one hand far upwards to the top. As she spoke, her large wings beat, and Shiarra felt them lift upwards with the movement.

When Leewana was finally spotted by those on the ground, a mighty roar arose. She set her large body on the high shelf, and Shiarra found them surrounded by her missing friends.

Before Shiarra's feet touched the ground, she was flung around in a hard hug, and Leian was kissing her.

"Shiarra!" Tresstéanna shouted while the others pushed in towards her and Leian.

"Let the girl down. There are others here who want to greet her," Col shouted.

"Not in the same manner," Stria said with a smile as she pulled Leian away just enough to hug the missing wizard herself.

"My turn!" Seth said and drew in for a quick hug and a peck on Shiarra's cheek.

"It is good to see you!" Tresstéanna said over the loud welcomes her friends were giving Shiarra. "Your book was right!" she said to Belent, and Shiarra saw her queen slap the sorcerer on his back.

"Book?" Shiarra asked as she was passed to Col for a quick hug. "What book…. Calob!" Shiarra interrupted her own question with a quick exclamation at seeing the nephew of Kriston standing before her.

"No, it is me, Colab," the boy said solemnly.

"We lost Meshi," Tresstéanna quickly said as she ran a hand up and down the boy's arm, as if to reassure him.

"Sash!" Shiarra said quickly as her mind cleared. "Quickly, we have to save him!"

"Sash?" Svlain said as she pushed to the front of the crowd that was gathered around the wizard. "Sash is dead. I saw him fall myself."

"No," Shiarra said with a shake of her head. "He is here, down below. He's attacking the giants' village."

"What do you mean? We were told he died fighting Dreail," Tresstéanna asked and grabbed Shiarra's arms.

"I do not know about that, only that Dreail changed him into a monster. The giants call him the Kagmar," Shiarra said as Leian's arm wrapped tightly around her. "Tresstéanna, you have to change him back!"

It took some convincing, but finally Shiarra, Leian, and Tresstéanna were settled on Leewana's back while the Protector held Kriston in her large arms. The four were insistent on remaining together, so they were the first ones to go down into the dark to save their friend.

It was hoped that Tresstéanna could use the globe to change their friend back, much like she had done for the Protectors themselves.

Shiarra hoped they arrived back at the village before the Kagmar disappeared back into the sandy shores. She set her mind that if they did not find him there at the village, they would track him back to where she had first seen him.

She hadn't needed to worry. When Leewana flew down out of the darkness and the village drew close, they could see that the fighting continued.

"The monsters are here!" Shiarra cried as they noticed that both sides of the village were lit up with battles fires. Lights and shouts rose into the darkness as Leewana flew towards the center of the village.

"Quickly, this way," Shiarra shouted as they jumped off the Protector's back.

"Wait!" Leian shouted as Shiarra raced towards the sounds of battle.

When she was quickly jerked around, she saw a terribly angry Leian facing her.

"You need to think before we race in there!" he shouted.

"I can do it!" Tresstéanna shouted but was quickly halted by Kriston.

"There is another way," Kriston said, pointing to one of the nearby buildings.

Looking up, Shiarra noticed it was a watchtower. It rose

above the roof lines of the nearby houses and would allow them to see everything below.

They found the giant door and large stairs, which took a while to maneuver. But once on the top, they spotted the Kagmar creature quickly. Its large red body was smashing through a battalion of giants.

"Can you change him from here?" Shiarra asked Tresstéanna, who shook her head.

"To change the Protectors, I had to touch them." She cast a look at Kriston. "We could do it," she said and a slow smile formed on her lips.

THE PLAN WAS SIMPLE, but still Kriston worried about it, and Tresstéanna.

After returning to the ground floor and finding the fastest path to where the fighting was, Leian and Shiarra headed off to his left while Kriston moved right and found the perfect spot. Tresstéanna remained on the straight path, and every time she vanished from his vision, he panicked a little.

Finally, when she gave the signal, he settled down and closed his eyes, then steadied his breathing. Using his birthright, his royal magic, he called forth his Beowulf.

As the wolf, he raced right towards the fighting monster. The Kagmar rose feet above Kriston's wolf head. Its red body shimmered in the cave's light as it attacked the giants. It was snapping at the large men with its claws, claws there were razor sharp and extremely quick.

Letting out a loud growl, Kriston sprang at the creature

when its back was to him. He scratched and bit at the monster. But the hard, red shell remained unharmed, and Kriston's wolf body was easily flung off.

But Kriston had guessed this would be the outcome of his first attack and, after flipping his long dark body, landed on all four paws. He braced for another attack, which allowed him to easily dodge a snapping claw. Then he ran around two large giants who were trying to use long spears against the creature.

His next attack was better aimed, and when Kriston sunk his teeth into the soft neck fold of the creature, he held on. His wolf body hung down along the creature's back, and his teeth kept him from falling. His claws still scraped the red shell for purchase as the monster spun around, trying to get its claws on its attacker. When a spear ricocheted off the red shell two inches from Kriston's muzzle, Kriston almost let go.

Damn giants are going to kill me, Kriston thought as he noticed movement out of the corner of his eyes.

Leian and Shiarra emerged from the far wall of a building and started blasting their magic at the creature. Kriston knew it was just lights and not killing magic, but still he flinched when a ball of yellow blasted the monster.

When the Kagmar turned towards the wizards, Kriston held on to the soft neck with his teeth and waited. When he felt something pull and tug at the fur on his back, he dug his teeth in deeper as Tresstéanna climbed up and over him.

"Hold on!" she shouted and raised the Globe of Corpuscle.

Kriston had one quick vision of the bright red orb before Tresstéanna had shoved it down upon the Kagmar's head.

Expecting a loud crack, or even a scream of pain, Kriston was shocked to see and hear nothing. The monster still spun around fighting; it still had a hard shell and odd face with deadly claws.

Tresstéanna sat atop Kriston's wolf back, clinging to his black fur. She raised the orb again but this time she shook her head and nestled the ball in between them. He felt a slight sting where the orb rested against his fur but kept a tight hold of the monster.

"Going to try this!" she shouted, and Kriston saw her eyes immediately go white with her magic. When the Kagmar's eyes turned white, Kriston held on and prayed.

He felt the creature give a mighty shake three seconds after its eyes milked over. When it stopped fighting and stood still, Kriston heard Shiarra shout for the giants to stand.

"Fall back, stop fighting, stand," she shouted as the creature doubled over, taking him and Tresstéanna along for the ride.

When they landed on the ground, Kriston's teeth no longer had a hold on the Kagmar. He felt himself falling away as Tresstéanna still clung to his fur. He tried to land under her and scrambled up when they hit the ground.

Seeing she was unharmed, he quickly turned to study the odd form before them. The Kagmar was no longer red, but an odd russet color. The hard shell appeared to be melting away, leaving raw skin behind.

"He is changing. You can come out if you want," Tresstéanna said beside him, and he immediately dropped his magic.

When he came back to himself, he was still sitting in the small alleyway between two houses about three blocks from where the fighting had taken place. Standing, he raced back to see that Sash was still bent over. His large form was shaking as he transformed back into his human form.

The giants nearby were pointing and shouting while

Shiarra and Leian relayed orders. Weapons still pointed at the changing figure, but no one attacked as the two wizards stood between the giants and the transforming Sash.

"Stay back, he is our friend," Leian shouted.

"Stand, keep your men away," Shiarra hollered at a rather large giant who gave her a quick nod and started barking his own orders at the gathered giants.

"Fall back, the wizard has this under control," the giant shouted just as a scream emitted from Sash's changing form.

Distracted, Kriston kept his eyes on the horrific transformation. Red globs of crusty skin melted away, and the claws retracted and formed into large fingers.

Big black eyes sank back into the head and transformed into a dark brown, while the sharp fangs retreated into small round teeth. When another scream came from Sash, the large man sank facedown into the dirt and remained still.

Unsure if his friend was finished changing back to himself, Kriston slowly approached and nudged the naked man with the toe of his boot.

"Sash, are you back?" he asked.

"I am," came a thick croak, much to Kriston's relief.

"She did it!" Kriston said with a smile and glanced up to praise Tresstéanna. Finding her missing, he quickly turned on the spot. Still not finding her in the crowd around him, he said to Shiarra, "Where is she?"

When Shiarra and Leian both shook their heads, he realized his mistake. She had used the time between his transforming from his Beowulf back to himself to slip away. She was headed to Dreail by herself.

"Cats!" he hissed. He quickly got his bearings and headed towards where he thought the water sat.

He ran like the devil was after him, racing past homes, buildings, and giants. Sweat poured off him, not from his exertion but from fear. He ran past the center of the village with its open court and down another street.

Finally seeing the water ahead, he doubled his speed. He couldn't lose her, not again.

When his feet drew close to the water, he slipped on the rocks to an odd stop and scanned the water's edge. There was a sharp drop, no more than ten feet down into the water. Rocks and dirt littered the ledge where he stood. He had only a second to notice the waters were bubbling, then he spotted her.

She stood thirty feet from him, naked on the ledge leading to the water's edge. Her magical knife, strapped to her left forearm, was the only item she wore. Her long hair was unbound, flowing down her slender back, and her arms were extended far above her head. She held the globe in one hand and fisted something in her other.

"Tresstéanna!" he shouted.

She slowly turned towards him and smiled. He noticed tears sparkled off her pale cheeks. Love and sadness filled her eyes. Then, before he could step towards her, she quickly took her fisted hand and held up the purple petal. After showing it to him, she quickly placed it in her mouth.

Shock crossed her face, and he took a running step towards her. But before he could reach her, her body transformed.

Her legs melted away, and her body flopped to the ground. The long shapely legs appeared to lace together and were replaced by a single scaly tail the color of soft blue glass. The scales formed just below her navel and shimmered in the faint light of the cave. The tail was twice as long as her legs had been, and she swished it back and forth in the dirt where she sat.

She still nestled the orb to her bare chest and glanced down at her own tail as she gave it a mighty swing. Her mouth opened and closed as if she was trying to speak or breath.

She turned her head towards him as she looked over her left shoulder. Her blue eyes grew large and round as her mouth tried to suck in air. Then, she quickly flung herself over the cliff and into the waters far below.

DREAIL, both mother and father to those created in the water domain, felt the intrusion of the one that did not belong. It had felt the changing of its newest creature, the Kagmar, its mixed child, one from the land transformed into one of Dreail's own making. It no longer heard this child and knew it walked once more outside Dreail's home.

When the water around Dreail's large form shivered with the invasion of the new creature, it smelled the water around its massive body. Its children felt the change too, for those surrounding Dreail screamed with the intrusion into their home.

"Find it," Dreail ordered, using the language its children understood.

Moving its long shark body back and forth, Dreail swam to where it knew its enemy would eventually go. It was within the dark opening immediately. Hidden down the narrow, flooded cavern rested the mother's cradle.

If Dreail thought hard, it could remember why the cradle was so important. It would have then remembered its mother, Genoa. It might have even recalled why it had been created and that its sole purpose was to defend its mother.

It would have recalled then its once beautiful form, a sea

creature with a long blue tail and fluttering fins that helped it swim in the water. Its impressive form had once had a human head and arms, all given and created by its mother.

Dreail might have recalled creating its first child, the Lady of the Tentril. She had been its first daughter, so dear to Dreail that it had often swam down the length of the cavern to talk with her.

But, since its changing, it knew only hatred. Its purpose had been changed to attack and reproduce monsters. This had been the only thing Dreail had done for many years now.

Yet somewhere inside Dreail's mind it remembered that this dark crevice held a place it must protect, guard with all its might.

It knew this, just as it knew this new intruder would seek the cradle. Evil magic held Dreail captive, magic which wrapped the large body of Dreail in the form of a red rope. It was this magic that kept the Protector spellbound.

Trapped in a form it had not been created in, changed from the beautiful to the hideous monster that now swam back and forth, it guarded the one place that held all the secrets of the world.

When it smelled the water again, it tasted blood and something else.

Mother, Dreail thought as its dark eyes scanned the black waters.

14

ONE DROP OF WATER

resstéanna knew what must be done. She had been told by Genoa that her path led down the flooded cavern of the cradle. She had been shown Dreail within the eye of Adulario. It had shown her a massive shark. Sharks lived in the water, which meant she had to travel down into the water. Safely.

As they had walked into the dark cavern of the Krack, her mind raced to all the possibilities. Yet only one solution presented itself to her. And it was a dangerous one.

She knew she would need to keep Kriston safe, just like she had done when confronting Adulario all those days ago. To do that, she would need to go alone to confront the last Protector.

She had seen her chance during their planning to transform Sash back to himself. Transforming Sash had caused her some confusion at first. When the globe didn't work, she had quickly changed gears and used her magic to talk to Sash.

She had found the trapped man immediately upon touching him. He was inside the Kagmar, screaming for release, trapped and unable to control his own body. She had used her magic to guide him out of the spell, successfully returning her friend to his natural form.

Using Kriston's Beowulf had been brilliant, and the time it took for him to change back and return had been needed. Yet this plan had caused her great sadness. She was breaking his trust in her and feared that, if she failed, he would never get over her deceit.

But to save Genoa, both goddess and planet, she had to sacrifice much.

After she had seen the change in Sash, and noticed Kriston's Beowulf disappear, she had immediately raced through the village. She'd headed away from Kriston and her friends, running towards the water and what awaited here there.

When she stood on the edge of the ledge, her courage failed her. Could she really do this? Alone?

Knowing time was fast escaping her, she took a deep breath and pulled the Globe of Corpuscle from the magical box, then stripped out of her clothing. She strapped her magical knife to her left arm and pulled the Orwic flower out of her pack. Setting the pot on the hard ground, she pulled a petal from the purple plant.

Her courage returned as she raised the globe and petal above her head. She was meant for this, her mind told her. She had traversed worlds and trials to stand here in this moment.

Maybe her travels in Earth would aid her in this endeavor. After all, she now knew what words she would utter for the Orwic's magic to return her safely to her natural form, if she survived.

When Kriston had appeared, her courage once again wavered. But her determination had taken over, and she'd quickly eaten the petal of the Orwic before he could stop her.

"Transform me into a mermaid and return me when my mission is complete," she murmured as she swallowed the petal.

Her time on Earth had shown her what a mermaid should look like, so she thought she knew what to expect. What she hadn't expected was the pain.

As it ripped through her, she fell to the ground and fought the discomfort. When her legs transformed, she almost dropped the globe because of the agony.

Realizing she could no longer breathe caused her to panic, but then she sent Kriston a last longing look and threw herself down into the water.

Breathe! Her body craved to breathe, but it wasn't air it sought. It was water.

She had only seconds to test her new tail and the gills that sat on either side of her slender neck. Then she was surrounded.

Seeing Dreail's children circling her kicked all her warrior training into action. She tucked the orb like a football, grabbed her knife from her armband, and slashed at the closest creature. When blood filled the water, she moved on to the next attacker.

Using her powerful tail, she swam, dodging and weaving in and out of the attacking monsters. But she found they moved just as fast as she could. If speed wasn't the way to win, then she would have to use her other skills.

She found one of the massive snakes nearby. She grabbed its long body with her arm, the one that held the knife, and wrapped it around the snake's tail. Using her own tail, she tried to steer it towards a small opening in the wall of attacking monsters. When the creature she hugged tried to double back along its body, she called forth her magic.

The Surpense was hers now. Its small black eyes turned white as she controlled it. She soon found that it wasn't the fastest swimmer and quickly abandoned it. She reached for a different monster, this one crab like, yet it too was slow.

As she was using her knife to slash at an attacking spider, she noticed out of the corner of her eye another powerful creature approaching and turned to face it. This one had a massive maw full of sharp teeth. Large gills ran along its misshaped body, which ended in four large tentacles covered in round suckers.

Come at me! she thought, holding Genoa closer, her knife at the ready once again.

Instead of cutting the creature, she faked right and used the knife to stab along its side. Keeping the blade imbedded in the monster's side, she ran her magic down the blade's length and into the monster.

Reading its mind through her magic, she discovered that the creature was a Gordam, and it desperately craved her flesh. As her magic slammed into it, it shook with the intrusion but used its powerful tentacles to swim away from the other creatures as it followed her commands.

She had the Gordam attack anything that came near, but worried that her knife was sliding out of the wound. She feared she would lose control of the creature, so she glanced around for another monster she could use.

When two large crabs swam directly at her, she pulled the knife out of the wounded Gordam and flung the magical knife at one while using her tail to smash the head of the second.

Spinning in the water, she felt a blast of water fly past her and turned in time to see a large sword sink into a third crab she had missed seeing. Shocked, she turned and saw Kriston swim past her. When he pulled his massive sword from the dead monster, she saw he had a dark green mermaid tail.

When he swam towards her, his handsome face was set in anger. Keeping her eyes on him, she reached her hand out and called her magical knife back to her palm. Seeing another attacker draw close, she used it to cut one of the nearby Surpense as Kriston cut into another crab.

She could hear Kriston muttering something as he used his sword on a crab. She was shocked to hear his voice and realized that she too could speak under the water. She emitted small grunts when she used her tail to hit anything that got close to her.

"I'm sorry!" she shouted, and Kriston turned to glare at her. "We have to go this way!" she shouted and pointed off to her right.

"Not without me!" he growled and angrily plunged his sword into a nearby Gordam while using his tail to bash in half a crab that had been attacking from behind him. Realizing there were more monsters then they could fight, she called to Kriston again.

"Quickly, there are too many! This way!" She swam towards Kriston and tugged on his free arm. He turned and pushed her head down just as a massive claw swiped at it.

When Kriston's sword had severed the claw, he grabbed her arm and pulled her to freedom. They swam in unison, swift and silent as the monsters chased them.

"I am sorry," she finally said as the gap grew between them and Dreail's children.

"We will discuss it later, if we survive." He cast her a quick look. "By the way, the tail looks good on you." His flash of a grin had her heart skipping a beat as they swam into the dark waters.

SASH FELT his body's transformation much like you felt a tooth ache. Pain rippled through his limbs as the hard shell retreated and his raw skin was left behind.

He heard Kriston and responded to his friend, but when he looked up, the man was gone. Confused, he glanced around and noticed he was surrounded by giants. Fearing their attack, he quickly stood and reached for his sword. But finding no weapon, or pants, he lifted his fists instead.

"That is not necessary." Shiarra's voice caused him to spin on the spot and locate the wizard. After confirming it was the wizard, he lowered his hands to cover his man parts.

"Beg your pardon," he said, and tried not to turn red at finding himself naked and in the presence of so many. "What has happened and why am I naked?"

"We have a good story to answer that question," Wizard Leian said with a grin as he threw Sash a bundle of clothing. "It is a monster of a tale." Both he and Shiarra snickered out loud, and Sash stared at them in confusion.

"Quickly, get dressed, and we will relay all the horrid details," Shiarra said as she turned her back on him and walked over to a very large giant.

Giving his head a shake, Sash bent to dress and found that his movements seemed stiff. It was as if he had been sick. Maybe that's what was wrong. He had been ill. But if so, why had he been naked, and where was he?

Scanning his mind, he thought back to his last memory. He recalled being with Svlain. He remembered the land nymph. But that had taken place in the desert. Looking around, he thought they were back in the Kylix, but how had he gotten here?

"Leian, where are we?" he asked as he buttoned up the borrowed shirt.

"The giants' village down in the Kylix," the wizard said with a shake of his head. "They are our allies now, but our foe is vast and dangerous." Leian shook his head and handed Sash some boots. "We have quite a battle ahead of us."

"They disappeared at the water's edge!" Shiarra said as she ran back towards them. "Their tracks go down into the water." She turned when a giant came forward holding two piles of clothing.

Sash recognized Tresstéanna's backpack immediately

when it was handed to Shiarra. When a small purple flower was turned over to the wizard, he heard her suck in a breath.

"Look! Two petals are missing," she cried.

Sash looked back and forth between the two.

"What in the king's name is going on?" he growled, and turned to Leian. "Where is Svlain and are those the queen's things?"

"Come, we will tell you everything while we march to meet the others," Leian said. After confirming Sash had finished lacing the boots up, he walked off with the giants following them.

Sash was astonished and ashamed by the story he was told next. He worried about the giants he had injured while in the form of the monster. But having no memory of these fights, he turned his mind to the tale of the palace and the battles Leian spoke of.

"So, the slaves are all free?" he asked with a smile. "The Otomi fighters really did it?" Giving his large head a shake, he smiled.

"It was all thanks to the great lady, Carrington," Leian said as they walked through the village and reached a tall wall. "They should be here soon, hopefully before the monsters attack again."

No sooner were the words out than one of the giants came running up to them.

"The monsters rally at the shore again," the giant said, and Sash saw a look passed between Shiarra and one of the giants.

"Hold them off," the giant ordered.

"Stand, do you know how long before they come?" Shiarra asked the giant, and he shook his head.

"We can hope they arrive before the attack gets too intense, but our numbers have dwindled. We have lots of injured," Stand said as Leian quickly stepped forward.

"I might be able to help with that," the wizard voiced as he turned to look at Shiarra, who nodded and placed a hand on Leian's arm.

"Knoll, take this one to the healer," Stand said and turned to study Sash. "Are you able to fight or are those muscles just for the ladies?"

Sash gave the giant a smile as he flexed his arms. "Give me a sword and you will find out."

"Good. Stemp find a knife for this man." Stand turned back to Sash. "Better make it a small one. He is a tiny fellow, after all." With a bark of a laugh, Stand placed a hand on his own hip knife and shook his head. "Better yet, take mine."

Sash found that what the giants called a knife was indeed sword size for him. After catching the weapon, Sash gave it a few swings and nodded.

"That will do." He looked up at the giant. "Better show me where the fighting is."

The fighting ended up on the other side of the town. Sash had to run to keep pace with the giants, but the movement helped loosen his stiff muscles.

"By the way, who are we fighting now?" Sash asked Shiarra, who kept stride with him.

"Oh, we forgot to tell you this part." The wizard lifted her dirty dress's torn slip a little higher. "The monstrous children of Dreail," she said quickly. She grew silent again as they ran.

"The ones from the lake?" Sash shook his head.

"Yes. Svlain was able to trap them down here and save the desert city, but now Tresstéanna and Kriston have taken Genoa down into the water to find the cradle, and we are left with the monsters." Sash knew this speech had worn Shiarra out. The wizard huffed and puffed when they finally came to a halt.

The barricade they stopped at was full of more giants. As they approached, Sash saw several near the door stand as they saluted Stand. This confirmed to Sash who was in charge, but when the giant turned to study Shiarra, Sash reconsidered this.

"My men will direct the approaching army here, but this fortification might be in jeopardy if we cannot hold the eastern wall." Stand turned to show them a map. "Here the water is deep, which allows them to amass before springing up."

Looking at the map, Sash saw the line indicating the separation of water and land. The village was outlined and then he saw the dam.

"Why does the dam still stand?" Sash asked as his eyes turned to Stand.

"It stands because we need it," Stand replied. He would have turned to dismiss Sash except Shiarra stepped forward.

"For what?" she asked quickly as she bent over the parchment.

Stand turned and looked at the wizard for a moment. Then, with a shake of his head, he drew out another parchment. "The giants down here have spent many years building this structure so we can live without control of the Grands. The dam helps irrigate and regulate foods."

The parchment showed a drawing of what the giants hoped the village would one day become. Sash noticed that in the drawing closest to the dam, there were lines of farms. Small dots indicated where they hoped their homes to be. There were irrigation ditches drawn on the map and a massive bridge leading over the lake, one that had towers and piers leading out into the water.

"Stand, peace has been made aboveground. The Grands no longer hold control over Midzark," Shiarra said as she picked up the drawing. "This hidden life is no longer needed. You and your people can return to the sun above."

Shaking his head, Stand turned to look at her. "Some of

my people have been banished." Stand turned to study his men in the room. "Some do not wish to return above."

"Then we must change their minds," a soft female voice said from the doorway.

Turning, Sash saw a large giantess step into the room. Several of the giants bowed, and Shiarra rushed forward. While Sash had been studying the giantess, Svlain had stepped into the room too. It was Svlain who Shiarra rushed forward to hug.

"My Grand," Stand said with a nod of his head.

"No, I am just Carrington now," the giantess said. She turned to motion to Svlain and Belent next to her. "These people have shown me the error of my ways." Turning, the woman addressed all within the large room. "Freedom has been won!" she bellowed, raising her fist to the air. "All are free and welcome back in Midzark."

KRISTON'S ANGER from being left behind by Tresstéanna had been intense. After running to the spot where she had vanished, he had been relieved to see, sitting on top of her neatly folded clothing, the Orwic flower.

Giving no thought to his own danger, he tore off his boots and pants and swallowed the small purple flower. Knowing a wish was needed, he immediately asked for the same wish Tresstéanna had used and jumped into the waters before the change to merman had been completed.

Anger had quickly been replaced by fear. Fear for Tresstéanna. He realized that she was surrounded by large monsters and feared he wouldn't reach her in time.

But as he swam, he saw her use several impressive moves on the monsters. This caused his anger to return.

"Should have told me," he mumbled as he fought his way to her. "Woman cannot keep doing this, should keep her tied up." He threw his large sword—with some difficulty because of the dark waters—at the attacking crab monster and continued his rant as they fought their way free.

Fleeing the attacking creatures had been smart, not that he would tell Tresstéanna this. But he knew they were outnumbered and at a disadvantage. There was no way to win any battle when it was two against… *How many of these blasted creatures were there?* he thought as the darkness engulfed them.

"Here, just ahead," Tresstéanna said, pulling her magical knife once more from her armband. Taking the hint, he drew his sword as a rock wall came into their vision.

"What of the last Protector?" Kriston asked, his eyes scanning the dark waters ahead.

When Tresstéanna shook her head, Kriston turned his attention to the swarming monsters behind them.

"They draw close!" he shouted, moving to block Tresstéanna from the advancing swarm.

"There!" Tresstéanna screamed. She lurched away from where Kriston swam.

"No!" Kriston shouted. He moved to follow her just as a large, dark figure crossed between them. "Look out!" he shouted, panicked when he could no longer see her, only the monster.

The creature was triple the size of any of its children and looked large enough to swallow him whole. Large teeth snapped in its wide jaw as it turned in Kriston's direction, its black eyes fixed on him.

"Tresstéanna!" Kriston shouted as the body of the

monster swayed and turned towards the last place Kriston had seen her.

Using his new powerful tail, Kriston swam to follow the monster. Slashing at its massive tail, he realized too late that the scales covering the shark were not ordinary ones. He drew his short knife after his sword bounced off the scales, which were like a metal armor.

Dreail swam away and showed no interest in Kriston. In fact, Kriston grabbed and clung onto the upper fin of Dreail's tail, and the monster stayed focused on Tresstéanna and the red orb she cradled in her arms.

"Swim!" Kriston shouted as Tresstéanna turned to face the approaching monster with Kriston clinging to its tail.

Her face was lit with the red glow of Genoa's orb. Determination covered her pretty face as her pale hair floated around it. She still held the Globe of Corpuscle, but it was no longer tucked against her breast. Instead, she held it out like an offering.

"Dreail, Genoa sent me to cleanse you and return you to your former glory," Tresstéanna shouted as the monster loomed towards her.

Feeling frustrated, Kriston slammed his short knife into the hard scales of Dreail's body. His frustration built as his knife slipped off the scales without causing any harm. Finding the scales were so close to each other that he couldn't even get the thin blade under the armor, he tried to tug and pull the monster off course. But nothing helped.

"Go! Swim!" he shouted again as they grew closer.

She shook her head once, and he cried out towards her when she swam right at the attacking creature, the globe held before her like a shield.

"NO!" Kriston screamed as she swam headfirst into the monster's large open mouth.

Distracted by what he had just witnessed, Kriston was

sent flying when Dreail gave a flick of his massive tail. He spun head over heels, flipping several times, and crashed into a massive rock wall. Blood poured from a wound on his shoulder as he tried to right himself.

When he heard a loud roar, he spun around in time to see the large shark wiggle and squirm yards from him. No longer did the dark grey scales hold the mysterious form of Dreail together. Instead a red glow emitted from the creature's skin as it writhed in pain.

"Tresstéanna!" Kriston shouted. He tried to attack the monster again, but the large side fins of the shark hit him and sent him sailing back into the rocks once more.

When he righted himself a second time, it was to a different scene. Instead of a large shark, the original form of Dreail emerged.

The creature was over forty feet long, including its large green tail. A human head and arms started the awesome form, but large fins fluttered along its back. Where hair should have been there were thin gill-like tufts that beat the water to help keep it afloat. The tail, which started below its chest, twisted into a large circle in the dark waters.

"Child," Dreail said, and Kriston looked into clear green eyes. No longer was Dreail trapped by the magic the evil wizard Fulder had encased it in so long ago.

"Where is she!" Kriston demanded as he swam forward. "Where is Tresstéanna!"

"She is safe. She is here." With this, Dreail reached into a large hidden pouch along its stomach and pulled out the balled figure of Tresstéanna, tail and all. "She has been brave and is unharmed."

Kriston didn't believe the creature and quickly swam forward to take Tresstéanna from its large hands. Running his hands along her arms, he found no injuries. When he pushed her long hair from her face, her eyes fluttered open.

"Did I die?" she whispered.

"No, but you sure gave it a try," Kriston said as he kissed her and then gave her a quick shake. "Never again!" he growled.

"Again? How many sea monsters do you think I'll run into?" she asked with a smile.

"Children of my mother." Dreail's interruption caused Kriston and Tresstéanna to look at the large Protector. "She awaits."

Dreail reached up and took the red orb from its necklace, which rested just below its throat.

"There, follow the cavern and you will find the cradle. Return Genoa to her resting place. I will wait for you here. But hurry, my powers of creation cannot change my children back."

Kriston turned to see a wall of black creatures fast approaching their position. "Cats!" he hissed, "they are still coming!"

He grabbed Tresstéanna's hand, and they swam quickly towards the black opening of the cavern, hoping they were fast enough to escape the wave of monsters swimming at them.

SASH SET the last of the explosive charges along the narrow walkway of the dam. He gave himself only a second to marvel at the wonders the giants had built in the Kylix.

Large stones had been squared and placed along the wide opening of the valley of rocks, successfully blocking the waters that flowed deep underground. A small grate allowed the waters to escape along the side of the structure. The grate had a flap that had hand controls that kept the water at a level the giants wished.

Hearing Knoll give a shout, Sash stood and wiped dust from his borrowed pants. He looked towards the giant and noticed that he was running towards where Sash now stood. When Knoll threw his left arm out and pointed, Sash scanned the waters. Towards the shore where the village now stood, he noticed movement.

"Cats!" he hissed as a wave of monsters crawled out of the waters and attacked the giant's home.

Without hesitation, Sash picked up the last of the charges and raced back along the dam. As he ran, he thought back to his plan. If the monsters needed the deep water to mount their attack, why not get rid of the water.

He knew the dam was not natural, knew that it must be broken, and the water returned to its natural flow. When Kriston and Tresstéanna managed to return the globe to its resting place, then the waters would be needed to cleanse the large tunnel of the Kylix.

Genoa couldn't clean what was blocked.

The plan had been simple, break the dam. But how? Stand had provided that information when he'd produced several large black orbs.

"We call them booms," Stand said as he studied a crate full of the black balls. "You light the fuse and boom!"

"Are they strong enough to take down the dam?" Belent asked as he reached to pick up one of the balls. When Stand blocked the sorcerer from touching the ball, Belent withdrew his hand.

"And more," Stand replied as they drew up plans for where the booms would be placed.

Sash had been quick to volunteer, and with the giant named Knoll and another called Lant, they set out. Belent wished to witness this marvel so he went with them.

Now Sash raced towards Belent, and the wizard glanced up and spotted the attacking monsters.

"Quickly," Sash shouted as Knoll raced past him.

As they reached the shore, Knoll skidded to a stop. "Here, hand me the line!" The giant bent down and twisted the six lines to form one large rope. "They will blow at different times, but we cannot help that."

"But they will blow?" Belent asked as he bent to study what the giant was doing.

"Yes. It will take a while for the fire to reach them. By then, we should be back at the battle." Knoll withdrew two large stones from his pocket.

He lit the rope, and Sash saw the fire quickly travel down its length, heading back to the booms set along the dam.

"How?" Belent asked.

"Oil dipped string," Knoll said as he grabbed the sorcerer. "Now move! We do not want to be anywhere near here when it goes!"

They raced back along the shore and after a few feet turned inland and followed the narrow pathway leading back to the village.

When they neared the wall of the giants' village, they ran into several smaller monsters. Sash spotted the giant spiders and snakes attacking the outer wall of the city.

Using his sword, Sash ran at the closest monster and severed its long sharp legs from its body. He felt a blast of Belent's magic blow into another near him and turned to wedge his blade between the sharp teeth of a Surpense as it tried to attack him.

Then using his fist on a snake, he pounded it down and then stomped on its head. After slicing the head clean off with his sword, he turned to meet the next monster.

Finding more creatures than he thought he could handle, even with Belent blasting at them, Sash started to worry.

When Knoll reached down and grabbed two of the large spiders by their round bodies and squashed them like berries, Sash gaped up at the giant. Without him knowing, the two giants they traveled with had managed to squish and kill the remaining monsters.

"There, now on to the battle," Knoll said as he wiped his hands on a rather large rag.

"Useful, these giants," Belent said as he wiped blood from a small gash along his brow.

Sash nodded and turned to follow Knoll inside the walls of the city.

When they returned to the fortification, they saw chaos. Sash knew there was order within this mess and watched as his eyes adjusted to what he was seeing.

Stand and the lady Carrington stood near the center table. Svlain and Wizard Col were leaning over the map while runners moved in and out of the room.

When Col noticed them, he smiled and motioned them forward.

"Were you successful?" he asked as both Stand and Carrington stopped what they were doing to listen to his answer.

"Yes," Sash said and turned to Knoll.

"It should be any minute now," Knoll said with a nod.

"Good. Take the big one and see how he can help with the left flank. Several of the small warriors are already there," Stand ordered. He turned to Col when the wizard spoke.

"Might as well have him take the other one. His magical skills will soon exceed my own," Col said with a wave of his hand.

Sash raced after Knoll, with Belent trailing behind, and headed towards the battle. The giants had cleared the rocky area between the water and their home, allowing clear visibility for when the monsters attacked. They had placed large barricades along the shore, which caused the monsters to bottleneck in two locations.

These barricades allowed the giants to control the oncoming attacks. Not entirely, but the flow of attack was somewhat regulated, like the waters of the lake were by the dam. Many of these strategies reminded Sash of what he had briefly seen in Kós Kóvar.

As they neared the battle, he heard the telltale sounds of fighting. Loud bangs and cries could be heard along with the screams from the monsters.

He watched the swift blades of Stria blow into a nasty crab creature as Hilar used a long staff to stab the creature to the ground. Seth flew by him and raced towards a snake while Timmons cut another with his long sword. Three giants moved between the quick dragon warriors and tried to help by stepping on any nearby snake or spider. They appeared to be having a hard time finding a quarry as the dragon warriors were quick in their attack.

"Keep some for us!" one of the giants growled as he moved to pick up a rather nasty squashy monster and threw it against a nearby rock.

"Over here!" Knoll shouted as Sash twisted in time to see Belent send a blast of magic into a nearby crab.

Drawing his sword, Sash nodded at the nearby dragon warriors and moved down the trail to see what destruction he could cause. He had three Gordams lying on the ground before the first boom rocked the cavern. Moving quickly to retain his balance, Sash looked towards the dam and noticed smoke and fire filling the far left of the structure.

"Here comes the next one!" Knoll shouted just as a blast of smoke and fire exploded from the dam, just right of the first one.

The cave rocked again as the nearby monsters screamed or hissed in confusion. With satisfaction, Sash stabbed the nearest one and turned to watch the waters of the underground lake dip slightly as it started to spill out beyond the dam.

Then another explosion rocked the cavern, this one more intense than the first two, and the entire Kylix shook.

Boulders from the cave's ceiling were shaken loose. House-sized rocks came tumbling out of the blackness, landing around those who battled far below.

Finding a pillar of rock slammed into the ground feet from him, Sash quickly glanced up in fear. As another, smaller blast sounded, and a third boom ripped into the dam, he saw Knoll shake his head.

"That big one was not us!" the giant shouted and pointed in the opposite direction of the dam.

Just then the darkness of the cave lit up with a flash of bright red. The walls of the cavern glowed as another large explosion blew through the air, causing more pillars of rocks to fall from above.

"What is that?" Sash shouted as he turned once more to look towards the new blast.

"It's Genoa!" Belent yelled as another red blast ripped through the air.

15

GENOA

Tresstéanna's tail pushed her through the water behind Kriston's form. She felt the water stir around them as her eyes scanned the approaching hole.

The blackness appeared to reach out at them and only the feel of Kriston's hand on her arm kept her from trying to flee.

What is beyond? she wondered and feared.

"Hurry!" Kriston's scream caused her to kick her tail harder.

The cave seemed massive. It felt wide and tall, but as she pulled the glowing orb forward, she noticed it was just the darkness that made the cave appear large.

Rocks glowed red in Genoa's light. The rocks cut the blackness in half with their sharp angles and ragged edges. She felt Kriston slow when the way forward narrowed.

Not wanting to get cut by the rocks, they slowed, and he let go of her arm to keep from smashing into a sharp formation.

"Be careful," he hissed, maneuvering between two rock formations that seemed to block the way forward.

"Here, let me hold the orb up so we can see better," she said. She moved around Kriston towards the front.

When the red glow from the orb lit up the way, they saw the cavern dipped downward. The water was clear, but the rocks seemed to close in on the pathway.

"Kriston, it narrows even more." She turned to face him. "You won't be able to squeeze in there."

Shaking his head, Kriston studied the cave. "I can manage," he said with a slight hesitation.

"No. I can, but you cannot. Stay here, protect my flank while I go in." She quickly reached up to place a finger over his lips. "You know you can't squeeze in there; it will be better if I go in alone. Stay here."

Knowing he was about to argue more, she quickly kissed him and squirmed between the large, jagged rocks. Once there, she turned to look back at him.

"I'll be right back." She gave him a smile.

She didn't want to acknowledge her fear of leaving Kriston, so used that smile to shield her feelings from him and herself. She turned and found the way forward was difficult to swim. She switched to pulling herself through the rocks and found this was easier.

Knowing tight spaces usually led to no space, she kept thoughts of claustrophobia from her mind and kept focused instead on the end results.

"Return Genoa, get the heck out!" she chanted much like she had chanted the prayer, "Don't get caught," all those days before on Earth when she had been trying to escape the library.

Crawling in the darkness with rocks ripping at her scales and arms, the only comfort she had was knowing that Kriston was feet from her. The glow from Genoa reflected her enclosed prison as she slowly moved forward, inches at a time.

"Are you still there?" Kriston's shout caused her to pause.

"Yes, it gets tighter down here," she answered. She pushed another inch forward.

"Are we sure that this the correct cave?" he yelled. Doubt and frustration filled his voice.

"Yes." She pushed the orb forward a little. When light erupted in front of her, she almost dropped the globe.

"What was that?" he yelled, distracting her.

"Hold on!" she shouted, and once again raised the orb. The light erupted again, and she smiled when she noticed it. "It's ahead! I'm almost there."

The light was a reflection of the orb's red glow on thousands of jewels just beyond her reach. She squeezed and tugged and pulled as she tried to reach the cavern ahead. But her way forward was barred by several large, pointed rocks. She felt her frustration build.

She took her magical knife out of its sheath and started hacking at the tips of the rocks. The tight cave made it difficult for her to swing hard at the stones, and she had to settle for smaller sweeps of her arm.

When she had finally smashed one of the tips of the pillars off, she heard a shout from Kriston.

"They are here!" he shouted, and she heard him grunt with exertion.

Knowing the monsters of Dreail had somehow gotten past the Protector and were now attacking Kriston made her movements panicked. When she went to smash at the rock this time, she cut a deep gouge in her right thumb.

Cursing the pain, and her fear, she finally felt her magic burst out of her in frustration. When the magic hit the rocks, a loud crack sounded, and she found the way forward clear of the enclosing rocks.

"Damn!" she hissed as she sucked her injury. "Should have done that move first."

Tucking Genoa's orb to her side, she swam into the crystal-filled chamber of the cradle.

Tresstéanna felt like Aladdin in the Cave of Wonders. Jewels and crystals filled the chamber she now swam in.

Her mermaid tail shimmered in the light's reflection, much like the walls did. Spinning in the spot, she saw rock crystals bigger than she was. Several spiraled and rose well above her head as they reached way up to the top of the cavern, well over a hundred feet from where she swam.

"Wow!" she said as her eyes scanned the variety of colors and stones that surrounded her. In the prior cave, Genoa's red orb had been the only light. It had bounced off the black rocks and kept everything eerie in its crimson glow.

Here, inside the cradle, the red was only one of the colors. Blue, yellow, green, and gold blasted her senses as she moved further inside the chamber.

Unsure where Genoa's orb had been settled, Tresstéanna twisted and turned while her eyes scanned the marvels of the chamber. But seeing only the bright gemstones, she hesitated.

"*Child,*" Genoa said as Tresstéanna held her in her hands, "*I am home.*"

"Where do I place you?" Tresstéanna asked as she continued to spin around, searching for the goddess's resting place.

"*Release me,*" Genoa said as the orb flashed a bright red glow.

Taking one last look at the globe in her hands, Tresstéanna opened her palms and let the orb float away.

The globe hovered for a second, then shot upwards to the ceiling. Without thinking, Tresstéanna swam after it. It rose high to the crystals lodged inside the top of the cave and floated right up to a small round opening. Instead of disappearing inside the opening, the orb attached itself to the crystal.

"Now to set things right," she heard the goddess say. She marveled that she hadn't needed to touch the orb to hear Genoa's words.

When the cavern started to shake around her, Tresstéanna was spun around in the water as fear enveloped her.

WIZARD LEIAN WAS USING his magic to heal some of the wounded giants when the fighting started. Healing allowed some of the warriors to return to the fight, while it kept others from crossing over in death.

Sweat poured down his back as he bent to right a broken bone as sounds of the fighting continued outside the town. The healer rushed from one bed to the other as he attempted to stop bleeding or mend bones.

A runner came and told Leian that Shiarra was safe. She was remaining in the headquarters. But when a blast of magic sounded from outside, Leian knew Shiarra had already left the safety of that room.

"Blasted woman is always running headfirst into danger," he grumbled as he bent over the next patient.

More injured were brought in, and he was assessing the first giant when he felt Genoa's magic blast through the room. Standing, he saw the glow of red magic dash through the dirt floor and quickly raced out to follow it.

"You!" he shouted to a nearby runner. "Which way to

headquarters?" He had quite lost his bearings. After being pointed in the right direction, he raced along the streets.

Two houses from headquarters, he ran into Shiarra. Grabbing her arms to keep her from falling over, he looked down at her wide eyes.

"Is it her?" Shiarra exclaimed. She smiled when he nodded.

"Yes. Tresstéanna did it!" he said as another wave knocked into them.

"What is she doing?" Shiarra asked as she grabbed Leian's shirt for support.

"Fixing things," Leian said. He pulled Shiarra into the doorway of the headquarters.

They found the others inside. Col remained standing, but Svlain had fallen over and was being helped up by Zain.

"What in the king's name was that?" Zain asked as he kept an arm around the land nymph's waist.

"It is Genoa!" Shiarra said as she braced herself against the table.

"The goddess?" Carrington asked as her eyes grew large. "Is she displeased?"

"No!" Leian said with a smile. "She is cleansing the cave."

"Should we evacuate?" Stand asked as a runner came into the room.

"Sir, the dam is broken, and the creatures are disappearing!" the small giant said, and then he quickly turned and raced beyond the doorway again.

Following the lad, they all ran down through the streets of the village. They raced towards the water and noticed the army of giants, Húriya, and Otomi fighters, including the dragon warriors from Genoa, standing on the shore, looking out to where there had once sat a large underground lake.

Giant and small men and women stood with their eyes downcast at what had once been a vast lake. No monsters were seen, only a clear blue flowing river. Mud and sediment were quickly being replaced by growing green and orange foliage. Flowers of pure white opened to the cave's odd glowing walls as the water washed away any of the remnants of the dam.

Rocks the sizes of houses and large buildings flowed down the stream and disappeared down the massive cavern.

"She is cleaning the Kylix," Leian said as Seth came and slapped him on his back.

"A good purging was needed," Seth said with a laugh.

"What of Tresstéanna and Kriston?" Svlain asked quietly, and a hush fell over the crowd.

Her words had all eyes turning to their right. Far in the darkness where the water's flow started, they noticed only flowers and brightly covered foliage.

Leian and the others from Genoa were joined by Ava the Zaeim and Carrington from Midzark. Also, with the group were Mayson and several of his men.

The large group immediately started walking the new shore of the river in search of their missing friends. Shiarra and Svlain were in a panic and had to be warned to remain calm and walk slowly in case they missed any signs of the two. Though the ground was covered by pretty flowers, there were still sharp rocks to navigate and, in several spots, the water was deep and the shore very steep.

They had traveled several minutes when Timmons gave a shout.

"There!" he said and all eyes were directed to where he pointed far ahead.

Shiarra rushed forward, flanked by Svlain, as the form of Tresstéanna emerged from behind a large rock. Seeing that the queen didn't have any clothing on, the men remained behind as the land nymph and wizard encircled their friend.

"Here, someone should bring her these," Col said, shoving the pile of Tresstéanna's clothing at him.

"Me? I'm a man!" Leian said, turning bright pink as he glanced anywhere but where the three women stood.

"I will take them," Carrington said. She grabbed the clothing and walked quickly over to where the women stood.

Leian kept his eyes diverted long after Tresstéanna walked down to their group, but after hearing her question about Kriston, he turned to study his surroundings again.

"He is safe," Belent said as he closed the cover to his new magical book.

"Are you sure!" Tresstéanna demanded and rounded on the sorcerer.

"He is no longer in the cave," the sorcerer said, but he could not provide any further explanation other than what the book had told him.

Unwilling or unable to take Belent's word that Kriston was safe, Tresstéanna tried to read the book herself but found the pages blank. In frustration and anxiety, Tresstéanna demanded they start the trek back down the Kylix immediately.

"Much must be prepared before we start," Col stated, and Leian nodded in agreement.

Supplies had to be gathered, equipment repaired, and talks with both Carrington and Ava finished before the group from Genoa could return home.

That first day after Genoa had been returned, Ava, Carrington, and Mayson agreed that a new counsel should be established for Midzark. Ensuring that peace remained, all races would join in the counsel, which would have seats not only inside the forest but also across the desert.

Trade between the two lands would start, as it appeared the desert was once again blooming, and the land was returning to its former glory. Rain fell out of the sky the first day Genoa had been returned to her cradle, and with the rain came relief from the heat.

"Will we be allowed to visit the mainland?" Carrington asked, her face hopeful and filled with wonder.

"We do not think so," Col said with a shake of his head. "The path is long and still holds the Protectors."

"But to discover the mainland and never be allowed to see it?" Mayson asked with a shake of his head. "How are we to remain here knowing it's out there, just beyond our reach?"

"It is not," Ava said with a smile. "Genoa has righted our home. If we follow her guidance then we can hope that one day she will break the barriers of our two worlds and reunite us."

Leian was amazed to discover that, within his small world, there were still things that could shock and please him. Finding friends where once monsters lurked was a lesson he would always remember.

Two days before the original band of travelers returned down the long cavern of the Kylix, the giant village had been abandoned. Those who had once called the cave home now returned up to Midzark as free people.

The cave was left for the giant ants who still made the cavern their home. No longer did they do battle with the giants for food or land, and with the return of the plants, the ants were able to exist comfortably.

The only person not willing to return on the journey was Colab. The young prince met privately with the queen and asked to remain behind in Midzark.

"He grew fond of Maraneal," Tresstéanna told wizards Leian, Shiarra, and Col along with Belent the night before they started their trek. "He asked that I explain his request to Kriston. Without Meshi, Colab didn't see a need to return to the mainland."

"It is good he found love," Shiarra stated as she squeezed Leian's hand.

"He has made a new home," Tresstéanna said with a nod of her head.

Leian didn't blame the young prince for wanting to stay because of love. He knew he would follow Shiarra anywhere and felt the pull so hard that before that night was finished, he insisted Tresstéanna complete the ceremony joining Shiarra and him in marriage.

Standing on the lip of the Krack, with all of Midzark shining in the early morning's light, Leian joined hands with Shiarra. She had been given a new white dress. Her long hair had been brushed back and bright flowers adorned her hair. The smile on her pretty face was something Leian would carry with him always.

The ceremony was simple, and all their friends gathered along the edge of the Hessite cliffs to witness the joining. The only one missing was her father, Sayer Phillip.

After the wedding, a quick toast was made by Col and then the bride and groom changed back into their travel clothes.

Goodbyes were said to those remaining in Midzark, and the travel down the dark cavern started once more. Leewana traveled with them until they reached the large forest roots two nights later. The roots had remained after Genoa's purging, but with the knowledge of their dangers, the group quickly and carefully traversed the odd forest.

Beyond the forest they discovered the dangerous spiders missing. Either Genoa had cleared the path or the smaller Jumna spiders had completely wiped out the larger more dangerous Black Haricot spiders. Either way, everyone was glad no sight of the spiders was found.

Fifteen days after setting foot back in the Kylix, they

reached the domain of Adulario. The large Protector greeted them after he arose from the solid ground.

His rock shape emerged and shook the ground as his impressive form took shape. Tresstéanna returned his blue eye to him and thanked him for its use.

"It is I who should thank you. You returned our mother and my siblings to our rightful forms," Adulario said with a bow of his head. "In appreciation, here is a token of our thanks."

He plucked a large stone from the side of the crown that sat upon his head. It shone bright blue and was the size of a small baby's fist. He presented it to the queen.

Gado the lizard had joined them on their return through the vast cavern. The lizard felt obligated, since the band had managed to stay alive. Also, with the purging of the cave's poison, the lizard had its original home back.

Following the lizard had been made easier now that the dangers of the cavern had been swept away. But still, rocks and caverns needed to be traversed, much to the frustration of Tresstéanna who worried day and night about Kriston. She had nagged Belent several more times about the prince's location, but the odd book only assured her he was safe.

"Safe? That could mean anything!" she grumbled one night as they sat around eating. Her words worried those closest and all would then turn their thoughts to the missing man.

Kriston found it hard to fight the large snakes while trying to remain in the tight cave leading to the cradle. He couldn't slash at

the monsters with his sword and take a full swing. Finally, he had to settle for short jabs at the heads of the snakes that neared him.

Grunting with his efforts, he worried about being stuck inside the small cavern as larger monsters blocked their exit.

When he felt a small blast in the cave behind him, his fear increased. Had the cave collapsed on Tresstéanna? Was she trapped and dying just feet from him?

His frustration built, distracting him, as an attacking snake swiped a cut across his forearm.

"Blasted creatures!" he hissed, and stabbed the monster in its eye. When it wiggled away in pain, there were two more to take its place.

"Let me!" Dreail's voice sounded and the water grew warm as the Protector used its magic against its children.

The first snake found its eyes closed to sight, while the second wiggled and shrunk to the size of a small worm. Amazed, Kriston turned and saw the large Protector's eyes peering down the long tunnel he and Tresstéanna had come from.

"These escaped my notice and got past me. There are no more down here," Dreail said as its large green eye peered at Kriston.

"Thank you," Kriston said. He nodded to the giant creature and turned to look back towards where Tresstéanna had disappeared just as the cave gave a mighty shake.

"Come out of there!" Dreail's commanding voice bellowed.

Instead of retreating, Kriston tried to squeeze between the rocks that kept him from Tresstéanna.

"No!" he shouted as he scraped and cut his way through the rocks. "I have to get to her!"

"No, child, she is with our mother now," Dreail said, and Kriston felt the water grow warm. Dreail was using his magic and water to blast Kriston's body out of the hole. Landing within the Protector's hands, Kriston fought to return to the cave that led to the cradle and Tresstéanna.

Another larger explosion blasted into them as the waters

around them turned red. Thrown from the opening, Kriston found himself tucked gently inside the Protector's grasp while they flew through the waters.

"Hold tight!" Dreail said as another wave of water hit them. "She sets it right!"

Unsure what the giant water creature meant, Kriston tried to see beyond the large hand that held him. As the rocks and water swirled beyond his protective enclosure, Kriston felt the swirling motion increase as consciousness finally left him.

When he awoke, it was to a soothing yellow glow emanating from beyond his eyelids. Unsure what had happened, he blinked his eyes opened and stared at the sun. It had an odd waver to it, and he realized he was underwater still.

Feeling his body float, he moved his limbs and felt the tail swish as he righted himself from a lying position in the dirt.

"What happened?" he asked, spinning around to glance at his surroundings.

"I brought you home," Dreail said from next to him.

Swimming to the large Protector, Kriston watched the creature and nodded. The large green fins beat while the curled tail remained steady in the water.

"Home?" Kriston asked and glanced around again.

"To Genoa. The mainland." Dreail pointed upwards. To Kriston's astonishment, he saw the familiar outline of the Cleveite Mountains far above the lake he and Dreail currently swam in.

"Home!" Kriston shouted, turning to face the creature again. "What about Tresstéanna? What of my other friends? You abandoned them?"

"There were things I needed to right," Dreail said as green eyes studied Kriston. "Your friends are safe now that our mother is home. But others outside were still in danger. My children had been set free by the breaking of the dam and our mother needed my help," Dreail said as if scolding Kriston.

"But how are they to get out of the cave?" Kriston asked. The Protector crossed his arms in impatience.

"Our mother will care for them." Dreail shook his massive head. "You were injured and since I was needed here, I carried you in my protective pouch."

Just thinking of the creature's large stomach pouch made Kriston uncomfortable, so he studied the water's surface as Dreail continued.

"Genoa has cleansed the cave and will guide your people back home." Dreail turned when a ghostly figure materialized near them. "Daughter."

"Cherished," the Lady of the Tentril said as her true form shined in the water.

Kriston noticed a smaller pale figure much like Dreail. The new figure was clearly female and, instead of fins at the lady's back, she had long flowing hair. "It has been years since I was blessed by your presence."

"My prison was long and difficult," Dreail said sadly. "But I was freed by the one you sent."

"Has our mother been returned?" the lady asked. She smiled when Dreail nodded. "Then all will be restored?"

"Yes, and more." Dreail turned to Kriston. "Mother has agreed that in memory of our trials a new species will be created."

Turning, Dreail bent forward and pulled two small figures from its pouch. The babies had tails and bore a striking similarity to Kriston's current form.

The first child was dark green—hair of green like Dreail's scales and green skin. The second was a dark purple with deep lavender eyes.

"These two will be a gift to Genoa's people. They will grow to rule the seas of this land. Grow and multiply, while commanding the waters far to the east." Dreail handed the two babies over to the Lady. "Teach them and take care. One day soon the people of the land will have need of them."

"What shall I call them?" the lady asked as she cradled the two in her arms.

"Bettina will be the mother to all Merpeople and Cargnet will be their father."

TRESSTÉANNA STEPPED out of the dark cavern for the last time and took a deep breath of fresh air.

The smell was familiar to her and as the sun hit her face, she couldn't help the grin that passed over her lips. Only the thought of Kriston kept a full smile from forming as she scanned the green landscape beyond the bleakness of the cave's rock opening.

"My queen, you have returned!" The shout arose from the small valley below the cavern's opening, and more shouts followed. As she stepped further outside the cavern, a huge shadow passed over her.

Before she had time to think, Su Na landed feet from her, shaking the ground with his landing.

"Su Na!" she shouted, and raced towards the dragon. Giving his massive golden head a hug, she tried to stop the tears as they fell and landed on his large golden scales.

"My lady!" Su Na said, wrapping one of his massive forelegs around her slender body.

"My queen!" came another voice, and Tresstéanna turned to see Wizard Cenzic slowly walk up to her. After he bowed, he turned to smile at the others. "Welcome home!"

"Cenzic!" Col said. He walked forward to shake the man's hand.

"Cenzic," Tresstéanna said. She walked over to stand between the two. "Have you seen Kriston?"

Seeing the confusion on the old wizard's face had her heart sinking. When he shook his head, his eyes returned to Col's. "Is the prince missing?"

"We last saw him deep within the Kylix but were told he was safe and out of the cave. We assumed he would be here waiting for us," Col stated as his eyes turned to where Belent stood.

"Belent!" Tresstéanna said, turning on the sorcerer. "Where is he?" she demanded.

Shaking his head, Belent reached for his book once more. The Trialth book remained empty, leaving them no clue where the prince could be found.

Much to Tresstéanna's dismay, she was quickly thrust into her duties and, before the sun set, found despair made her weak.

"Tresstéanna, you must eat," Shiarra stated as she shoved a bowl of soup before her.

Tresstéanna had taken to her tent after sending scouts out to search the surrounding area for Kriston. Shaking her head, she leaned over the map once more. "If I do the Finders spell wrong it won't work." She held the single button of Kriston's that she had yanked off his discarded shirt. It was the shirt he had left beside the water's edge all those days ago, and she gripped it in her hand now like a lifeline. "Thirty days!" she said with frustration. "It's been thirty days since our fight with Dreail and the last time I saw him. I had hoped he would be here waiting for me, but they haven't seen hide nor hair of him."

She knew her words would cause confusion in Shiarra, but at the moment she forgot her friend was there.

Taking the button, she spread her hands over the map of Genoa and tried again. Her first two failures had been caused by her own frustration. So, after taking a deep breath, she tried the complicated Finders spell again.

The words were easy, but the hand motion and magic were beyond her. But still she tried. This time, she felt her magic rise up out of her core. When a faint green glow emanated along the maps' edges, she squealed with pleasure.

"There!" Shiarra said, pointing to a small circle just east of their location.

"Where, I don't see the rip," Tresstéanna shouted, studying the map.

"I saw it. Your magic was faint, and the spell only lasted a moment, but I noticed a tear there above that little circle."

After holding the map up, Tresstéanna still couldn't see anything. But willing to take the wizard's word as truth, she marched out of her tent and grabbed the reins of Star, her yellow horse.

"You cannot go alone!" Shiarra called after her as Tresstéanna kicked Star into a run.

"The hell I can't!" Tresstéanna yelled over her shoulder. If Shiarra was right, Kriston was only a mile away.

The run along the new river's edge was quick. Flowers and grass now grew where once black poison had seeped and bleed. No longer did the Vi Porta smell of death and decay. The black ooze that had almost killed her months ago was now missing, replaced by Genoa.

Bending far over Star's neck, Tresstéanna felt the cool wind of the approaching night hit her face. Tears leaked from her eyes, caused by the wind and speed with which she urged the horse.

"Hurry!" she said as images of Kriston flew through her mind. She had left him, she remembered. Left him to crawl through a tight space. Left him to the monsters that had attacked them from behind.

She felt guilty about leaving him, and this guilt had eaten

her alive during the long trip back down the Kylix. It had consumed her more than the worry for Kriston. She knew Kriston could handle himself in most situations and, deep down, she knew he was safe. But the guilt ate away and soured her stomach and gave her a headache. So overwhelming was the guilt that she found it hard to eat or sleep.

Now, as she raced east, she saw the clear lake and was shocked to see it was the same lake she had almost died at months ago. It was the lake the black poison had pooled in, the one she, as Té, had used her magic against to allow Col and the dragon warriors to safely pass beyond.

"Kriston!" she shouted as Star slid to a stop at the lake's edge.

Looking around, she saw that the lake's waters remained still. There was no sign of life along the water's edge, and she panicked.

He had to be here!

Marching around calling his name resulted in nothing. Feeling frustrated, she stomped to the water's edge when a loud plop sounded feet inside the lake.

Turning, she studied the dark waters. She heard another plop and saw a small ripple ten feet from where she stood.

Thinking the disturbance was only a fish, she was shocked when a small rock hit her in her left shoulder. Rushing forward, she jumped into the water and saw Kriston just below the water's surface.

"Kriston!" she screamed and dove down to him. He wrapped his arms around her and smiled, but needing breath, she quickly kicked back up, so her face was above the surface.

"Why are you still a merman?" she shouted and felt frustrated when he shook his head. "Ugh! Did you use my same wish when you ate the Orwic petal?"

Again, Kriston shook his head. If he tried to talk, she

couldn't hear it, so she kicked her feet and legs while trying to think.

"I asked to be a mermaid until my mission was complete!" she said and looked down at him. "Kriston, what is your mission?"

She watched him shake his head and smiled when it came to her.

"Kriston, I'm safe!" she shouted, and before she was finished talking, the water around him started to bubble. Legs replaced the long tail and she saw his mouth open once before his head raised above the water and he took a big breath of air.

After wrapping his naked lower half in one of her horse blankets, they journeyed back to the main camp, both riding Star. Kriston kept his arms tightly wrapped around her waist, which was simply fine with her.

This reminded her of the first time she had met Kriston, when he'd captured her all those days ago along the shore of Mirror Lake. A smile crossed her lips when the memory came to her mind and as they drew near the camp, shouts of joy could be heard.

"I think we should get married on the shores of the Mirror Lake," she said. She smiled when he chuckled.

"Agreed," he said, drawing her closer. "Soon!"

EPILOGUE

The wedding of Kriston and Tresstéanna took place the last day of fall that same year. The trees along the shore had turned a bright orange and red while the warm crisp air hinted at cooler days and long nights.

Genoa had adopted Midzark's calendar, along with their time recording. So, in the fifth month, named Topkiá, on Jesta, the 67th day, the two royals were wed.

Friends and family gathered around them under a large golden tent on the shores of Mirror Lake. It was the same spot where she had first met Kriston.

Tresstéanna wore a long golden dress with an elegant neckline and bodice. Her pale hair was worn up with thin tendrils around her glowing face. A golden crown matched that of her new husband, but hers had a large blue stone called the Liberty stone, which sat upon its center.

Kriston wore his best dark black trousers with a short green jacket. His hair had been trimmed and his green eyes remained fixed on his bride as he said his vows.

Col officiated and Wizard Cenzic walked the bride down

the aisle. The wizard carried the elemental staff given to him by Genoa as a symbol of the queen's triumphs.

The wedding day was so magical that she found it hard not to smile. The sun shone and the birds joined in on the celebration.

Food and drinks finished the ceremony, with the feast continuing well into the night.

Several swans had gathered along the shoreline to see the magical queen wed her prince. Deer and gentle creatures drew near and the only figures missing were the large owls. But since they were nocturnal, Tresstéanna didn't fault them for missing the event.

Several of the nearest towns sent their Sayers, including Shiarra's father, who had been overjoyed by his daughter's marriage to Wizard Leian.

Days before her own wedding, Tresstéanna had officiated over Svlain and Zain's wedding. The two had finally agreed to wed, and then had traveled to the lake to witness Tresstéanna's own wedding. They told her they would travel back to Rigel City, then they would go to the Cliffs of Faro. Their life would be one spent between the two, using Zain's dragon Llis for the long journey.

Tresstéanna thought the plan wonderful and was pleased to see her two friends so happy.

Kriston's nephew, Calob, who was now king of Matera, had journeyed to the lake for the wedding with his vast entourage of counselors. These advisors included Captain Crain and Commander Stoltz. Stoltz brought most of the resistance fighters, including his new wife, a very pretty lady named Merna.

Calob had been saddened to hear of his twin brother's troubles in Midzark but showed relief when he heard that Colab had found love.

"He is truly happy?" Calob asked them the night before the wedding.

"He is. Without Meshi, he felt he could guide the people of Midzark, and with Maraneal, I think Colab will find happiness," Kriston said, patting the boy on the arm.

Tresstéanna had been pleased when her mother had arrived two days before the wedding. Mero the Push Tu, leader of the Scarents, had been accompanied by three other Scarents. Tresstéanna had immediately rushed into her mother's open arms and smiled when a tear leaked from the woman's odd eyes.

"You have found the happiness I once had with your father," Mero said as she embraced her daughter.

"I have." Tresstéanna smiled. "We make our home closer to you. We started the plans for the castle we will live in west of here. We make Pinewoods our home now. We'll call it Castle Pines."

"You will be closer?" Again, tears leaked from the Scarent's eyes as she hugged her daughter again.

"It's the heart of Genoa," Tresstéanna had told her mother, but deep down she knew differently.

Genoa was much bigger than the orb she had carried for so many days. She was even bigger than the land she called home. Genoa was the missing element she had searched for her whole life. Genoa was family, friends, and loved ones.

THE SWAY of Star's steps eased Tresstéanna's discomfort as they moved along the water's edge.

Rubbing her swollen belly, Tresstéanna felt a little kick,

no doubt one of Zander's feet. The lad was impatient as he lay cradled inside her womb. This thought caused her to smile as Kriston guided Rath closer.

"This is too much for you and the baby," he said with a scowl on his handsome face.

"Nonsense." She smiled at him. "Besides, the babies like the movement."

Watching, she noticed the moment her words sunk in. His green eyes grew wide with shock, and his face paled slightly.

"Babies? More than one?" he croaked as his face turned another shade paler.

"Two, yes. A boy and girl, to be exact." She took the hand from her belly and reached over and patted his arm to comfort him. "But they will not be appearing for some time yet."

Laughing when he rode up, Col studied the two as he pulled his own horse close. "Finally told him?"

"He will get over it soon enough," Timmons said from behind them as they drew closer to their destination.

"Maybe, but wait until he has to change twice as many nappies," Seth said with a smirk. "You know all about nappies, don't you Timmons."

"How is Rayshell?" Tresstéanna asked, ignoring the snickers from around her.

Timmons smiled and puffed his chest out when he told her that his wife was fine. "The baby has his first tooth!" he pronounced, as if the child had accomplished this feat through bravery or skills.

"I'm sure Rayshell is proud," Tresstéanna said as her horse crested the last ridge.

Spotting their destination, the group grew quiet, and Tresstéanna thought back to the message from Genoa several days ago as her eyes scanned the area.

What had once appeared to be a massive maw of an evil mouth now shined in the afternoon light. Flowers and vines covered the cave's entrance, giving it a whimsical appearance now.

Drawing closer, Tresstéanna noticed that all the land's scars had healed in this magical place. The entrance to the Kylix stood bold and beautiful as the small band of travelers approached.

"Are they here yet?" Seth asked.

"I don't think so," Tresstéanna replied as Kriston helped her down from Star's back.

"We are!" Svlain shouted as Zain's brown and teal dragon landed near the horses.

Hellos were said, including hugs and kisses, but the group kept casting their eyes on the massive cave's entrance. When sounds could be heard inside and a light shone from the darkness, Tresstéanna moved quickly forward.

The first to step out of the cavern was a tall giant girl. Long dark hair was braided down her back and her eyes were round and full of wonder.

"You must be Charlotte," Tresstéanna said with a smile as Carrington followed, steps behind her daughter.

"Are you the white queen?" Charlotte asked as she stopped and stared.

"Remember your manners," Carrington scolded as she grasped the girl's hand, who then quickly bowed.

"Welcome to Genoa," Tresstéanna said with a smile and a slight bow of her head.

When Colab stepped out of the dark shadow of the cave, he was followed by his pretty wife, Maraneal. Next came Ava the Zaeim, her Gaura robe wrapped around her. Several other people followed, some giants.

"All are welcomed to Genoa," Tresstéanna, queen of Castle Pines, said with a large smile.

ABOUT THE AUTHORS

JJ Anders is the pseudonym used by the powerhouse writing duo of NY Times & USA Today bestselling author, Jill Sanders and her identical twin sister, Jody. Hailing from the Pacific Northwest, these two talented ladies have merged their creative forces to craft an amazing new fantasy series that will leave you begging for more.

With over sixty bestselling romance books and counting, Jill alone is a force to be reckoned with, boasting thousands of glowing reviews with a cumulative 4.7 star rating. Jody's powerful imagination and newfound love of writing has spawned the thrilling new world and enchanting characters of Genoa. As a furious reader and devoted mother, Jody's passion for storytelling reaches full bloom by teaming up with her talented twin to bring her magical stories to life for the enjoyment of readers everywhere.